Praise for *Murder's No Votive Confidence*

"A charming mystery with believable, likeable characters. Check it out."
—*Suspense Magazine*

"Charming . . . With this great cast and setting, *Murder's No Votive Confidence* was a very enjoyable take on the country house mystery."
—*Criminal Element*

"This is a perfect summer cozy with a lush setting and a fun heroine."
—*Parkersburg News & Sentinel*

"A cozy with candles, conspiring couples, and a cat—what could be a better combination? Christin Brecher's debut mystery has all those and more."
—Kaitlyn Dunnett, author of *Clause & Effect*

"A scentsational new series! Christin Brecher's charming debut, *Murder's No Votive Confidence*, glows with a seaside location, a candle shop, and a kitty that will melt your heart. I_____ting characters and a twisting _____ ____ you intrigued to the very _____
—Krista Davis, _____ ___

"A charmingly fu_ _____ _____ and turns and _____ _____rs. *Murder's No Votive* _____ ____ooked from the first pages."
—Kirsten Weiss, author of *Bleeding Tarts*

"The first book in the Nantucket Candle Maker Mystery series by Christin Brecher burns bright with a delightful protagonist, realistic characters, and an intriguing plot—a breath of fresh Nantucket air!"
—Barbara Allan, author of *Antiques Ravin'*

Also by Christin Brecher

Murder's No Votive Confidence

Published by Kensington Publishing Corporation

Murder
Makes Scents

Christin Brecher

KENSINGTON BOOKS
KENSINGTON PUBLISHING CORP.
www.kensingtonbooks.com

KENSINGTON BOOKS are published by

Kensington Publishing Corp.
119 West 40th Street
New York, NY 10018

All Kensington titles, imprints, and distributed lines are available at special quantity discounts for bulk purchases for sales promotion, premiums, fund-raising, educational, or institutional use.

Special book excerpts or customized printings can also be created to fit specific needs. For details, write or phone the office of the Kensington Sales Manager: Attn.: Sales Department. Kensington Publishing Corp., 119 West 40th Street, New York, NY 10018. Phone: 1-800-221-2647.

Kensington and the K logo Reg. U.S. Pat. & TM Off.

First Printing: March 2020
ISBN-13: 978-1-4967-2141-9
ISBN-10: 1-4967-2141-1

ISBN-13: 978-1-4967-2142-6 (eBook)
ISBN-10: 1-4967-2142-X (eBook)

10 9 8 7 6 5 4 3 2 1

Printed in the United States of America

To Tommy and Carly
With all my love

Chapter 1

I was in heaven.

I was in Paris.

I was at Cire Trudon, one of the city's finest candle stores.

Most visitors to Paris look forward to the cheeses and breads, the art, the bridges linking the Left and Right Banks, the sparkle of the Eiffel Tower at night. I was in Paris to enjoy all of those highlights, plus a few more. As proprietor of the Wick & Flame, my candle store on Nantucket Island, I had my own enchantments to enjoy.

This beautiful autumn morning, I had already made a pilgrimage to Diptyque, the internationally renowned French candle company. My senses alit, I'd followed my visit with a stroll through the Tuileries Gardens and over the Pont Royal, where the Bateau Mouche floated below me on the Seine. Once across the river, I'd visited Quintessence Paris, a one-of-a-kind establishment which leads customers from room to room of a grand home to enjoy candles designed for each living space.

I had particularly wanted to visit Quintessence Paris because it is run by a woman from a perfume family. I'm also the daughter of a perfumer. In fact, I was in Paris because of my mother, Millie Wright. The World Perfumery Conference was taking place this week, and they had invited her to speak on a panel entitled "The Art of Scent Extractions."

When Millie had called me three weeks ago to propose I meet her in Paris, I knew that the invitation was an unspoken apology. This summer, she'd had plans to come home, a rare event, but then she'd cancelled at the last minute. An opportunity had come up to visit scientists in the rainforest to learn about indigenous scents. Something about absorption traps. All very scientific. The trip had ultimately led to her invitation to speak at the conference, and I think she wanted me to see that her detour had been worthwhile.

I'd had one caveat, which was that she had to return with me to Nantucket for a visit as well, but the truth was, she and I both knew I would accept her good-will gesture. A *sorry* is nice, but Paris is Paris, and this was one case where our sense of adventure aligned. Millie is happiest roaming the world, seeking unique and exotic scents to create perfumes. In contrast, I find my buzz on Nantucket, running my store, the Wick & Flame, and tackling my candle creations. I'd also solved a murder a few months ago, so I argue that you can discover the mysteries of the world right outside your front door.

Now, I was among candles of every size, color, and scent at Cire Trudon. I reverently admired a display of tapers, piled in tidy rows by color against the back wall. Then I marveled over an elegant circle of bell jars which encased sophisticated scents on a round table in the middle of the room. I lifted a jar from a candle called Byron, melting into its peppery scent, and thought how wonderful the aroma would be during a winter's day on Nantucket. Thirty miles off the coast of Massachusetts, my hometown was a chilly place in February, and a warm scent does wonders for body and soul. My nose sated, I crossed the store with the quiet reverence one saves for museums, to admire their pièce de résistance. On a credenza at the far side of the store was a remarkable group of wax busts featuring characters in French history, tempting customers to light the wicks atop their heads. Marie Antoinette stared at me, daring me to try. As if I would. Her molded hair was too fabulous to mess with.

The sales associate politely indulged me while I took a few snaps of the candle busts on display. As I zoomed in on a stern-faced Napoleon, my phone pinged a photo from my boyfriend, Peter, who was back home. His lopsided grin and the lock of blond hair over his forehead reminded me of his boyish charm, while the look in his eyes made me miss his warm embrace. I smiled at the image of him holding up four fingers, and I sent a thumbs-up selfie back to him. We'd recently hit the four-month mark in our relationship, and we were feeling pretty smug about ourselves. I hated to jinx myself, but life was good. In addition to the magic of new love coursing through my veins, my business had been strong enough over the summer that I'd felt confident to leave for a few days abroad. Even the timing of the trip was perfect, since everyone back home had begun to remind me that my birthday was coming up. Thirty. I might have been imagining it, but the reminder was often followed with a look that made me feel like I had spinach in my teeth.

"May I help you?" the sales associate asked. From her subtle pout, I realized that I'd crossed a line when my attention had shifted from her candles to Peter's text.

"*Non, merci*," I said, practicing my accent. I checked the time. It was later than I'd realized. With one last tour of the establishment and a friendly "*au revoir*," I picked up a healthy pace to meet Millie for a snack at a café across the street from the conference center on the Left Bank.

Today was the end of the conference, and after my mom's presentation we'd be heading back to Nantucket, but Millie and I had likely patronized a year's worth of cafés over the last few days. We'd had a ball sitting at small, round tables, unlit Gauloises cigarettes dangling from our lips for a cinema-noire effect as we drank our café cremes and people-watched. The parade of high-style, fabulous couples walking hand in hand, and even the dogs enjoying croissant crumbs from the pavement beside the cafés, was captivating.

It took a few minutes longer than I anticipated to reach what had become our favorite haunt, Café Bonne Chance, because I had to wait by the Odeon as a caravan of black cars, with a motorcade on each side, passed by. The much talked about Peace Jubilee was being held the following week in Paris. Already, the city was filling up with important foreign leaders for strategic meetings and with citizens from all walks who had opinions to voice. It was an exciting moment to be in the city. Unlike other peace summits, leaders from small kingdoms, in some cases from remote areas, were invited to share insights into how they promoted peace. Including these new voices at the table had created excitement around the globe. I couldn't help think what good sports the Parisians were. The closed-off streets, the demonstrations, and the obligations that came with such an undertaking made me appreciate the simplicity of my small-town life.

When I finally arrived, Millie was already seated at an outdoor table with the coat check lady from the World Perfumery Conference, Olive Tidings. The two women both loved the spot for breakfast and had become fast friends over the last few days while enjoying their morning pastries. A stocky British woman, Olive wore skirted tweed suits every day. She was warm enough on even the chilliest occasions with no more than a matching fedora.

"*Bonjour,* Stella," my mom said with outstretched arms as I pulled up a chair.

We kissed on each cheek as if we were French. We both knew how silly we'd look with such formality back home, but we could not resist. In honor of the panel, Millie's fabulous red hair, a Wright trait that contrasts starkly with my dark, wild mane, was pulled into a soft updo. She wore a thick, navy sweater secured with big black buttons, high black boots, and bright red lipstick. She was a striking woman whose story-telling skills were even more enchanting. Her audience was in for a treat.

"Maybe it's because we're leaving later this afternoon," said my mother, "but the croissants are particularly delicious today. I ordered one for you."

"I couldn't agree more," said Olive wholeheartedly, over a bite of her own pastry. She waved at two men in business suits who returned a friendly greeting as they passed us. Through her job at the coat check room, Olive had seemingly met everyone.

"I think this week was a sign you need to travel more, Olive," said Millie with a speech I knew she liked to make to anyone she thought she might convert to her nomadic lifestyle. "I can see you like people and places too much to be cloistered in that school all the time. And people love you."

Millie and I found it endlessly fascinating that the conference's coat checker was actually a literature teacher from an all-girls boarding school in England. After twenty years of teaching, Olive was on sabbatical and had always dreamed of visiting Paris. After three days of rich, French foods, however, she'd realized she wasn't a lady of leisure. Noticing an ad in *Le Monde* about the conference, she'd applied for a job and landed one working at the coat check.

"I always say, greet people with a smile, or your day will be rubbish," Olive said. To prove her point, she smiled across the sea of customers at Café Bonne Chance, and nodded at one woman who caught her eye.

"To smiles," said Millie.

The ladies clinked their cups. I ordered an espresso and shared my morning's excursions as they peppered me with questions and enjoyed my photos. Finally, Olive looked at her watch.

"I'll say my good-byes to you," she said, rising from her chair. "And head off to make some others. I had a lovely time meeting you this week."

"I never say good-bye," said Millie. True, but after six months without coming home, I knew there were some folks back on Nantucket who felt they'd seen the last of her. "And remember what I said about travel. *Mi casa es su casa.*"

"Thank you," said Olive. "But be careful what you say. I have a lot of time on my hands."

We hugged and said our good-byes, and Olive Tidings took off ahead of us in thick-soled shoes.

"We should head over too," said Millie, after finishing her croissant.

Picking up her black bag, which contained perfume samples she planned to highlight during her presentation, Millie linked arms with me, and we headed to the last day of the World Perfumery Conference.

Three blocks later, the sliding doors of the conference hotel opened automatically. We entered the lobby, which was filled with people with rolling bags and name tags, all of them carrying folders of some sort or another. Posters lined the walls with advertisements for new perfumes. Some of the brands were familiar, mass-market products, and others were for the kinds of companies that catered to the industry— mixers, distributors, packagers. The heart of the conference was taking place down a long, wide corridor covered in a deep red carpet, off of which were meeting rooms, large and small.

I pulled out my phone and flipped it to video. I'd been making short, documentary-style clips of the trip all weekend, and this was the highlight I couldn't miss.

"How does it feel to be a scent-extractions expert?" I said to my mom. "Look at the camera."

"Hi." She waved.

I was about to ask her another question, but the lobby was crowded and noisy with people bumping into each other as they headed to their panels or meetings without so much as a "pardon." I decided I'd try again later at a better location.

My mom and I entered the conference's main area where people registered or met for impromptu meetings in one of several lounge areas. We headed to a map displayed against one wall which outlined the day's events, so that we could confirm how to get to her panel. While I located where the meeting was to take place, and where we could find a rest stop along the way, Millie opened her bag on a bench beside me and looked through her inventory one last time. She took out her vials, examined them carefully, and opened one or two. She was a perfectionist when it came to her work, and her black bag was like an on-the-go lab. Similar in size and shape to a doctor's bag, she'd had her prized accessory custom designed around the time I was born by a leather maker at the San Lorenzo market in Florence, Italy. That bag had been around so long, I sometimes wondered if it held some deeper meaning for her. Between my name, my wild mane of hair, and my Mediterranean complexion, I sometimes fancied as a child that I could be Italian. Millie, however, had always been quiet about my father's identity.

When I'd figured out the lay of the land, I turned on my phone's camera again.

"Let me get a video of you in front of the map," I said.

Millie gathered her belongings and struck a pose like Vanna White on *Wheel of Fortune*.

"Welcome to the World Perfumery Conference," she said to the camera, her arms gracefully directed to the map. "Here you will see—"

Her speech was interrupted by a collective cry from the far end of the conference's reception area. A woman screamed, a man yelled something in French, another person cried out in Japanese.

As panic grew like a wave among the crowd, my mind went immediately to the worst. Shootings. Terrorism. I heard others around me express the same fear, which made my blood run cold. My beautiful morning, and our excitement about the afternoon's panel, had suddenly been hijacked by chaos.

"What's going on?" my mom said.

"I'm not sure," I said. I considered that we should run for cover, as many around us were, but my instinct to fight usually wins over that of flight.

Suddenly, I saw a group of people forming by the Grand Ballroom. They were yelling and calling for help. Their circular formation suggested that a single person lay within their midst. In moments, the fear that had spread across the crowded lobby shifted to the sort of curiosity that accompanies drivers on a highway who want a glimpse of an accident. We were grateful it wasn't us, hopeful help would come quickly, and slightly morbid in our desire to see the scene unfold. My mom and I took a few steps forward.

"Probably a heart attack," she said.

"I hope the French paramedics are fast," I said.

"*Meurtre*," someone cried from the middle of the crowd.

My French is rudimentary at best, but there are words which, when said a certain way, and given the right context, can be universally understood. This was one of them.

"Did he say murder?" I said, but I did not need to wait for an answer.

The crowd in front of the Grand Ballroom parted. I saw a hand reach out, followed by a head. I watched as a man, about my age, crawled forward in my direction. Instinctively, I reached out my arms. He looked up for a moment and caught my eye, but he did not say a word.

In the moment our eyes met, I saw that he was neither handsome nor ugly, neither flashy nor shabby. He was average on every level. The sort of person who could fade into a crowd and even into a small gathering, except for one thing.

There was a knife sticking out of his back.

Chapter 2

Seeing a man collapse with a knife in his back had been so surreal, I would not have believed it had happened except for the frenzy that ensued. In an instant, the World Perfumery Conference ended. The gendarme rushed into the conference center and began to cordon off the room. I heard the sound of sirens and looked through the large paned windows of the hotel, where I saw the flashing lights of firetrucks, police cars, and ambulances. A man in a blue uniform began to bark loudly at all the bystanders. Immediately, we were herded like cattle into one of the hotel's empty ballrooms. Many of the unlucky witnesses to the crime rushed into the room offered to us, presumably to escape the scene.

I moved more slowly, as I was fascinated by the proceedings. I watched as officers, wearing a variety of uniforms, converged around the man's body and scattered across the hotel. Some spoke into walkie-talkies. Others traversed the building to relay information and give instructions. Although the scene looked chaotic, there was efficiency in the way the police, fire department, and emergency medical care teams worked.

At the door to the ballroom, I put my arm around my mother, who had been tugging me to move more quickly. I turned back and took one more look at the crime scene. My last image was of a man in a blue uniform, who passed us with a body bag.

I'd seen a murdered man before, last spring, but I'd never seen a man die.

The victim had made eye contact with me before his last breath. There had been a personal connection. I had seen the small knife, no bigger than a letter opener, moments after it had been thrust into his back. I felt sickened and angry that someone could do something so horrible to another human being.

"Dirty business," I heard a man to the left of me say, "but only a matter of time before something like this happened. There's a black market for new scents."

"It was a lovers' quarrel," someone to the right of me said.

"I saw him the other night. He worked in the kitchen," said someone behind me. "Must have been a disgruntled employee."

Dozens of other theories began to circulate among the crowd in languages familiar and unfamiliar to me. I watched as some onlookers cried, others took pictures, and still more spoke on their phones, looking annoyed, distressed, or sometimes excited. I recognized a couple of familiar faces from the week, but no one who we'd particularly befriended. I didn't think anyone looked guilty of murder, although experience had taught me that someone willing to commit murder could hide in plain sight.

While we were in lockdown, police officers circulated our group, checked bags, and asked every one of us for our identification. I was amazed, from the snippets I could hear, by how different everyone's perception of the scene had been. I listened as the victim was described as both young and old, and even, by one person, as a woman. An older lady not far from me claimed the murdered man was speaking Italian, which I was certain was untrue. A man with a mustache said he heard the victim mumbling incoherently to himself when he first stumbled into the crowd. Everyone spoke with certainty, but I realized that no one had seen the scene the same way.

After about forty minutes, it was our turn. I handed an officer our passports, because Millie had mostly lost the ability to speak. Clutching her black bag on her lap, she had seated herself on a folding chair from the moment we'd entered the room.

I confess, her reaction surprised me. Very little flusters my mom. Until that moment, the list had only included cats. The woman was like Indiana Jones, running around the world in search of adventure. A cat, however, terrified her. Legend had it that my old great aunt, Frances, had had a terror of a cat when my mom was growing up. The poor creature was sickly and grumpy and hissed at everyone, but my mom had taken it personally. Now, I added murdered bodies to her list. I was grateful for involuntary muscles, because I don't think she would have breathed without them.

"Open your bags, please," said the officer after he'd checked our passports.

Reluctantly, Millie opened her bag. The man gave a cursory look inside.

"Did you see anyone suspicious at the conference today?" he said, finally getting down to business. His notepad was out, but I could tell he wasn't expecting anything particularly informative from an American woman and her distressed mother.

"No," I said. "My mother was on her way to speak at a panel. I wish I'd noticed something that could help you. All I can offer is that I thought the victim's behavior was the most interesting."

"Why do you think so?" he said, not looking up from his pad as he scribbled down yet another well-intentioned statement.

"The man didn't utter a word before his death," I said. "He made no accusations. We were all surrounding him, but he did not point a finger or share a clue."

"Perhaps having a knife in his back distracted him," said the policeman. "Had you seen the man before today?"

"No, we hadn't," I said.

"Thank you," said the officer. "Does your mother need medical assistance? We have medics on hand."

"I'm fine," said my mother, recovering her voice.

The officer nodded to her and handed me a business card before moving on.

I toyed with getting my mom help but knew she wouldn't accept it, so we both waited to be released. I tried to make small talk, but she needed silence. The waiting made me antsy. The only thing I wanted to do was slip out of the room and back to the conference area in hopes of seeing something that could help me understand how and why the attack had happened. After a few minutes, I told the guard at the door that I was claustrophobic and needed to leave the room for a few minutes. He told me to sit down. A few minutes later, I tried a jail break when he coughed, but came face-to-face with a new officer joining the room who blocked my exit. Even my appeal to use the bathroom failed, as there was a luxurious powder room in a cordoned off hallway that was nowhere near the crime scene.

After an hour with no success, everyone was finally released. During the perfumers' mass exodus, I tried to catch at least one glimpse of the crime scene. The area in front of the Grand Ballroom, however, was now tented and covered as officials entered and exited.

Stepping through the hotel's sliding doors, we left one world and entered another. The fresh air was a relief, but on both sides of the hotel's doors the press had formed behind barriers. They took photos and called out questions as we passed, in hopes that someone would answer them. Some did.

My mom and I avoided the paparazzi and headed to our small hotel, four blocks away, by foot. Although she was still quiet, I was glad she embraced the walk, and I took it as a good sign. Thankfully we'd already packed our suitcases, because we needed to hustle to the airport for our flight home. Honestly, I was so grateful to the concierge for making sure a cab was waiting for us out front when we left, that I gave him every euro I could spare in thanks. I promised the same to the taxi driver if he could get us to the airport in time.

We quickly learned, however, that his task would not be so easy. I picked up some French curses from our driver as I realized that the unexpected ending to our trip to Paris would have one more act. We had only gotten as far as the Tenth Arrondissement when we found ourselves in the most unique traffic jam I'd ever experienced.

"Look at that," I said to Millie as I stared out the taxi's window.

A caravan for the Peace Jubilee featuring a man on an elephant, both of them bejeweled in equally regal attire and flanked by flag-baring officials on horseback, held up several blocks in every direction. I was not familiar with their purple and blue flag, but that was one of the wonderful things about the upcoming summit. Nations small and large had a seat at the table. I considered that in a short span of time, I had encountered the darkest act of violence at the conference and the brightest commitment to friendship from my taxi.

Although I was fascinated by the parade, we had nonrefundable tickets and we couldn't miss our flight.

"One, two three." I counted to keep my cool.

As you can imagine, we barely made it to our gate in time. We had no bags to check, but the security line was slow and our gate seemed like a mile away. Millie and I are not cut out for marathon running, and we were sweaty messes by the time we reached our seats.

Once aboard our plane, my mom and I mostly stared at the flight maps on the seats in front of us, lost in thought. I tried not to think about the murder. Sure, I wondered why the man was murdered, who had done it, and how someone had been able to stick a knife into his back without a witness. I wanted to look up details of the unfolding story, but, more importantly, I didn't want to upset Millie all over again. My mother still clung tightly to her black bag for comfort, sometimes as if it were a baby, other times as if she were the baby and it was her security blanket.

Without the news to distract me, I thought about

the fantastic sites, scents, and tastes I had experienced over the last three days. I was also finally able to appreciate the elephant parade we'd witnessed when we'd left town. Having been in the city as it prepared for the Peace Jubilee, I realized I had a special connection to the upcoming event. I looked forward to following its progress, and hoped it went well. There was something so magical about the prospect of many hands reaching out in peace.

When we landed in Boston, a stoic Millie and I resumed our marathon efforts to another gate in order to take a small plane over to Nantucket.

"Feel any better?" I said to my mom when we settled into a row of seats at the gate, where the other passengers were mostly powering up their phones and laptops before boarding. "We're an ocean away from murder."

"Absolutely," she said.

We smiled at each other, but I knew we were both pretending. That's when I decided enough was enough. We'd had an amazing trip and a long-awaited reunion. I was not going to let the final moments of our visit, however gruesome, negate the experience we'd had.

I stood up, and lifted both my bag and Millie's.

"Come on. Let's take the ferry home," I said to her. "We need the sea air."

"You're a genius," said my mom, joining me with a renewed spring to her step as we headed away from our gate to find a flight to Hyannis, on the Cape.

As a kid, whenever we had big decisions to make, or when we simply were low on cash but needed a "vacation," we'd sometimes take the Nantucket ferry to the Cape, round trip. The journey across the ocean and back was always a transformative experience for both of us. For less than forty bucks each, the salty sea breeze had the magical effect of clearing our heads, the lapping of the waves against the boat's hull washed our cares away, and the sounds of the motor, the dogs, and the idle chitchat of folks became its own soothing music.

Excited by this new plan, we changed our flight's destination to the Cape, where the Steamship Authority was only a few minutes away. It was amazing to me that due to the time change we were able to make an early evening ferry. The moment I stepped aboard, I felt as if Nantucket was waiting for us with open arms. The sky was still light, and seagulls flew above us as the ferry's deep horn signaled our departure. We climbed to the open deck up top, and after a few minutes we began to genuinely relax. I knew we were going to be fine when my mom smoothed her hair and nodded across the deck with a smile.

I followed her gaze to see a man about her age in a blue windbreaker and a plaid cap. My adrenaline must still have been running high, because he looked to me like the kindest man I'd ever seen. He tipped his hat by way of a greeting.

"I know him," said Millie.

"Really?" I said with a smile and a peck to her cheek. "Have some fun. I'm going to grab a coffee."

I spent the rest of the hour-long ferry ride inside. I was happy that my mother was enjoying herself above, plus I was finally able to learn more about the Paris murder. I poured through the coverage of the event that had taken center stage in the world news.

Immediately, I noticed the headlines, which stated

that the murderer was someone named Rex Laruam. I clicked on one story to get the details.

Officials in Paris have confirmed that the killer of an American government official at the World Perfumery Conference in Paris on Wednesday was Rex Laruam. Known as the King of Shadows, Laruam is an anarchist behind many attacks against global peace that have taken place in the last decade.

A US government source, who asked for anonymity, said that Laruam went to the World Perfumery Conference to intercept classified documents on a flash drive, which were being transferred between French and US agents. These documents are related to the upcoming Peace Jubilee in Paris. Laruam is still at large, but the documents were recovered, and are now believed to be in Morocco under tight global security.

I couldn't believe it. Both the violent murder and the beautiful parade I had witnessed in Paris only hours ago had been opposite sides of the same coin. I looked at the horizon for a comforting glimpse of Nantucket's skyline. Seeing only the sea before me, I returned to the news story.

The files Laruam was seeking allegedly pertain to the arrival of a queen from a remote kingdom in the South Pacific, whose identity, known to only a few organizers, is being protected until the Peace Jubilee. The kingdom's participation at the Jubilee has been considered an important symbol of global unity because their people have never engaged in war. Scientists and psychologists are also fascinated by the fact that their

*people live to be a hundred years old, on average. They
live humbly, but there's no poverty among the citizens.
The documents Laruam was seeking detailed locations
of the queen's passage to Paris, specifically where security
is stationed along the way. The security team is thought
to include a handful of American agents.*

I went on to read that the small nation rarely engaged with the outside world. Immediately, I understood the significance of that fact. If anything went
wrong while they were at the Jubilee, they'd probably
never reach out to the "modern" world again. Meanwhile, those who had supported an effort at global
peace would look ineffectual. That was a scenario
which would have made some factions, like the Rex
Laruams of the world, quite happy to see play out.

I was wondering why the documents had ended
up at the World Perfumery Conference, but the
press seemed more interested in why such important
documents had been stored on a flash drive. This old-
fashioned approach to security seemed to catch the
imagination of the press as much as Laruam did. I
had to agree that the strategy seemed unusually risky,
especially since I had seen the outcome firsthand.

Suddenly, I felt the ferry shift into a lower speed,
which signified that we would soon reach Nantucket.
Sure enough, I looked up to see the white bell tower
of the tallest building in town, the First Congregational Church. As we passed the jetties of the town
beach, I made my way to the upper deck to find my
mom and her friend in deep conversation, their
heads bent easily toward each other as they laughed
over something she said.

I approached with a smile to match theirs.

"Stella, this is Nathaniel Dinks. He was two years ahead of me in high school," said my mother.

"I recognized her immediately from across the deck," said Nathaniel, shaking my hand.

"Nathaniel's here for Frank Marshall's birthday celebration," she said. "We were all in high school together."

"I know about the event!" I said. "My best friend, Emily, is a party planner. She was hired to organize the celebration. Tomorrow until Saturday, right?"

Frank Marshall's three-day reunion birthday was Emily's first job since she'd had her daughter four months ago. Frank lived part-time in Boston and part-time in Nantucket, after he had become a huge success running a business solutions company. He and Emily had planned a great list of activities for the event. I knew Frank was flying to Nantucket tomorrow on his private jet. All of the guests except for Nathaniel, and another man named Leonard Bartow, still lived on the island.

"I haven't seen the gang in maybe twenty years," said Nathaniel, "but we text during college basketball season and stuff like that. My wife died last year, so I was really touched to get the invite."

"I'm sorry about your wife," said Millie. I nodded, sympathetically, along with her.

"Well, Frank's a good guy to get me back here," said Nathaniel. "I'm thinking it's a sign I should move back home. I miss fishing. Maybe the fire department can use me as a volunteer."

My mom flashed me the slightest look, which I immediately recognized. She liked this man of action. I was delighted. The idea of her settling down on

Nantucket had never occurred to me, but here was someone who might entice her to stay.

"Since Frank's party starts tomorrow, why not join us for dinner tonight?" I said.

"We'll have a party," said Millie, brightly.

Mission accomplished. The ferry had definitely unleashed the old Millie I knew. There's nothing like several hours of travel and a party, but I was game.

"I'd love that," he said, looking surprised and pleased.

As the ferry rounded Brant Point at the entrance to the harbor, the passengers on board and a few beachgoers on the shore waved to each other. I looked over the railing and across the waters at a large sailboat moored in the harbor. A woman was on the deck, looking at our band of arrivals through binoculars, and I was happy to be returning to an island where something as simple as a ferry's arrival was still exciting.

When the deck hands finally tied the ferry to the docks, I immediately spotted Peter waiting for me. I sped down the gangplank ahead of Millie and Nathaniel to give him a heartfelt hug and kiss.

"I've caught up on all the news," I said, enjoying his warm embrace. "Fair warning, I'm sure I'll be puzzling over the Paris murder for weeks."

"You're a reporter's dream girl," he said, tugging me closer to him.

"I take that as the highest of compliments from you," I said since Peter is a reporter for the local newspaper, the *Inquirer & Mirror*. "Also, we're having a party tonight."

"Awesome," said Peter without hesitation. "I'll make my famous cheese spaghetti."

"I'll bring wine," said Nathaniel, arriving beside us with a small wheelie suitcase.

"I'll drink it," said my mom, looking ready for some fun after our long trip home.

I beamed when Peter hugged my mom and kindly shook hands with Nathaniel. As Peter tossed our bags into his trunk, I opened the passenger door, happy to see he hadn't forgotten my special request. To my delight, I was attacked by a furry monster.

"Tinker," I said to my cat, who purred and climbed all over me as if he had thought he was never going to see me again.

My mom muffled a scream, and not too tactfully.

"Don't worry," I said to her. "Peter brought Tinker for a reason. I wanted to give Tinker a quick hello before he heads over to the Wick & Flame, where he will be sleeping during your visit."

"Millie, I'll drive you and the bags over to Stella's," said Peter.

"And I'll drop Tinker at the store and be right behind you," I said.

"That's a great plan," said Millie, handing her black bag to me. "And while you're at it, can you put my perfume samples from the Amazon in the safe? After Paris, I'm feeling superstitious."

"What did we do without Amazon?" said Nathaniel with a look of appreciation for the retail behemoth.

"No, *the* Amazon," said Millie with a giggle. "They're from a trip I took. I'll tell you all about it tonight."

My mom got in the car with Peter and threw air kisses to both of us, while Nathaniel and I headed down the red-brick sidewalks of town. Nathaniel secured Millie's bag on top of his so that I could hold Tinker.

"I feel like we've been away forever, but it was only a few days," I said. "The difference between our cobblestone streets and Paris's grand boulevards is really striking."

"But it was Nantucket's whalers who supplied the oils that lit Paris's street lamps, once upon a time," said Nathaniel.

All of us who've grown up on Nantucket have some pride in that fact. When you grow up in a town like ours, which has a sailor's map showing the distance from its location on Main Street to places around the world, you value these things.

"Twenty years since I was last here, but the Jared looks exactly the same," said Nathaniel as we reached the hotel on the corner of Centre Street. The Jared Coffin House is a historic red-brick mansion built by Mr. Coffin, who was a ship owner during the island's prime whaling days. These days, there are dozens of mansions on Nantucket, but his was one of the first.

"Thanks again for the invitation tonight," Nathaniel said, nodding a greeting to a bellman who approached. "It's my lucky day. Millie was one of the prettiest girls in school when I was there."

He turned to me and rubbed Tinker's back.

"She still is," I said with a smile.

"Yes, she is," he said.

I looked behind Nathaniel for our bags, but they were in the hands of the bellhop who was heading up the stairs.

"Sir?" I said to the retreating bellhop.

He continued up the stairs without seeming to hear me.

"Sir?" I said, reaching him. "You have my bag. I'd be in a lot of trouble if I lost it."

"Excuse the confusion," said the man, all business, and already at the entrance to the hotel.

"Got it!" I said to Nathaniel as I headed back down the stairs.

"Perfect," he said. "See you tonight?"

"Looking forward to it," I said, as I continued down the block.

At the other end of Centre Street was my store, the Wick & Flame. I could make out my small storefront with its paned-glass window, homey and welcoming. Once outside, I paused to appreciate my store. Humble in comparison to those I'd visited in Paris, its white walls were covered in shelves, and were filled with different colored and scented products. I smiled with pride.

I waved at a woman behind the counter inside, who looked a bit like a bee dressed in black pants and a yellow, hand-made sweater she'd knitted. Cherry Waddle. A local resident who is also a loyal student of my candle-making classes, I'd entrusted my store to Cherry while I was away.

I always keep a different candle lit on my counter to highlight a new product. When I entered, I noticed that Citrus Lime was featured today.

"Welcome home!" said Cherry. She came toward me with a huge hug.

I hugged her back, feeling like we hadn't seen each other in years, as Tinker sprang from my arms in order to keep from being crushed between us.

"The pink window display I came up with has been a hit," Cherry said, motioning toward my front window. I'd left the store filled with autumn hues, but Cherry had had her own ideas. "What do you think?"

"Very creative," I said.

"I have some other thoughts," she began, and dove right into a full update about her sales and my stock and a few new ideas she had for the store.

As she spoke, I put Millie's bag into a safe we'd had since I was a kid. These days, it sat behind my register, covered by a blue, block print tapestry. I used the old metal container as my deposit box when I didn't have time to go to the bank, and also as a table for my tea stand. When my job was done, I poured a cup of tea and lingered as Cherry continued to fill me in on my days away. I had an ulterior motive for taking my time. I wanted Peter and my mom to get to know each other at home, without me hovering around them.

By the time I left Tinker in Cherry's care, I was feeling very clever about my plan at home. I also, however, had the strangest feeling that someone was watching me. Living with a cat gives you that kind of sixth sense. I turned back to the store to see Cherry smiling and talking to Tinker as she closed up for the evening. Then a police car pulled up beside me with its lights flashing.

Chapter 3

"Want a ride home?" said Officer Andy Southerland, one of Nantucket's finest, and one of my oldest friends.

"Perfect timing," I said, appreciating his offer as I jumped into his car. "I have such good stuff for you."

"A little Eiffel Tower Christmas ornament?" he said with a brotherly punch on my shoulder.

"No," I said. "Better. A murder case."

"I heard," he said. "I'm surprised you didn't stay there to find the killer."

"There are things like civilians not getting involved in murders," I said, quoting a lecture he'd given me last spring, after I'd helped him solve a case.

Then I showered him with a detailed description of our last moments in Paris as he drove out of town and toward home.

I could tell by the way Andy playfully lifted the side of his mouth that he was not listening to my version of the story as an officer of the law. Rather, he was enjoying my storytelling skills, which I'd argue were appropriately detailed, without an overkill of suppositions. He had a question for me here and there, too, so I knew I'd gotten his attention.

"I wonder why the hand-off was at a perfume conference," I said.

"Maybe because it was a big crowd," said Andy, thoughtfully. "It might have been easy to do business."

"Do you think you could find out?"

"Nope," said Andy, turning the steering wheel. "We need to let the pros do their job, my friend. Nantucket is far away from Paris, Morocco, and Rex Laruam. I'm happy with that. Mostly because that means I won't have to worry about you getting into trouble."

"Bah," I said as we pulled up to my place. "You worry too much. We're having a party tonight. You and Georgianna should come."

"I wish we could. I'd love to see Millie, but I'm on duty," he said. "And Georgianna's got a juicing class. It's her new thing."

"I'm glad to know that if you ever marry her, you'll be regular forever," I said, closing the door and waving as he pulled away.

In contrast to the excitement of my close encounter with global espionage and exotic kingdoms, I headed to *Leftovers*, my aptly named home, which is an apartment above the garage at my cousin Chris's house. Nantucket homes often have names advertised on quarter boards above their front doors, and *Leftovers* suited my place perfectly. I'd been living there since I came home from college. I didn't plan to stay there forever, but eight years later, I was still here. Aside from a paint job and some knickknacks I'd picked up at the Hospital Thrift Shop on India Street, which is known for great finds, I hadn't done much to the place. My decorating efforts went into the Wick & Flame instead. In the meantime, I had the good company of Chris, his wife, and their two young sons right across the yard.

I walked upstairs to the comforting sounds of Peter and my mother.

"Peter and I think it's silly that you don't want a birthday party," my mom said as I arrived on the landing to my apartment. "In three days, it will be Saturday, and you'll be thirty. If that's not a perfect combination for a party, I don't know what is. You're only thirty once, you know."

"You say that every year," I said, carrying my small suitcase to my room.

"And every year it's true," she said when I returned. "Case in point, you'll never be twelve again. Or fifteen. You should celebrate. We won't get you a cake, but we're all going to make toasts at the party tonight."

"That seems like a fair compromise," I said, trying to look like I had no idea that they were all planning a surprise party for me on my actual birthday. I hadn't solved a crime once before without picking up some skills. In spite of many hushed whispers and misdirects among my friends and family, I'd figured out before I'd left for Paris that there was something in the works. I will give the gang credit, however. They had not tipped their hand on where the party would be held. My guess was Chris's backyard. He threw a great barbeque, and everyone knew I was hooked on his burgers.

Meanwhile, Millie and Peter's conspiratorial smiles would be worth a few extra toasts at dinner tonight. And as Peter left to buy the American cheese, spaghetti, and milk he'd need for his favorite dish, my mom gave me a devilish look.

"He only moved to Nantucket in May," I said, too casually. "Let's see if he can make it through the February Blahs."

I know that people from the mainland can struggle with the isolation of island life. I've had my heart bruised in the past because of it. Peter Bailey was a free-spirited guy. It was something I loved about him, but I wanted to make sure he was really satisfied with a life writing for a local paper on a small island. Truth be told, I was also not entirely sure I was ready for anything much more serious than what we had. Emily said I was crazy, but she was home with her four-month-old daughter, and I've noticed over the years that people like to lure others to their side once they've transitioned to marriage and parenthood.

"He may surprise you," said my mom as she headed to the shower and I started to prepare for our party. I hated how she could sometimes read my mind.

I didn't have much time to dwell on my relationship, however. An hour later, at least a dozen hands were passing plates of cheese spaghetti and other potluck delights across my small living room. Emily arrived with her husband, and beelined over to Nathaniel Dinks and another man he'd introduced to us as Lennie Bartow. I noticed right away that Lennie lacked Nathaniel's cheerful demeanor. Although they had been in the same high school class, he looked older, and definitely more intense.

"Look at us, Lennie," I heard Nathaniel say. "We're just a couple of guys on the town."

"As long as we get home early," Lennie said, walking

with a limp to my improvised buffet. "I have a couple of business calls to make."

Life of the party. Ten minutes later, I found Lennie in my bedroom, on one of his calls. I hoped for Emily's sake that the rest of Frank Marshall's guests would be easier to entertain.

Chris, my cousin, had arrived with his two boys and, to our surprise, two extra guests. Chris was a mess when he walked through my door. He had the boys to himself for the weekend while his wife was at a college reunion. The few wisps of hair he had left on his head were already sticking up in different directions.

"Stella, please meet Laura and John Pierre Morton." Chris gestured to the couple beside him. "They are staying with us for the next three days. Our first Airbnb guests. They booked this morning."

I knew that Chris and his wife had recently decided to try their hand at Airbnb to make some extra money, but I decided that Chris had confirmed the booking before he'd thought it through. Now, he was playing innkeeper during his already busy weekend with the boys. I realized that a free meal at my place with no dishes to clean was his idea of heaven tonight.

"It's a treat to be Chris's first customers," said Laura, "and for us to be invited to your party."

"I agree," said John Pierre with a friendly smile.

"Are you French?" I said, detecting a faint accent.

"What are the chances?" said Millie, coming to my side with two glasses of chardonnay, which she handed to the couple. "We were just in Paris."

"We're from Canada. Outside of Quebec," Laura said as Millie launched into a full description of our trip.

Laura listened, kindly. I admired her lavender duster which covered a flower-print dress. She was probably in her early forties, but her outfit, topped with a small dragonfly hair clip on one side, gave her the timeless elegance of having stepped out of a painting. John Pierre, beside her, wore a blue-checked shirt and jeans. There was a touch of high-low glamour to the couple, and I could see why Millie was drawn to them.

By eight o'clock, my home was filled with great friends and more Wrights than I could count.

"Poor Lennie," Millie said to me as we refilled the cheese tray. "He's aged a lot. I'd never have recognized him, but he's still the same sweet soul."

"I don't remember you ever mentioning these guys," I said.

"They were older," she said. "Not in my gang. By the way, you'll need to keep your backroom free at the Wick & Flame tomorrow morning."

"She's invited me and some others to hear the presentation about the Amazon that she was going to give in Paris," said Cherry, coming to our side to inspect the refills.

One thing I loved about my mom. She might not be around much, but when she was home, she jumped right back into the swing of things. While Cherry reviewed a list of friends she planned to invite to Millie's lecture, I looked across the room at Peter. He was balancing an orange on his nose for the amusement of Chris's boys.

"That man's smitten with you," Cherry said to me with an all-knowing look. "I wouldn't be surprised if he popped the question sometime soon."

"Stop, Cherry," I said, willing myself not to blush.

Fortunately, I was saved by the bell. My doorbell.

I scanned the room, felt that everyone invited was accounted for, and then took the steps down to my front door.

"We need more wine over here!" I heard someone say.

I opened the door. Before me stood Olive Tidings.

"I know," she said. "Surprise!"

"Come in," I said, forgoing the double kisses to each cheek and throwing my arms around our friend.

"Don't worry," she said, hugging me back. "I'm not a stalker. But Paris lost its luster after I found myself at a conference with a murdered man. I remembered your mother's suggestion that I go somewhere new, and that your *casa* was my *casa*, so I bit the so-called bullet and caught a flight here. I'm staying at the Jared Coffin House in town. It's just up my alley. Historic. Like me. And you don't have to babysit me. I'm here for a few days, then off to Boston."

"Are you kidding?" I said. "This is the most wonderful surprise. Come in!"

"Olive! Is it really you?" said my mom from above as we headed up the stairs. "What a wonderful surprise. Everyone, meet our dear friend from our trip to Paris."

The crowd raised a glass in cheer at our newest arrival, and the party continued with various toasts of "Welcome Home!" and "Happy Birthday" all night. It was after eleven by the time the crowd dispersed. Chris brought all the newcomers in our group to see his home on the way out. He's a contractor and had renovated his old house to perfection. He was understandably very proud of his work.

"If you're thinking of moving back, Nathaniel, I have a property you should look at," Chris said as they headed out my door. "The owners suspended work halfway through construction, and I wouldn't be surprised if they sell."

"Leave him alone," Millie called after them. "You'll scare him away."

"I don't think so," said Lennie.

Emily was the last to go, and Peter offered to drive her home since her husband had left earlier to relieve the babysitter. When I shut the door behind them, my mom and I fell onto my double-sized mattress. A few minutes later, she was snoring, her body stretched diagonally, and I was thinking from my two inches of bed space that Tinker was living like a king at my store in comparison.

Sitting up, I texted Peter to see if he was still awake. There was no answer. Sleep, however, still eluded me, and after a few more minutes of tossing and turning, I got up and headed to my sofa. That solution was no better, because my back was stiff from the airplane and now the cushions felt too soft. Finally, I scribbled a note to my mom, and tiptoed down the stairs with my coat and car keys. There was a comfy chair in my workroom at the Wick & Flame. A few hours of sleep there would be better than a sliver of mattress and stereophonic snoring.

When the wheels of my bright red Beetle hit the cobblestones of Main Street, they sounded like bombs going off in the otherwise silent town. Fortunately, the population on Main Street at this hour was zero, so I didn't feel too badly. Turning the corner onto Centre Street, I parked in front of my store. As I approached, the moonlight lit my breath in the cold night air. Fall was upon us.

I hadn't taken more than one step inside the Wick & Flame when I noticed the mess. Tinker, evidently, had disliked his lodgings. My candle displays had been knocked over, his water bowl spilled, and some receipts on my counter were now on the floor. Across the room, I saw his shining, green-saucer eyes staring at me.

"Bad boy," I said to him in a whisper.

Tinker swished his tail across the floor. He casually walked over to me as if the scene was my fault. I supposed it was. I'd never left him overnight at the Wick & Flame. Lesson learned. He circled my feet in what I decided was his apology. I picked him up, appreciating his warmth, and decided not to worry about the mess tonight.

Carrying Tinker into my workroom, I settled into my comfy chair with a blanket and Tinker to keep me warm. Immediately, I started to drift to sleep. My dreams were starting to take hold of me when something urged me to wake. I tried to pat Tinker, thinking he had nudged me. A moment later, I stirred again. There was no doubt about it. I heard the bell over my door jingle slightly, and then stop.

Chapter 4

I opened my eyes in the dark room.

I listened, but heard nothing. Maybe something. I couldn't be sure. Gathering my courage, I rose, and with Tinker beside me, tiptoed toward the closed door that separated us from the shop. I knelt and looked through the keyhole. I could not see anything moving, so I stood, turned the knob, and opened the door about an inch.

The room was untidy, as I'd left it, but empty.

Flicking on my light switch, I went to my front door. To my surprise, it was unlocked. It was highly unusual for me to forget to lock the door, but I'd been admittedly distracted by Tinker and his mess when I'd arrived. Maybe I'd forgotten? It was possible, but not something I'd ever done before. Sizing up the room, I didn't think anything had been taken, although it was a little hard to tell. I now regretted not putting the room back in order before I'd gone to sleep.

In an effort to keep my imagination from getting the better of me, I tapped a Frank Sinatra playlist on my phone and let the big band sounds of "Come Fly with Me" brighten the mood.

"Tinker, between the travel, the murder, and the non-stop movement of being in Millie Wright's company over the last few days, I've let my imagination get the best of me." I fished out a pile of receipts that had slipped under my cash register.

Tinker was indulging my cleaning mission by sitting upright on my counter and watching my every move. When "Fly Me to the Moon" began to play, he padded over to my store's window, and I followed. I smiled at my window display, filled with Cherry's pink candles, including a bright pink, lacquered candelabra I'd purchased at Bookworks, the bookstore on Broad Street, nearby. I was straightening one of its candles when I saw movement across the street. At first I thought it might be a tree, rustling in the wind, but something made me take a second look. Tinker stopped licking his paws.

"Did you see that?"

He responded by pointing his ears and twitching his whiskers in the same direction of the shadowy human form I was now sure I'd seen across the street. I searched the sidewalk again, but the figure had disappeared.

"Tell me you made this mess, and not an intruder," I said to Tinker.

My cat looked back, noncommittally.

I tried to forget the incident as I continued to tidy up, but I could not ignore the fact that I'd perhaps left my door open for a petty thief to enter my store. I could not find anything missing, so I was wary of calling the police, but it was highly unusual for someone to be creeping around town at this time of night. After a few more minutes of debate, I decided to at least report what had happened. If there was a petty thief around town, the police should know. When a car pulled up in front of my store a few minutes later, I was happy that Andy was on duty.

"You OK?" he said, scanning the mess with laser-like precision when I opened the door for him.

"Nothing was taken," I said. "I don't think. I have to be honest. Tinker made the mess."

Andy looked at me funny.

"What happened?" he said.

I told him.

"How're you doing?" he said when I'd finished.

"What do you mean?"

"It's just, you saw someone get murdered."

I crossed my arms and threw him a look. Tinker, who was between us, curled into a tight ball.

"Out," I said.

"You said it yourself," he said as I hustled him to the door. "Nothing was taken, and Tinker made the mess. I know Millie snores, but maybe you need some sleep."

"Out," I said again. For my tenth birthday, I'd had a campout, and Millie had snored all night to our endless amusement, but right now it irritated me that he remembered.

"OK, OK," he said, half out the door.

"If I'm dead in the morning, you'll be sorry," I said, and closed the door.

"Go home," he said through the window.

Outside, Andy turned on his flashlight and looked up and down the street. He might have given me a hard time, but Andy was a serious officer who would never leave a stone unturned if someone might be in trouble. He walked the full length of the block and back, then knocked on my door. I opened it a smidge.

"No sign of anyone," he said.

"Thanks."

He turned off his flashlight and got back into his car. I suddenly felt bone tired. If a thief wanted to take the thirty-seven dollars in my cash register, he could have it. Turning the lock and switching off the lights, I headed to the backroom and fell asleep in my chair, hugging Tinker to me.

I slept soundly until the sunlight hit me from the room's window, and I heard knocking on my store's door. Rubbing the sleep from my eyes, I walked to the door, happy I'd cleaned up last night. My mom stood outside with Chris's Airbnb guests, John Pierre and Laura Morton. In true Millie form, she'd already made new friends.

"Clothes," she said when I let them in. She handed me an outfit she'd picked out and started to unfold chairs I keep in my backroom. "Please do something about this cat. My panel starts in half an hour."

"Your store is beautiful," said Laura. "And we can't wait to hear your mother's lecture."

"Thanks," I said, depositing Tinker into the small bathroom off my workroom where I knew he'd be happy to take a nap. Everyone looked so content, I decided not to mention last night's incident.

"Your place is great," said John Pierre, scanning every inch of the store. I was delighted to see him inhale each scent with genuine pleasure, and even happier when Millie joined him in doing so. I knew she was pleased to find a few candles that were derived from her perfumes. In fact, I was hoping to collaborate with her on a few more products while she was in town. She was more than happy to have retired from retail, but she loved a good project.

By the time I'd finished dressing and was describing my method of wicking a candle to Laura, there was another knock on the door. I turned to see Cherry, along with a couple of her friends who were also my best candle-making students. They like to call themselves the Candleers, a name I loved so much, I had plans to add a candle with that name to my product line—something with rose and lilac. Rounding out the crowd was Nathaniel, his friend, Lennie Bartow, and Olive Tidings.

As Millie's guests piled into my store, she knelt by our safe.

"That's very antiquated security you have," said Olive, peering over her. "World War Two stuff, I'd imagine."

"It sounds like you have some rare products from the Amazon, Millie," said Laura. "Perhaps you should have more protection."

"Only Stella and I have the code," said Millie, pulling the safe's iron handle and opening its door. "I don't think we'll have any troubles on Nantucket."

"If I'm helping out at the store, perhaps I should have the combination too," said Cherry.

"Stella, can you remove samples four through seven and pass them around for our guests to enjoy?" Millie said as she ushered people into the backroom.

"I'd take the safe's combination with me to the grave," said Cherry as she passed me, looking somewhat disappointed to be left out of any component of the Wick & Flame.

"Gather round, everyone. Welcome to an overview of the sophisticated ways in which scent extractions have developed, courtesy of the brilliant scientists I met in the Amazon," Millie said.

Our guests all took seats and applauded, although I'm not sure any of us really knew exactly what "scent extractions" were. Meanwhile, I passed the vials numbered four, five, six, and seven around the room for everyone to smell.

"Did you know that the rainforest," she began, "shelters almost nine-tenths of all forms of known and unknown life?"

We all shook our heads and murmured appreciative remarks.

"As such, it is home to biological treasures that deserve to be treated with the utmost care," she said, as if beginning a fairy tale. "These treasures also include those on the olfactory level."

Cherry's hand shot up. "What does that mean?" she said without waiting to be called upon.

"It means that there are a host of novel and extraordinary scents to be uncovered in the rainforest. And for years, scientists have searched for new, attractive aromas. In my discussion, I will reveal some of the ways that scientists are using methods to capture these scents. For example, a single flower can be placed in a glass vessel of adapted size and shape without damaging the flower. The scented air surrounding the flower is then drawn through the adsorption trap by means of a pump."

The crowd was hooked. As Millie spoke about her fascinating trek into the rainforest, particularly of the day she watched a small blimp with a large version of the pump she'd described descend upon an area of unique fauna, each and every person in my workroom soaked in her speech as if they were privy to highly classified information and a fascinating tale wrapped in one.

I slipped away when I heard a knock on my door and spied Emily. Six older gentlemen stood behind her, peeking over her shoulder. I turned my sign to OPEN and let them in. The quiet of the crowd in my workroom was immediately replaced by their boisterous greetings. I noticed they sent a few sloppy waves and giggles toward Nathaniel and Lennie.

"Thanks," Emily said to me. "Frank Marshall and his pals. They met Frank at his private jet after a few morning Bloody Marys. I told them Lennie and Nathaniel were here. I have a van out front to take them to golf."

"Boys," I heard Millie say, "you should tend to your friends."

I turned to see Nathaniel and Lennie quietly slip out of her presentation, and then I closed the workroom door so the guys could greet each other. As they warmly embraced and chided each other for being unrecognizable in their old age, Peter arrived at my door with a pencil and a pad of paper sticking out of his shirt pocket. The man is always ready for a good story.

"Am I missing something?" he said, poking his head inside.

"A Nantucket High School reunion, and my mom's lecture on Amazonian extractions," I said. "She's today's featured guest at the Wick & Flame."

I rang up a votive candle for the birthday boy. Then, I moved on to help a woman who had entered the store behind Peter. I've noticed that when a few people are browsing the store, my foot traffic grows exponentially. In my early days, I would ask my family to visit over the course of the day to keep the Wick & Flame looking crowded until the news of my business spread.

I sometimes wondered if people caught on to the fact that my clientele was mostly red haired, but their help did the trick.

"Do you have time to do something fun today? Maybe a ride on your boat?" I said to Peter, but then I realized the woman I'd been helping had left the store without taking her change.

Before Peter could answer, I popped out of my front door to call after her.

The woman was walking quickly, but I followed her. I had her five dollars and twenty cents in my hand. As I rounded the corner, I saw her stop in front of my favorite coffee shop, The Bean. She was on her phone and looking at the ground as she spoke, so she did not see me. She had black hair, pulled through a gray baseball cap, and was wearing black leggings and a black windbreaker. Nothing special, but there was something familiar about her that I had missed in my busy store. As I approached, I realized she was the woman I had seen looking through binoculars from her boat while I was on the ferry yesterday.

Although I got closer, she kept her back to me.

"The operation is on track," I heard her say. "Mission accomplished. There were unanticipated obstacles during recovery, so I will make sure the site is sanitized before I exfiltrate."

Before I could tap her on the shoulder, my coat landed on mine. I turned around to see Peter.

"Whatcha doing?" he said.

"Did you hear that?" I said.

I turned back around, but the woman was gone.

Chapter 5

The combination of the woman's quick departure from my store and her phone conversation intrigued me.

"How about a walk?" I said, and headed down the street at a brisk pace to see if I could find her. I did still have her change after all.

"For the record, I've had more romantic walks before," Peter said, following me.

I thought I saw the woman head into the Hub, the town's newspaper store, but my view was blocked by a group of ladies who were chatting on the sidewalk.

I took Peter's hand and pulled him farther down the street with me.

We entered the Hub, but the woman was nowhere to be found.

"What's up with you?" Peter said, refusing to budge another inch. "Cherry's managing the cash register, in case you were worried."

"What do 'mission' and 'exfiltrate' mean to you?" I said.

"Nothing," he said. "Why?"

I stepped outside of the Hub for one last look, but the woman was nowhere in sight.

"Listen," said Peter, and I realized he looked serious.

"I was thinking, for your birthday, I know you don't want a party, but can we have a special dinner that night, just the two of us?"

I knew he was asking me to dinner so that he could get me to the party. Up until that moment, I'd enjoyed playing along, but now I couldn't stop thinking about the woman.

"We should get back to the store," I said.

We started up Main Street.

"Is that a yes?" he said when we arrived at the door to the Wick & Flame.

"To what?" I said.

"Dinner."

"Yes," I said. "Absolutely, yes."

Peter was smiling at me. I could see he was excited about his success at having secured a way to get me to the party.

"I'm looking forward to it," I added a kiss to suppress my smile.

"So, what were you saying about a ride in the harbor?"

"I'm thinking after witnessing a murder and being up for over twenty hours yesterday, I should probably relax a bit."

"I like your thinking," he said.

Our embrace was broken as my morning's guests now began to stream out of my store. First, Millie exited with the birthday boys.

"The men have invited me to golf," she said as Emily motioned for their van to pull up.

"She's one of us," said Lennie.

I guessed that after hearing her Amazon speech, Lennie had caught Millie Fever. He now slung his arm around my mom in a way that seemed to bother Nathaniel and amuse Millie.

"Thanks for hosting us, Stella," said John Pierre, as he exited next with Laura and Olive. "We're going to take one of Barrett's Tours around the island."

"They've kindly agreed to take me with them," said Olive, looking pleased about the outing. "We get to see all of the highlights, and there's a special stop at one of the cranberry bogs. A preview of your upcoming Cranberry Festival."

As the Mortons and Olive headed toward the Barrett's bus stop, the door of the Wick & Flame opened a third time. Now, the Candleers joined the sidewalk scene.

"We'd like you to run a candle-mold class for us, inspired by those wonderful photos you took of the heads in Paris," Cherry said.

"Start tomorrow," said Millie as she boarded the van. "Then I can join too."

It was no surprise, but with Millie in town I knew we'd have a party every day. It wasn't often that I had the opportunity to include my mom in one of my classes, so I immediately agreed we should start bright and early.

When the morning crowd left, I settled into my workday. I had some paperwork to catch up on and a steady stream of customers, but during the occasional lulls, my thoughts drifted to the Mysterious Woman's phone conversation, especially given the shadow I'd seen across from my store last night. I looked through my store window more than a few times in hopes of seeing her again. By closing time, I was happy for a diversion when Millie and Nathaniel showed up at my door.

"I won the putting contest," said Millie, with a bow. "My prize is that Nathaniel has permission from the guys to join us for dinner. I'm starving. Let's join the early-bird crowd."

"I'm hungry, too," I said, texting Peter to see if he could meet us.

Millie looked through the open door to my workroom, and suddenly took an abrupt step back.

"Shoo, cat," she said. "Stella? You promised."

Tinker was perched on my worktable. He had behaved admirably all day, and now gave Millie a friendly look and swish of his tail. I could see by the way he stood and then leaned against his paws that he had plans to befriend my mom. Big plans. Having picked up on Millie's disdain, he was ready to prove his charm.

He began by jumping off the table and padding over to her, where he circled her feet by way of a greeting. Unfortunately, he'd lost her from the moment he'd left the table. The more he tried to prove his charm, the more Millie inched backward toward my workroom, her hand reaching behind her for the door. By the time I was able to intervene, she had had enough. She dashed out the Wick & Flame's door with Nathaniel behind her. The two were halfway down the block before I'd flipped my sign to CLOSED and turned the lock. Walking behind them, I noticed that after a day of golf they were now comfortable holding hands in public.

Fortunately, I had my own date. Over dinner, Peter and I honestly had a hard time keeping straight faces while the newest couple on Nantucket chatted about things that made no sense to us. If Millie and Nathaniel had broken into a secret handshake, I wouldn't have been surprised.

"I can't believe you didn't see that lady at The Bean today," I said to Peter over my last French fry. "She was on the phone when you met me. There's something strange about her."

"I didn't notice anyone but you," he said, with a wink that told me he was channeling Millie and Nathaniel's mush.

"Aren't you sweet," said Millie. To be honest, I was surprised she'd heard anything we'd said.

"Dark leggings, dark baseball cap? Dark hair?" I said. "She was talking about an operation being on track and referred to it as a mission."

"How clandestine," said Nathaniel. I could tell he thought he was playing along with some far-fetched story I was telling.

"Be careful," said Peter. "Stella has a knack for following up on clandestine things. Before you know it, she'll be sending you on an investigation to find the lady."

"Millie warned me," said Nathaniel.

My mother waved me off as I flashed my eyes at her.

"I tell everyone," she said. "It's in the genes. We Wrights don't like to let things lie when they don't sit well with us."

The waitress arrived and returned Nathaniel's credit card, which he'd somehow slipped to her without our noticing. This time I joined my mom in gushing over Nathaniel. Peter looked polite, but I could tell he felt I'd jumped ship.

"Dessert is on us," said my mom. "Ice cream at the Juice Bar. Where's my sweater?"

We all searched for her navy sweater with the big,

black buttons. Under the table. Beside our chairs. Alas, it was nowhere to be found.

"I'll swing by the Wick & Flame. You probably left it there," Nathaniel said.

"Brilliant idea," I said. "Here's the key. Then we can have a minute to talk about you over our coffee."

We tortured Peter with girl talk for a few more minutes before we finally left the restaurant. As we stepped outside, Nathaniel was crossing the street with the sweater in hand. In spite of his chivalry, I thought he was starting to look a little tired. I understood. Millie could be hard to keep up with.

"Found it," he said.

"Thank you," said Millie with a wave.

Unfortunately, Nathaniel's adventures were not over. At that moment, I knew I'd forgotten to relay to him a critical piece of information: Tinker never gives up. Behind Nathaniel, my cat pranced along, happily wanting to join the party after successfully darting out of my store, unnoticed. He does that, the rascal. Millie had just stepped off the curb and taken her sweater when she caught sight of my furry friend.

"Oh no," she said.

I knew in that moment that we were all in for some trouble. Main Street is not a road to traverse with speed, especially in heels, which Millie was now wearing. The entire street is paved in cobblestones of all shapes and sizes—some high, some low, some bigger than others. Off she ran, however, with her sweater flying behind her like the flag of one of the Peace Jubilee's attendees. Nathaniel, not having realized that Tinker was behind them, looked understandably concerned by my mother's outbreak. He followed her down the street and jumped from stone to stone as if

they were hot coals. Neither stood a chance. Tinker is
fast. Three car lengths away, my cat jumped into Millie's
arms and began to lick her.

"Nghahh!" Millie cried, loudly, as she fell backwards,
still struggling to free herself from Tinker's affections.

As Millie backtracked, she bumped into Nathaniel
who was still hurtling toward her. Suddenly, both were
falling to the ground. They hit heads as they did, and
lay, unmoving, in the street. Tinker looked at me,
aware that something had gone wrong. He skulked over
to a car tire, his eyes wide with concern.

Within seconds, Main Street filled with people
coming forward to see what the commotion was and
who the two people lying in the street were.

"Call an ambulance," I heard our waitress say.

"Oof," said my mom, rubbing her head. I could see
a bad cut on her knee where her pants were now torn.

Nathaniel sat up, rubbing his wrist.

A moment later, I heard the sound of an ambulance heading toward us. As I looked toward the
source of the siren's blare, I noticed something unexpected. While people on the sidewalk headed toward
the commotion, one person walked away. I knew by
her outfit that she was the Mysterious Woman who'd
fled my store. She dropped her head and continued,
down the street. I took a few steps to follow her.

"Hey," I said.

She looked up and caught my eye. Then she disappeared into the night.

Chapter 6

"Stella, I think I should get home to finish the stew," said my mom.

I turned back to my mom with growing concern. Millie Wright had never made a stew in her life.

"Gosh, the moon is full tonight," she added.

A medic arrived beside us. We all looked up. There was no moon in sight, only a streetlight.

"Could be a concussion," the medic said to me.

He began to ask her if different parts of her body hurt. Thankfully, Millie replied "no" to each question, but she still was not making any move to sit or stand. After being questioned, she began to sing "Moon River."

Over her voice, I heard a grunt. I turned to see a medic beside Nathaniel as well. His sleeve was rolled up, and he was holding his arm, but he seemed more concerned about Millie. The moment he was bandaged, he raced to her side.

"Is she OK?" he said to the medics as they transferred her onto a stretcher.

"Sir, I'm going to need you to get on a stretcher too," said the medic. "We'll need to have a doctor look at that arm and give you a concussion test."

"I don't need that. I can walk," he said, and stepped into the ambulance on his own.

"You're going to be OK," I said to my mom as she was readied for transport.

"Of course I will, you sweet Pookie Bear," she said. "But I'll need a change of clothes. I can't make much out of a hospital gown."

The idea of my mom in her lipstick and her hair in an updo, somehow making a hospital gown into a negligee made me feel deep down that she was going to be fine. I stepped into the ambulance and waved to Peter, who was holding Tinker, as the doors shut, and we drove away. Seated between the two patients, I put in a call to my cousin, Kate, who is a nurse at the Cottage Hospital. One of the benefits of being from a big family is the variety of places we work. I was relieved to find out she was on duty.

When we arrived a few minutes later, the medics quickly brought the pair inside. I hadn't even stepped fully out of the ambulance when the Emergency Room doors shut behind them. I followed, but when I entered the hospital there was no sign of Millie or Nathaniel. I was handed a pile of papers to fill out. After a few minutes, Peter arrived.

"I brought Tinker home. Are you OK?" he said, folding me into him.

The doors to the waiting room opened, and Kate entered. Kate has a tendency, with her blunt haircut, firmly held lips, and small round glasses, to look serious, even while eating an ice cream. Peter and I held our breath on instinct.

"She's resting comfortably," Kate said. "She has a bad concussion, but it could have been worse. Last summer we had to helicopter two people off island after spills like hers. She's asleep now, but you can poke your head in. We're keeping her overnight."

"OK," I said, unnerved that her injury merited a stay at the hospital, but happy we were not heading to Mass General. "What about Nathaniel?"

"He sprained his wrist," she said as we walked down the fluorescent-lit hall to Millie's room. "He won't let us give him a concussion test. The two had quite a crash though, so we told him without the test he'd have to stay overnight for observation. He's a stubborn guy, but he said if he could stay in Millie's room that would be OK. What do you think?"

"Fine by me," I said.

"He's kept to her side like a moth to a flame."

"We should call his relatives," Peter said. "He grew up here."

"I know," said Kate, "but he told us his parents died, and he was an only child. He didn't mention any kids."

"Poor guy. I'll tell Emily," I said. "At least his friends should know."

Kate opened the door where my mom lay fast asleep, snoring as usual. I was never so happy to hear her snore. There were two beds in the room, and Nathaniel lay in the other, still in his street clothes, looking as if the confinement was torture. He had a bandage around his wrist, but otherwise looked no worse for wear. He silently waved.

"I'll stay the night," I said, heading to Millie's bed-side.

"Actually, you should go home. I'll call you when she wakes up," said Kate, touching my arm. "She might be like this until tomorrow afternoon. A concussion is a bruise to the brain. She needs to let it rest."

"I'll call you if anything changes," said Nathaniel. "I'm fine. I feel like a goof. I was trying to show off and rescue her from Tinker."

"You are a gentleman," I said. "Thanks."

"Wait," he said, reaching into his pants pocket with his good hand. "Here's the store key. I forgot to give it back with all the commotion."

"What's that expression? No good deed goes unpunished? I think you proved that one tonight," I said and gave him a hug.

"Could've been worse," he said.

I wasn't sure how, but I nodded like he had a point. I was reluctant to leave but with Nathaniel's reassurances, Peter eventually got me out the door. He drove us back to town so I could get my car, and I shuddered as we passed the now-quiet stretch where our night had gone from fun to trouble.

"Do you want some company?" said Peter as we pulled up to my Beetle.

Did I ever.

It was only about eleven o'clock by the time I'd taken a warm shower and sipped the tea Peter kindly made for me. We sat on my sofa with Tinker at our feet, and Peter stroking my hair and making me laugh. The next thing I knew, I woke to the rise and fall of Peter's chest. As far as I could tell, he'd had the full weight of my head on him all night.

I breathed a sigh of relief. There had been no phone call during the night from the hospital. That could only mean good news. My mom had clearly not taken any turns for the worse, and she was likely still sleeping.

I was wondering if I should move, or if any sudden shift would wake Peter, who seemed to be in deep stages of REM sleep. I had started to slip back to sleep myself when Tinker took a silent leap to the kitchen windowsill and stared, intently, at the ground below. I fancied maybe he'd heard a deer outside. Putting a blanket over Peter's sleeping body, I tiptoed across the room to join Tinker. Deer spotting was something we liked to do in the morning. I looked out at the rising sun and took stock of the last few days. They'd been a roller coaster, that was for sure.

First, my mom and I had seen a man with a knife in his back who had subsequently died. Next, I'd been spooked by the idea that someone had broken into my store. Then, I was sure a woman who'd left my store without change had been up to no good. Now, my mother and Nathaniel were in the hospital. Nothing was ever calm when Millie Wright was around.

Tinker put his paw on my window as Peter stretched, still asleep, on my sofa. I looked below, but there was no deer. I saw a piece of paper, however, fluttering in the breeze on my door. It was likely a note from Chris, and I felt badly I hadn't texted or called him before falling asleep last night. The Wright news machine is a strong one, and there was no doubt that my entire family had heard the story about Millie and Nathaniel's accident by now. I crept down my stairs taking my phone with me to scan a list of texts with good wishes from friends and family for Millie. Tacked to my door, I also found a folded piece of paper.

When I opened it, I saw a typed note.
I began reading.

Stella Wright, Heard about your mother's
concussion. If you value her life at all, find the
formula she has hidden by tomorrow evening.
Further instructions will follow regarding
delivery. Do not show this letter to anyone,
especially the police, or, quite simply, you will
find your mother dead.

"What's that?" said Peter from behind me, with a
sleepy kiss to the back of my neck.

"Nothing," I said, clutching the note.

I flashed him a smile, took the stairs up to my apartment two at a time, and headed straight to my
bathroom.

"Are you OK?" said Peter, following me and knocking on my door.

"Yup," I said. "All good. Brushing my teeth."

I turned on the faucet and sat on the edge of my
tub. As I reread the note again, my phone rang. It was
Andy.

I was tempted to share this morning's death threat
with the police, so I answered.

"Hi," I said. "You'll never believe this."

Before I continued, however, I glanced at the note.
The words *you will find your mother dead* hit me. I decided to keep my mouth shut. For now.

"I heard about the accident," he said. "How's your
mom and her friend?"

Grateful for his friendship, but fearful I might say
too much, I gave him a hasty update about Millie's

concussion. When I clicked End, I looked at the note again.

I've learned in my lifetime to accept the unusual when it comes to Millie Wright. When I arrived at college, for example, she'd accidentally applied to one of the institution's oldest secret societies, after thinking she was merely helping participants in a freshman orientation activity. How does a mom pull that off?

None of her exploits, however, had ever included anything dark. I had no idea about a formula, or why it was worth a threat to my mom's life, but I did know one thing. I'm not the kind of person to take a death threat lightly. You mess with me like that, and I kick into overdrive.

I opened the bathroom door. Peter was seated on the edge of my bed, wrestling with Tinker.

"I have to head over to the hospital," I said.

I needed to have a chat with Millie. I needed to hear from her directly what she had brought home from the World Perfumery Conference that was not hers to take.

"Do you want company?" he said, with Tinker licking him from some sort of quarter nelson hold.

"Maybe later," I said, truthfully.

We snuck in a good-bye kiss that lasted from my bedroom to my front door, but I scooted him out the door. When he left, I looked at Tinker. He twitched, then sat on my mom's blue sweater. I could tell he felt responsible for the accident. He's a clever cat that way.

"Don't feel badly about last night," I said as I scooped out his breakfast. "You were just trying to make a friend. I think Millie has bigger problems than you, buddy."

I thought about that statement as I drove to the

hospital. I reconsidered my early mornings in Paris when I'd overslept. Despite my best intentions, I'd lay wide awake each night with jet lag and then sleep the mornings away like a bear who'd eaten enough baguettes to get through a winter's hibernation. My mom, on the other hand, was up and out the door each morning to the conference. I'd assumed she was attending panels along with the other attendees, but perhaps she'd had business of which I knew nothing. I realized there were a couple of times during our weekends where she'd hung up from a phone conversation when I'd entered the room. I'd suspected her furtive behavior was related to plotting my surprise party, but now I wondered if something else was going on.

By the time I walked into my mom's hospital room, I was ready to see her in a whole new light. One look at her sleeping figure, however, and my heart ached. There was no way that Millie Wright was in any trouble she had consciously made for herself. I knew my mother was tenacious about her quests for new scents, but I never knew her to be a thief or to do anything untoward. Whatever mess she had gotten herself into, it had been by accident.

"Mom?" I said, and touched her shoulder. She snorted and snuggled even more deeply into her blanket, but I needed to talk to her. I rubbed her shoulder again.

"Good morning," said a soft voice.

I looked across the room to find that Nathaniel was up. Still in his clothes from last night, he was seated in the guest chair by the window and reading *Moby Dick*, a Nantucket favorite. He smiled his twinkly smile and held up a finger to hush me.

"I could read this whole book in the amount of

time your beautiful mom can sleep," he said. "Your cousin, Kate, said she's probably going to keep sleeping all day. Her vitals are strong, so there's nothing to be concerned about, but she's headed for a huge hangover when she wakes up."

My head ached, just thinking about it.

"How do you feel?" I said.

"Like someone with two left feet," he said. "I still can't believe I fell. I couldn't sleep a wink, so I found this book in the waiting room."

"Has she said anything?" I said.

"Only once," he said. "Something about the Amazon."

I nodded and wondered if her ramblings had to do with the note.

"You look more tired than I do," said Nathaniel.

"Jet lag," I said. "And worry."

"Don't worry," he said. "She'll be up and at 'em before you know it. By the way, I forgot to tell you. Remember last night you were talking about that woman?"

I had that feeling where your stomach drops but the rest of you keeps standing. I nodded.

"I saw someone who fit her description near your store when I picked up Millie's sweater," he said. "She was probably returning for her change."

Nathaniel's comments made me realize that there was one person whom I could connect to every ominous moment since our homecoming. The Mysterious Woman I'd first seen from the ferry who had left my store in a hurry to answer a call about a mission, and who I'd spotted again last night. A missing formula sounded like a mission.

"I think she was a sailor," I said, remembering how she had taken off when I'd seen her last night. "She's probably long gone by now."

I wondered.

Kate opened the door.

"We're letting you go," she said to Nathaniel, checking his chart. "The doctor will be here shortly to give you some instructions about your wrist."

"You might discharge me, but I'm not leaving Millie like this," he said, looking over at my sleeping mom. "And don't tell me I can only come at visiting hours, or I'll complain of head injuries and wrist pain to get myself readmitted. Once I rejoin the guys, they'll insist on coming here with me to visit her. They are not a quiet crew."

My phone buzzed and Peter's face lit my screen.

"Hi," I said while Kate and Nathaniel battled out their differences in soft whispers.

"How about a trip on the *Yacht* before work?" he said. "We never got around to it yesterday."

I liked the offer because it was sweet, but also because I decided it was time to meet the Mysterious Woman. If she was behind the note, I had more than a few strong words for her. I knew that Millie could drive someone crazy enough to resort to madness, but we had much better ways of solving conflict on Nantucket than jumping to death threats. I'd figure out the problem, and come up with a solution.

"Great idea. See you in thirty," I said, and quietly hung up.

I did not feel at liberty to tell Peter about the strange letter, but I was comforted by the thought that he was helping me, even if he didn't realize it.

"Staying in this room all day needs to be approved by a family member," Kate was saying in a no-nonsense tone.

Nathaniel looked at me. I felt a flood of relief at the

thought that he was willing to watch my mom while I dug her out of trouble.

"You're a good friend," I said to him. "But you must promise me one thing."

"Shoot," he said.

"Call me the moment she wakes up."

"You've got a deal," he said, looking pleased to have a job. "I'll keep you updated."

We swapped phone numbers. I kissed each of my sleeping mom's cheeks, and walked out with Kate, happy to have so many eyes upon her.

"I think he's got an old-person-who-knows-what-he-likes kinda crush," she said, pushing her glasses up her nose as she assessed the situation.

"What lingering effects might she have?" I said.

"Nausea, headaches. With the right amount of rest, she'll be fine. Don't worry about her."

Easy for her to say.

Before meeting Peter, I stopped home where I was relieved to see that no other notes had been pasted to my door. I ran upstairs and opened my junk closet, which holds everything I own but don't use on a daily basis. Shoved in the back was snorkeling equipment and a wet suit I occasionally use when I surf on a chilly day. I put on the wet suit, threw on sweatpants and a hoodie over my gear, and shoved some flippers into my bag. I also slipped the letter and five dollars and twenty cents, the Mysterious Woman's change, into a Ziploc bag and then into my waterproof pocket.

It was only eight in the morning when I arrived at the town harbor where Peter was waiting for me. It was only my second day home, but Millie already had me hopping.

Chapter 7

"The *Yacht*, my lady," Peter said when I arrived to the town docks. A boat, white with a green stripe, and not much larger than a dinghy, was rising and falling in the water. Peter reached out a hand and bowed.

"Sir," I said with great formality as I took his hand.

With all the fuss, anyone might think I was stepping onto a tender to take me to a much larger boat, but this was the main attraction. The *Yacht* was no more than our humble transportation's name. Peter had stocked it with cheese and crackers, knowing it was my weakness at any time of day, and we wasted no time heading out on the water. About ten minutes later, as we bobbed slowly past Children's Beach in the harbor, I spied the woman's boat, a real yacht, among others of equal size. The fact that she was still moored in our waters added to my hunch that she had written the note.

I pointed to Brant Point, where the ferry rounds the island's well-known lighthouse.

"Let's head over there," I said. "It's a good day for a dip."

"I didn't bring my suit," he said, picking up some speed as he brought us around the bend.

We passed the woman's boat. I did not see anyone on the deck.

"I can jump in with my skivvies on," Peter said, shutting off the motor and dropping anchor, "but I'm interviewing the owners of the Culinary Center about their new classes after this. I guess they won't mind if I'm wet."

"They might mind if you're shivering. It's pretty cold," I said as I stripped down to my wet suit and put on my flippers. Reluctantly, I dropped my phone into my bag.

He dipped his hand into the water. I could tell he agreed. I dove right in.

"I'm going to find us a penny, for good luck," I said, when I came up for air. "You enjoy the morning sun before your workday. This birthday girl needs some mindful meditation in the sea."

"Enjoy, crazy girl," said Peter with an approving smile. "Find us a fortune."

There's a superstition on Nantucket that you will ensure your return to the island if you throw two pennies overboard from the ferry bound to the mainland, specifically while rounding Brant Point. When I was about sixteen and desperate for a car, I'd snorkeled under the surface to see about that fortune. I hadn't found anything, but I maintain it was a respectable idea.

After watching me splash about, Peter stretched out on his boat to enjoy the sky, which is one of his favorite things to do. Knowing he'd be content for a while, I focused on the Mysterious Woman's sailboat and dove under the water again. Growing up surrounded by the sea, I was taught at a young age to be a strong, fast swimmer. When I rose three full breaths later, I was in front of the stern of a boat about thirty-five feet long. Its name, *Hatchfield*, was painted along the back, and there was a ladder hanging from the boat into the water. I peered back toward the *Yacht*. Peter was still relaxing. I listened, carefully, but I did not hear any noise coming from the deck of the *Hatchfield*. I seemed to be alone, with only the sound of the water hitting the boat's gently rocking hull to keep me company.

I slipped off my flippers and tied them to the side of the ladder. Then, I climbed aboard. I comforted myself with the knowledge that if something really ugly went down, I could get Peter's attention with one extra-loud scream. This would be my absolute last recourse, however. I didn't want to bring Peter into my mother's chaotic life unless I had to.

"Hello?" I said.

No one answered.

The boat had white, cushioned banquettes lining both sides of the stern, and a double door at middeck in front of the ship's wheel, which indicated a cabin was below. I decided that anything of interest must be downstairs, because it certainly was not on the empty deck. The space was clean, tidy, and void of any extraneous items. Taking a deep breath, I knocked on the cabin door. When there was no answer, I pulled at the doors. They opened easily.

"Hello?" I said again.

All was silent. Undeterred by her absence, I decided to learn more about this woman. I closed the doors behind me, climbed down the steps, and flipped on a light switch.

A lantern over a table at the back of the small cabin lit the room. I realized I was dripping everywhere, so I grabbed a dish towel from the galley, and I wiped the floor. Like the deck, the interior items—a table, a corner banquette, and the items of a small galley— were bolted to the boat, to minimize interior movement while at sea. Again, I did not see any personal items. I opened the mini fridge in search of something that might tell me about the Mysterious Woman. It contained a couple of bottles of water, three protein bars, and a premade salad from Stop & Shop.

I looked at a door to the right of the table which led to the boat's one berth. It was closed. I dropped the towel to the ground, and shuffled on top of it, so that I left no trace behind.

Grasping the doorknob, I pushed. The door opened with an unfriendly creak. I cautiously poked my head inside the room. No one was there.

I saw one personal item, a knapsack, on the floor, in front of the built-in bed. The bag was gray, and nondescript. Nothing anyone would look at twice. There was a sleeping bag, also gray, rolled up and tied to the side of the bed, as if ready for the boat to take off at any moment. I stepped into the room, the door shutting behind me with a nasty bang. I knew no one was on board, but the noise stopped me in my tracks for a moment. But just for a moment. I had things to do. I peeked in a small closet and in the two drawers under the bunk. All were empty.

Still poised on my little towel, though I was now drip-free, I zipped open the bag. On top was a clear pouch containing basic toiletries. The only thing of interest was a hairbrush, in which a few strands of hair were wrapped around the bristles. With some dismay, I studied the bristles. They were blond rather than the dark shade of the Mysterious Woman's hair. I started to feel I'd made a terrible mistake connecting the woman I'd seen in town to the one who lived on this boat.

Below the toiletries bag, I saw some basic clothing, leggings and T-shirts mostly. I lifted them. I'm glad I did because I made a satisfying discovery. A black wig. A noteworthy twist.

With renewed conviction, I now forged ahead by opening the front pocket of the backpack. Immediately, I felt I was about to hit the mother lode. Inside the compartment was a soft, white packet with a zipper across the top. It was thick and seemed to contain several items.

Of course, I opened it.

One look inside, and I was sure I'd found the author of my morning's threatening letter. And then some.

"What do we have here?" I said. I looked at a bundle of passports from different countries, which were bound by a simple rubber band. That wasn't all. Beside them were stacks of different currencies, also simply bound. I opened the passports to find photos of the woman I'd seen in town, but with slightly different looks and many different names. For a whole new set of reasons, I wondered again what my mom had gotten herself into.

I was about to put the soft envelope back into the knapsack when I saw the candle the woman had purchased from me, shoved into its innermost pocket. When I pulled out her votive, a photo fell out with it. It was a picture of a blond woman, smiling happily into the camera. Her arms were around a man who seemed equally happy. Behind them were snow-covered mountains, and their cheeks were both pink from the cold and maybe from love by the looks of them. I held the photo away from me and squinted a little. If I'd seen the photo in any other context, I'd never have believed it was the Mysterious Woman or the woman in the passport photos. The lady in the photo was radiant, filled with life, and her hair curled from under her cap as if leaping out of the picture. She was the opposite of the woman on Nantucket who had slipped out of my store and had skulked around town. The two people, however, were one and the same.

I put everything back into the knapsack and decided to get off the boat immediately. I wanted some of Peter's cheese, maybe a good luck penny, and a chance to puzzle out what I'd found. This was all much more than I'd bargained for.

Unfortunately, I had stayed a minute too long. Suddenly, I heard the hatch to the cabin open. Given the passports, the money, and the wig I had found, the Mysterious Woman was now the last person I wanted to encounter, especially as a trespasser. I'd come to the boat filled with blind rage about the note. Now, I had to admit the shortcomings of my plan. Like mother, like daughter, I had acted quickly, trusting I would be able to navigate my challenges as they arose. Instead, I was up against someone more dangerous than I had imagined.

I looked around the room for somewhere to hide. The drawers under the bunk were too shallow to shelter a fully-grown person. The closet seemed risky. Given my options, I decided to remain beside the door, by its hinges, so that if anyone opened it, I'd at least be concealed.

Outside my room, I heard someone take the steps down into the cabin. I heard breathing, but I could not tell if it was a man or woman. I pressed myself closer to the wall and tried to slow my racing pulse. I heard a floorboard squeak the tiniest bit, then I heard a quiet step across the room. Next, the room went deadly silent. I looked at the doorknob, waiting for it to turn.

OK, OK, OK, I mouthed to myself. *It's OK.*

It was not OK. I watched the knob turn, without anywhere to run or hide. The door opened, slowly, and a gun reached around the side of the door. It wasn't the first time I'd stared down the barrel of a gun, but that didn't make it any easier.

"Don't shoot," I said, raising my hands.

From around the side of the door, the Mysterious Woman, wet from a swim, peered at me. She was now blond, but she did not look like the happy woman in the photo. Instead she looked furious. I still held her knapsack, which didn't help.

"You?" she said, as if I were a small child who'd taken a seat at the grown-ups' table.

She dropped her gun to her side, retrieved her bag, and pulled me into the cabin where she sat me down in a not very friendly way. She knew I'd seen her secret stash, and she'd already pulled a gun on me, so I didn't think an excuse along the lines that I'd boarded the wrong boat by accident would work. I decided that having come this far, I'd take her on. Given the circumstances, I seemed to have nothing to lose.

"Why have you followed me around since I've come home?" I said, looking up at her from my seat.

The woman stared hard at me. She didn't say a word.

"If the *mission* I heard you talk about has anything to do with a threat on my mother," I said, "we have a problem."

The woman aimed the gun at me again and sat down across from me.

"What threat on your mother?" she said, steadily, from behind the barrel of her gun.

It's hard to bully a bully when they have a gun aimed at you, but it was now my turn to keep silent. I crossed my arms to make my point.

"Are you kidding me?" she said. "I know how to torture people seventeen different ways. I will show you each one if you don't tell me about this threat."

"Fine," I said and pulled the Ziploc bag out of my wet suit. Seventeen different ways was all I could think about. "This threat."

I handed her both the letter and her change from her purchase at my store.

Forgoing her change, the woman extracted the letter from the baggie, and read it. She stood and paced the small cabin. I was not sure what to make of her. On the one hand, she was willing to torture me; on the other hand, she seemed to have a lot on her mind that had nothing to do with me or the formula.

"He's here," she said, as much to herself as to me.

"Who?" I said.

The woman looked at me.

"Aside from leaving your flippers outside, you did a good job tracking me down," she said. "I'll give you that."

"Who is here? And what formula does he want?" I said, hoping to capitalize on the street cred she'd given me.

"He wants the formula I took from your mother's black bag two night ago," she said, confirming my suspicions about the sounds I had heard in my store two nights ago.

Chapter 8

The confession was an interesting move. I wondered why this stranger, who had a stash of passports and a gun, would share that information with me. She hadn't made the statement in a way that sounded like a taunt or a threat. And if she had the formula, she wasn't the author of the note.

I decided her admission was a slight opening for a future between us. She was as worried as I was about the author of the note, whoever he was. Perhaps we could put our heads together.

"I need that formula," I said calmly. "Someone's threatening my mother's life for it. Why don't you tell me what's going on? Maybe we can help each other."

I could tell she was deep in thought, so I stopped talking. Honestly, I'm not sure I had a choice. Finally, she sat back down directly across from me, with the table between us.

"My name is Agent Sarah Hill. I'm with the United States Government," she said. She unzipped the top of her wet suit and pulled out what looked like a school ID holder, black with a clear window through which I could see a small document. She handed it to me.

I took it. I realized I was looking at a badge. On the

left side was a holographic image of an American flag, and beside it was the title for a United States bureau that referred to international and national security. Centered on the form was a photo of the woman in front of me, with the name Agent Sarah Hill below it. There was also a number which probably corresponded to a file on her, likely something highly classified. I'd had no idea who I might have found on this boat when I'd decided to visit, but a secret agent had not been on my list of possibilities. I handed the badge back to her, not sure if I should feel better or worse about the news. I still had no idea if she was friend or foe.

"I heard you speak about a mission," I said, trying again. "Is the formula your mission?"

"Yes," she said. "I'm going to tell you the following, so you understand how important the formula is, and by doing so I am entrusting you with national defense secrets. Please acknowledge that you understand."

I nodded, automatically. The gesture seemed to suffice because Agent Hill shifted to a stiff, military posture at the table, as if she was conducting a governmental agency debrief. For now, I decided to trust her.

"The formula," Agent Hill began, "is connected to the man who was murdered at your perfume conference in Paris. He was my partner, and he was killed when our mission was compromised."

"Wait a minute," I said.

I held up my hands and shook my head in confusion. Agent Hill waited patiently as I got my head around the fact that the note from this morning tied back to the dead man in Paris.

I started to speak, but it was all starts and stops.

"This has to do with the Peace Jubilee?" I finally

said. "And the guy, Rex Laruam, who was trying to steal your files?"

"Yes," she said.

I sat back in my chair. In my wildest dreams, I hadn't expected to cross paths again with the murder I'd witnessed in Paris. At most, I'd planned to follow the story from afar, over morning coffees with Peter.

"To be clear," I said, "this is not about my mom's scents from her trip to the Amazon?"

"It's about your mother's black bag, not her trip to the Amazon or the samples she collected while she was there," she said.

I didn't like the conversation I was having, but I was relieved to know that my mom hadn't stolen a secret formula from the Amazon.

Agent Hill reached into her wet suit top once more, and now pulled out a small vial of pale-yellow liquid she had apparently taken from my mother's bag while I had been asleep in my workroom. She held it possessively, but I studied it carefully. The vial looked exactly like the kind my mother used for her samples. Its contents could have been any one of the formulas she carried around at any given time. There was one difference, however. When I had handed out vials four through seven at Millie's presentation, they had small labels around them with numbers to keep track of them. This one had no number on it.

"My partner died for this formula at the conference in Paris," she said.

"I thought he was protecting a flash drive."

"He wasn't. The information he was after was in an encrypted code hidden in the scents of this formula. When the scents are decrypted, they reveal unique flora scents found only in highly classified locations."

The formula was an encrypted list of scents. A code. Millie would love that idea. I wished she was with me now.

"As you've read," Agent Hill continued, "the data points Laruam was seeking, and which are contained in this formula, mark the path that the queen of a remote South Pacific island will be taking to the Peace Jubilee. The queen entrusted America with the list so that we could send protection for her small entourage. Her kingdom does not have the kinds of security our world demands."

I reached out to touch the vial, but Agent Hill put it back into her wetsuit.

"I don't understand how Millie and her bag fit in," I said, wishing I could see the formula again. I couldn't believe the power the small vial held.

Agent Hill clasped her hands together, and I gathered that she was becoming reluctant to continue, but I needed the whole story. Now.

"Unfortunately," she finally said, after some consideration, "when my partner picked up the formula under cover at the conference, he discovered our mission had been compromised. Rex Laruam was on to us. We had to abort. To protect the vial, he slipped it, at random, into a bag, which happened to be your mother's."

"We travelled all the way home with a secret code in our bags?" I said, stopping her. My fascination turned to fury. "You talk about protecting the queen. What about us? Rex Laruam could have killed us."

"Rex Laruam was supposed to follow our decoy lead and head to Morocco where a team was ready to capture him," she said. "The stories you read in the news about the document's location were a small part of other carefully planted leaks and misleads meant to lure him to us. We thought we had him this time."

"But instead he's in Nantucket," I said, trading my realization that I could have been in danger my entire trip home for the realization that my town might now be in danger. "Call your team and pick him up here. Sounds like this is good news for you. Nantucket is a small island. How hard can it be to find him?"

"Even if I could, it wouldn't be so easy," she said. "For one thing, we have never seen him. We have no idea of his identity, or even his nationality. For another, the goal of our mission, to protect the queen, is being conducted without the use of modern technology."

I was starting to lose my patience. Like the newspapers, I was ready to question the choices that had been made in protecting the code.

"In a high-tech world, sometimes old-fashioned methods are the most unexpected ways to go," Agent Hill continued, as if reading my mind. "We chose an unprecedented plan to throw him off. We shut off surveillance cameras at the hotel, which we feared he could hack, and we used the formula to hide the code instead of an electronic communications protocol. It was working too. You may think, given the outcome of my partner, that it was a foolish plan, but we had success with two other hand-offs that morning. When we discovered Rex Laruam was getting suspicious, we went to Plan B."

"We were Plan B?"

Agent Hill nodded.

"You were chosen at random, so that you would be impossible to trace," she said.

"Then how did you find us? And the formula?" I said.

"Fortunately, my partner was able to relay a message to someone from our agency before his last breath. He said '*red hair, black bag, mother.*' It took some work to confirm your mom's identity, but once we did, I was able to get the jet down here, ahead of you."

"Looks like Laruam has his own jet, too," I said. "And how did he find us? I was right there, by the injured man. I didn't see him say a thing to anyone."

"We thought, hoped, that Rex Laruam didn't see him say anything either."

I realized, by the way Agent Hill now spoke about her partner, that the two had been more than business associates. I thought of the photo in her bag.

"And yet, here we are," I said, sitting back down.

She nodded, stiffly.

"Why are you telling me this?" I said.

"I was sent here to recover the formula while everyone else went to Morocco. The problem is, to keep the lowest profile, I came here alone. I don't even have access to communications with my team. When I made my call yesterday, I was reprimanded for breaking protocol and my phone was erased."

"So, they've been setting up a trap for Laruam in Morocco," I said. "And we've got him right here, with no help?"

She nodded.

"My instructions were to recover the formula and lay low, right here in Nantucket, until Sunday," she said. "The queen is planning to begin her journey to Paris on Monday, and Nantucket was deemed to be the simplest, most unsuspecting, place to keep the formula until the moment it was needed, as extra precaution. Now, however, I have Laruam, you, and your mother to worry about."

"When he doesn't show up in Morocco, won't they send someone here to help you?" I said, hopefully.

"No," she said. "They've been getting intel, likely sent by his moles, that he's en route to Morocco. No one is worried about me."

"Then we have a lot of work to do between now and Sunday," I said. "You have the formula. Now, let's get this guy before he gets my mother."

Agent Hill shook her head, adamantly.

"My mission is to recover and protect the vial," she said. "Now that I know Laruam is on the island, the vial is no longer safe here. Fortunately, he does not know I am here. If he did, I'd already be dead. But I'll need to leave as soon as possible. My problem, however, is what to do with you and your mother."

"I can't believe that you'd let the person who killed your partner roam around this small island without trying to find him," I said.

Agent Hill cast a fearsome look at me, but I persisted. I knew deep down she wanted this man caught more than anyone—aside from me. As long as he was on the loose, I felt sure that Millie and I were in danger.

"Let me help you find him," I said. "Come on. You were snooping around my store at least twice yesterday. You must be curious."

"I was near your store because it's a circus there," she said. "Standard procedure is to make sure an agent leaves behind no trace of an operation. You, however, were sleeping in your store when I secured the vial. I didn't even get to lock the door. It's my job to make sure the site was clear of any hint of me."

At least I now understood why she'd been hanging around my place.

"When will your mother be released from the hospital?" she said.

"I think by the end of today."

"Then you and your mother will come here, so I can protect both of you, and the vial, from my only position of strength. This boat. We'll set sail tonight for one of our port safe houses until I can get help."

I was deeply concerned about Agent Hill's plan to put us under house arrest as a solution to our problem.

"You may find this hard to believe," I said, "but Nantucket Island can provide all of the solutions to your international espionage problems. You don't need to sail to safe houses, fly to Morocco, or flee from Paris when you have a small town like ours . . . ma'am."

Agent Hill didn't answer, but I wasn't going to leave my town while a madman was free on Nantucket. There had to be a better solution.

"Take my mom, but let me be your boots on the ground," I said, using the only military term I knew. "I'm no spy. Laruam would never suspect me of working with you. I can be your eyes and ears on the island while you get help."

"Absolutely not," she said.

"I've probably already met him," I said.

I was hoping to appeal to her covert operations instincts, but as the words spilled out, I realized the ugly truth that I probably had met the villain.

"What about the guests staying with my cousin, Chris?" I said, exploring the statement I'd made.

"The Mortons. From Canada. They showed up at my cousin's as Airbnb guests after a call out of nowhere yesterday. And Olive Tidings, our British friend. She showed up out of the blue too. She worked at the coat check in Paris, met everyone, and became friends with loads of people. Maybe she's Laruam. The fact that your partner picked Millie, out of everyone, might have been a lucky break for Laruam if he, or she, is Olive."

"I said no." Agent Hill spoke firmly, but I could see by the way she shifted her hands that she was tempted.

"I can come back to the boat tonight, with my mother, and let you know what I've found out about them," I said.

"Under my order, you will not pursue Laruam," she said with a conviction I decided I could not change. "You and your mother will return tonight, under cover of darkness. You will leave your phone at home since he might try to use it to track you. Come to Brant Point with a flashlight. Flash it three times, so that I know it's you. I'll come pick you up on the shoreline with the boat's dinghy. If you do not come, I can charge you with treason. Do you know what the sentence for treason is?"

I didn't, but Andy had lectured me quite a lot by now about letting the pros do their work, and I respected them all. I stood up, prepared to follow her directions. There were rules to follow, even if I did not like them.

"And in the meantime, be careful," she said, standing with me. "Rex Laruam does not know where the formula is. He is looking for it. And, to your point, he has likely integrated himself into your world."

"So, look around, but you didn't tell me to?" I said.

"No," she said. "But if I had boots on the ground, as you say, I'd certainly look into the three suspects you mentioned. I don't like the sound of them."

Agent Hill stared hard at me. She didn't even blink. Message received.

"OK," I said. "Millie and I will see you tonight."

Agent Hill turned to her fridge and opened the door without a word, so I took it as a sign that our meeting had ended. I climbed up to the deck alone. Once in the sunlight, I looked at the familiar skyline. On the *Yacht*, I could see Peter's raised knee while the rest of him still lay outstretched along his boat's bench. It was as if nothing had happened, but I felt that my whole world had changed.

Shimmying down the ladder, I slipped into the water where my flippers dangled from the side. I put them on and swam back to him.

"Hi," I said when I resurfaced.

Peter raised a baseball cap that he'd been using to shield himself from the autumn sun.

"Any luck with the pennies?" he said. "Can you pay for our fancy birthday dinner tomorrow night?"

"Weren't you worried about me?" I said, thinking how a good boyfriend should have checked to see if his girlfriend was OK after disappearing for so long.

"Nah," he said. "Why?"

"Oh, no reason," I said, grabbing his outstretched hand and pulling myself over the edge. "I mean, maybe when someone disappears into the sea for as long as I did you might get worried."

"First, I don't worry about you," said Peter with what I'd normally accept as a compliment. "Second, you were gone for, like, twenty minutes. I assumed you swam to the shore, and I figured you were having fun."

"Twenty minutes?" I said. Time really does have the ability to slow to a crawl when your life is flashing before your eyes.

"Are you cold?" he said.

I should have been cold, but I had stepped into the shoes of Agent Hill to find Rex Laruam and my blood was boiling.

"OK," he said, looking a little injured. "Want to go back?"

I nodded, thinking that tonight I would have to leave Peter again and head to an unknown safe house to protect my mother and the formula. I wondered how long I would be gone. I was glad I hadn't told Peter about the note or my trip to see the Mysterious Woman. If I had, he would have been carted off with us. I wouldn't have minded the company, but I didn't think it would be a healthy next step in our relationship.

Peter raised the anchor and started the motor, and we headed back to town. As we did, I draped my hoodie over myself and rolled my sweats into a ball. I knew I was being unusually quiet, but I had a lot to consider.

"Couples should be comfortable in silence, right?" I said, noticing his confused expression.

"Sure," he said, looking even more confused. "I love quiet. Whatever."

I don't know how it had happened, but Peter and I seemed to be in our first fight. I couldn't unpack the idea at the moment, but there was now definitely something amiss between us.

Chapter 9

I checked the time as we pulled back to the docks. It was just after nine o'clock. With a kiss to Peter that I can only describe as "off," I walked to my store one way while he headed to his interview another way. As I turned the corner onto Centre Street, I saw Cherry and the Candleers outside my store.

"Stella," said Cherry, waving. "It's Stella."

"Stella," said Flo, Cherry's best friend. "We were worried."

I assumed they were speaking about my mother's accident. That was the sort of news that would have reached them hours ago.

"We came for class, but you weren't here," said Flo.

I'd completely forgotten about the candle-mold class I'd agreed to run, but Cherry and Flo were flocked by three other women wrapped in various versions of crafts they'd made. One had a long, knitted scarf. One had a needlepoint purse. Flo, like her friend Cherry, wore a hand-knit sweater of the same pattern, but in a shade of green instead of yellow.

I loved the Candleers. And I knew I'd love our class, too, but I did not have an hour to spare today. I hated to do it, but I lied.

"Ladies," I said. "I've got to head to the hospital."

"Did your mother wake up yet?" said Flo.

"No," I said, and I looked to the ground.

"Then you are teaching your class," said Cherry. "Come on. Let's go."

She hustled me through the door, with the other ladies behind her. Glancing at the tapestry over my safe, I looked for signs that Agent Hill had stolen the formula from Millie's black bag. I couldn't identify anything out of place. It was unnerving for me to think that I might never have known she had visited. On the other hand, her expert work gave me faith that Rex Laruam had no idea that this young and efficient agent was on Nantucket.

"I'm not being hard on you," Cherry said to me. "I just know you. When you're busy with your candles, you relax. That's a good thing to do when a loved one is sick. Clears your mind. Remember the time you figured out where you lost your earrings during Basics 101?"

After having searched every purse, pocket, and drawer in my life, I'd remembered they were in my glove compartment while we'd poured our first candles together.

"I get that way when I'm chopping onions," said Flo. "Carrots? Nothing. Cucumbers can be my downfall. But give me an onion, and I can solve anything."

Perhaps Cherry and the girls had a point. I had jumped on board the *Hatchfield,* charged by fury over the note. Since then, I'd learned that Millie and I had stumbled into a case of international espionage. I'd met a real spy. And I now had Agent Hill's tacit authorization to investigate the identity of Rex Laruam. Spending some time at my own "headquarters" seemed like a good idea.

"OK," I said. "Let's do it."

My decision was greeted with a round of applause and support. I brought the group to the workroom in the back of my store and turned on the light.

While the ladies settled in for class, I slipped into the bathroom to change into some dry cleaning I'd left in the store before leaving for Paris. I'd forgotten to pack the outfit—a black jumpsuit—because I'd been busy ironing everything in my wardrobe with the deep conviction that I would keep up with the Parisians' style. Emily and I believed the French could wear anything elegantly because they iron unexpected things, like jeans. My ironing project was a noble ambition, but on my first day in Paris I'd seen a baby in a carriage give me a once-over, and I swear the babe lifted an eyebrow when she got to my turquoise wool cap, a hand-made gift from Cherry. Or maybe she wanted it. It's a great hat.

Inside the tiny bathroom, I carefully unzipped my wetsuit, frankly quite appreciative that no one had questioned me about my swim. People were definitely cutting me some slack, and it made me all the more protective of my hometown. I felt a need to do whatever it took to keep it safe. There were dark forces among us, and I vowed to keep them at bay.

I changed from my wetsuit into the jumpsuit, which was formfitting here and there except for a ruffle at the bottom of the pant legs. It was meant for a night out, not for a candle-mold class. Added to the fact that the sea water had ravaged my hair into a wild mass of curls, I looked like I could go clubbing. Fortunately, I always have a few products in the cabinet, so I was able to brush my hair and put on some make-up. I pulled my hair back into a ponytail with one of the rubber

bands I always keep on my wrist, added a few bobby
pins for good measure, and gave myself a serious
once-over. I decided I looked something like a spy
myself. I held two fingers toward the mirror, as if they
were a gun, but the look was too close to home. Instead,
I opened the door to my students.

"Hellooooo," I said over the whistles and catcalls
the ladies tossed my way.

I had to give a loud whistle myself to finally quiet the
room. I appreciated the women's admiration, but I had
a candle-mold class to teach. As an introduction, I passed
around the photos on my phone from Cire Trudon and
told them about the inspiration I had for our workshop.
Rather than use premade molds, which you can buy
online or in a store, we were going to make our own.

"Oh, dear," said Flo, when it was her turn to look at
my camera. "Oh, no!"

Her hand flew to her mouth.

"What is it?" I asked, retrieving my phone.

I realized that Flo had reached the end of my candle
photos and had landed upon the video I'd taken of
my mom playing Vanna White at the World Perfumery
Conference. Without knowing it, I'd kept the video
running as we'd approached the murdered man. The
video that had started with our excitement about
Millie's panel had ended with a dead man. Looking
closely at the last shot, I could now see that the man in
Agent Hill's smiling photo on the boat and the dead
man at conference were, without a doubt, the same man.
It was not surprising that I hadn't made the connection.
The hunk in the photo would be impossible not to
notice. The man on the floor of the World Perfumery
Conference was a washed-out version of that man. I

watched the video again, in search of Agent Hill, but I could not find her anywhere in the crowd.

"Maybe you should send this video to Andy," said Flo, bravely composing herself.

Normally I would have agreed, but for at least the next few hours, I wanted nothing to do with the police.

"In order to make our molds," I said, getting back to work. "We'll choose objects we'd like to make into candles and cast them in silicone. Take this, for example."

From one of my cabinets, I pulled out a silicone mold I'd made a few years ago from, of all things, the cast my orthodontist had made of my teeth before I had braces. I still thought it was pretty funny. My students began to come up with ideas for their candles as I poured melted wax into the mold of my crooked, adolescent teeth. Cherry immediately decided to make her mold from a Lego building her grandson had built for her. As the Candleers talked to each other about their ideas, I felt a wave of calm wash over me. Cherry was right. This was exactly what I needed to do.

Now on my own turf, I considered what I knew. To start with, Rex Laruam was on the island in search of a secret formula Millie had unwittingly transported from Paris to Nantucket. Agent Hill had taken it from my store two nights ago, which meant she had beat him to it. She believed, as did I, that Laruam would be both a newcomer to the island and to Millie's inner circle. Olive Tidings, John Pierre Morton, and Laura Morton fit both criteria. All three of my suspects had also been at Millie's presentation, and could have peeked into her bag while I'd been chasing after Agent Hill. If they'd looked, they would have noticed that the vial was already missing. Laruam also knew that Millie had been in an accident and presumed that I was a legitimate path to the formula, hence the note.

I delivered my toothy candle from its mold to positive reviews from my students. As they passed it around, appreciating how I had made the wick look like a piece of dental floss, I considered my suspects.

Olive Tidings seemed like she would devour mystery novels, not plot them, but I really hoped international anarchists had not camped out at my cousin's house, especially with his two young sons. The Mortons, however, had had the easiest opportunity to pin a note to my door this morning. They were right across the yard. Honestly, none of them looked as if they could pull off the kind of mission Agent Hill had described, but I had to be impartial if I wanted to discover Rex Laruam's identity.

I smiled at my students, and gave them their assignment for next week, which was to choose the items they wanted for their molds.

"Thank you for this wonderful lesson," Cherry said to me as we finished cleaning up. "And—special treat—I'm watching the store for you today. Go home. Take a nap. Visit your mother when she wakes up. No arguments. It's my birthday present to you."

Her announcement set off a new round of chatter among the ladies. They wanted to know what I planned to do tomorrow for my big day as they nudged each other and added an occasional wink. They were terrible at keeping a secret.

"Thank you," I said. "All of you."

Cherry's offer to watch my store was perfect, but not because I was planning to go home and take a nap. I left the comfort of the Wick & Flame to investigate my suspects. I had many advantages that the intelligence agents did not. I knew my island; I had eyes and ears everywhere. While Laruam was in my territory, there was no way I would let him get away.

I was two steps down the street when I saw Peter coming from his interview at the Culinary Center. We weren't officially in a fight, but I knew that our smiles to each other were a little forced.

"Wow," he said, eyeing my getup. "This is a new look. Maybe I should start a fashion column."

"Oh, this old thing?" I said with a twirl.

As I spun, I pulled from my bag a leftover Gauloise cigarette from the pack my mom and I had used for effect at Parisian cafés. I stuck it in my mouth, and let it roll across my lips. It was the final touch I needed for my spy look. I pinched his cheek and turned on my heels to my car. I felt dressed for a high-speed drive, but instead I had my small red Beetle, which I had to drive at a careful pace. I did not want to be pulled over by the police for speeding while I was looking for an international anarchist wanted for murder.

About a quarter of a mile to my house, I noticed a silver Buick driving toward me. It was Chris's second car, an old, worn-out sedan with a loud muffler, that was rarely used. As it passed by me, I noticed John Pierre in the driver's seat, and realized that Chris had offered the car as an amenity to his innkeeping services.

I made a U-turn and began to follow John Pierre. I stayed a good distance behind him, but I managed to keep his car in sight as we moved through traffic. We were driving toward a hub of commercial stores out of town, like the post office and the big Stop & Shop. I wondered where he might be going. Finally, I had an inkling. Ahead I saw Nantucket's Marine Home Center. He pulled in.

So did I.

Chapter 10

Marine Home Center, where John Pierre was parking, is the megastore of Nantucket. Originally a lumberyard, it began expanding in the 1950s and is now spread across a cluster of buildings. You can buy anything there, from a refrigerator to a decorative pillow. The downside is that, like my trips to Target on the mainland, I can never walk inside without losing at least an hour, and I've never walked out without a few things I'd had no idea I "needed" before entering.

I parked the Beetle at the end of the lot so John Pierre didn't see me, and then lifted my phone to take a photo of him, thinking that Agent Hill might appreciate as many visuals as possible during our debrief later this evening. Then I stopped myself. Agent Hill had said that her team had foregone the use of even phones as part of the effort to get ahead of Laruam. I decided that while I investigated any of our suspects, I would, too. I lowered my phone and shut it off.

In spite of the danger to my wallet, there was no way I was going to sit in my Beetle and second guess why John Pierre had decided to visit Marine Home Center. Once he got out of his car, I followed, a good distance behind him. He grabbed a shopping basket from out front and went inside.

I had no idea what to expect as I walked into the store, but soon realized that my surveillance would be slow moving. John Pierre browsed almost every aisle of the store at a snail's pace. At each turn he made, I was half an aisle behind and peeking around corners. Even if he was a regular guy, and not an enemy agent, I feared he would soon notice he was being tailed. Therefore, in the paint department, I grabbed a case of twelve silicone tubes, which I needed for my candle-mold class. If he caught me spying on him, I'd at least have an excuse for being there. The box, however, weighed about ten pounds, which made the tailing a little harder, especially when he left the building and headed across a path to the gardening center.

Traipsing a good distance behind him with my load, I watched as John Pierre finally put one item in his basket, a sturdy pair of gloves. A little farther on, he studied the display of pruning shears. He picked up a pair, turned them over in his hands, and then put them back in lieu of a larger set. Finally, as he headed toward the cashier, he grabbed a roll of strong twine from a shelf he passed. I had horrible thoughts of what John Pierre could do with those items, especially as they related to the threat against my mother.

"Can I help you?" a voice said from behind me.

I turned to see a saleslady from Marine Home Center who was beaming with friendly support.

"That's quite a heavy item you have there," she said. "Let me get you some help."

Before I could stop her, the woman was calling to a young, strong aide to cart my selection to the register.

"It'll be right here when you're ready," she called

out. "I love your outfit, by the way. I could never pull it off."

Her remark that I was carrying a heavy box had been loud, but not particularly interesting. Her announcement that I had on a striking outfit, however, made heads turn, including John Pierre's.

"Stella?" he said, from the checkout counter.

"Hi," I said, managing a smile. "Fancy meeting you here."

"I'm picking up some gardening supplies," he said, raising his basket as proof. "I told Chris I'd help him with some groundskeeping before his wife comes home. He said she's been struggling with the weeds, and I thought I could surprise her. I have a green thumb. So does Laura. We run a farm in Canada, so it's hard to keep us from working the outdoors."

I felt like his explanation was longer than it needed to be, but I was intrigued by his story that he ran a farm. I didn't know exactly what I expected farmers to look like, but it wasn't the Mortons. They were casual, but somewhat trendy. John Pierre looked more like he'd work in advertising than farm the land.

"Where's Laura?" I said as he finished paying.

"She's crazy about the stores you have in town," he said, and moved aside for me to check out. "I haven't seen her this keen to shop since we went to the markets in Delhi three years ago. Unfortunately, I think your stores are a bit more expensive."

"I'd agree," I said, swiping my card.

"I'm going to get us lunch before I pick her up," he said. "Then we're going to explore your beaches."

"They're beautiful. Any time of the year," I said, wondering what his other errands might be. It would normally be hard to tail someone in my Beetle, but

Chris's Buick was so loud, that I could track its noise from at least three cars back in traffic.

"Let me," he said, taking my purchase.

We walked out of the store with our packages. John Pierre helped me load mine into my car. He seemed much more like a polite Canadian than an enemy spy. We said good-bye, but I pretended to have something very important to stare at on my phone, so that I could delay pulling out onto the road. From over my screen, I watched John Pierre enter the Buick and toss his package into the passenger side of Chris's old car. He put on his seat belt, pulled out of the parking lot, and made a turn. Waiting for a couple of cars to pull ahead, I trailed him as he snaked toward the Stop & Shop.

I started to think he was probably picking up a picnic lunch for his trip to the beach this afternoon, and here I was wasting time. I changed my mind, however, when he drove right through the market's parking lot, exited on the other side, and headed back toward town.

Using the cover of large SUVs to keep my small car hidden, I followed him as we passed the Old Mill, until he turned onto a quiet street, where there was a pocket of historic houses I particularly love.

I couldn't make the same turn without John Pierre noticing me, so I pulled into a parking space and lowered the windows. I could hear his car slow down and then stop. Encouraged, I got out of the car, and continued on foot. A block away, as I'd guessed, I saw his car. I watched him get out with his Marine Home Center bag in tow. Then he, too, continued by foot.

Technically, John Pierre could walk to town to meet Laura in about ten minutes from our location, if that was his goal, but there was no reason to park so far away.

I followed him, hiding behind the hedges of houses. At the end of the block, I had one close call where my foot hit a stone a decibel too loudly, but fortunately a tree shielded me from view. After about two blocks, John Pierre stopped in front of a house. Its hedges were unkempt, and some shingles had fallen off of its side. I imagined it must be an eyesore to the neighbors, but to the random passerby it looked merely forgotten. I made a note of the address so that I could ask my cousin Liz, who works in the real estate business, to check on it.

I took cover by a hedge with a hole in it that gave me both a view and a hiding place; I watched as John Pierre stood before the home's front gate for a moment or two. After a quick look up and down the street, he unlatched the gate, and then walked down a short path and up three stairs to the front door. From his pocket, he pulled out a key which he slipped into the lock, and then he entered the house.

I couldn't believe my luck. My first surveillance was turning into a good lead. If John Pierre had easy access to a house, why stay with Chris? I was eager to see what he was doing inside. I looked up at a tree beside the front gate, but decided that climbing it for better viewing access would make noise and attract attention. Next, I sized up the shrubbery in front of the house. It was half dead along the right side, and I wondered if I could squeeze my way through in order to peek through the windows. Again, however, I doubted I could pull off such a move without attracting attention.

In the end, I slipped up the steps of a house across

the street, in the hope that it raised me high enough so that I could get a good look over the hedges and inside John Pierre's house. There was no car in the driveway, so I gambled that the owners were out, and I'd be undisturbed. The steps ended at a small porch. I pressed against one of the structure's pillars and peered across the street. Success. I could see inside.

I could not see John Pierre, but I kept my eyes trained on the windows, barely blinking. My best view was of the house's dining room. After a minute of study, I realized that the furnishings looked like a good quality given the state of the rest of the house. I considered that our local Rafael Osona Auctions would have a field day with some of the antiques inside.

After a few long minutes, I saw John Pierre enter the dining room. He circled the dining table once, and then left. I was leaning so far forward at this point that I almost fell over the railing of my hiding place and into the street. It was maddening. I had no idea what he was doing in there.

Finally, John Pierre reentered the room with several newspapers in his hands. I realized the top one was a copy of the *Inquirer & Mirror,* which featured a story that Peter had written for the most current issue. I watched as John Pierre laid it on the dining table. He left the room once more, then returned with a laptop. I hadn't seen him carry the papers or the laptop inside, but my line of sight hadn't been ideal. I might have missed it. Or he might have carried them in his bag from Marine Home Center. If John Pierre was Rex Laruam, I realized that he could be using this house as his headquarters. He sat at the table and turned on his computer, which he stared at carefully, as if he was reading a document.

After a few interminable minutes, he closed the laptop and stood up. I did not see what he did next because a car turned onto the street two blocks away. Afraid I might look suspicious, I struck a nonchalant pose and looked at my phone. When I recognized the approaching vehicle, however, I jumped right over the side railing and onto a bush. Then I hightailed it down the street, but it was too late. The car followed me and reached me within one block.

"You have a twig sticking out of your hair," said Andy from his open window. He was off duty in his usual jeans, T-shirt, and baseball cap. His arm hung casually out of his car window, but there was always something of the policeman in him.

"Hey, Andy," I said, pulling out the offending stick as if things always ended up stuck in there.

I kept walking.

He kept driving next to me.

"Good thing I'm not working," he said. "That's the sort of walk that tells me you're up to something."

I stopped and gave him a "you're crazy" look.

He stopped and gave me a "who do you think you're kidding?" look.

At that moment, I heard a door open to a house behind me. For fear that John Pierre was leaving, I resumed my walk, heading straight for my car.

"See you later," I said to Andy.

"Stay out of trouble," he said, and pulled away.

When I started up the Beetle, I drove around the corner to where John Pierre had parked, but there was no sign of his car. I had lost him.

Driving past the house once more, I heard the sound of clippers. I looked up to see a man, tending to the hedges next door. I imagined John Pierre's place had become such an eyesore for the neighbors that the higher the hedges, the better.

"Hi," I said to the man. He was probably in his mid-fifties. All I could see of him was his head and shoulders. I couldn't see his face clearly as it was covered by a baseball cap. Although he had clippers, and John Pierre had just purchased a pair, I didn't think they were the same man.

"Nice day, isn't it?" He said.

"It is. I hear they're opening up the old place," I said. "When was the last time someone was here?"

"Funny you should ask. I just saw a man leave. I don't think I've ever seen anyone here before," he said. "And I've been working for the Fowlers for years."

He stopped clipping to take a sip of water. I thought he studied me as he did. I was dying to take a look inside the house, but I would have to wait.

Chapter 11

Kicking myself for losing John Pierre, I drove to an intersection and stopped behind some cars. The traffic was a far cry from the thick congestion in Paris, but the waiting was equally frustrating. I had moved up only one car's length when, to my surprise, I saw Olive ride past on a bicycle. It's not that I didn't think she was capable of riding a bike. Of the three suspects Agent Hill had encouraged me to keep an eye on, Olive was likely the sturdiest of all. What caught my interest, however, was that she was wearing pants. They were tweed, of course, but I'd never seen her in anything but a matching skirt and jacket with a serious blouse peeking through. The last day of the conference, she'd added a hat pin to her fedora, but that was about it.

The driver behind me honked. I pulled ahead. A few other bikers and cars shared the street, so I knew Olive would not see me. She kept a respectable pace, and so did I. She used proper hand signals at turns and rang her bell when she passed someone. When we pulled into town, she got off of her bike and walked it along the sidewalk, per town rules, until she reached the Jared Coffin House. Her behavior made me even more skeptical that she could be a suspect, in spite of the fact that she had worked at the murder scene in Paris.

I parked my car a couple of buildings away from the hotel where Olive was leaning over to lock her bike on the hotel's rack. I was about to switch my energies to finding Laura Morton when the strangest thing happened. Her hair shifted about an inch down her ear, hat included. I'd never realized Olive wore a wig, but I supposed ladies her age might. Under any other circumstance I'd have left it at that, but now I wondered if Rex Laruam was in disguise. My concern grew when I noticed the accessory she had tied to the bar of the bike. I had not been able to see it from my proximity behind her in my car, but now I saw that she had a shovel, about two feet long, tied to the bike. Immediately concerned for my mother's safety, I called Kate.

"I just left her room," said Kate, likely noticing the worry in my voice when she'd picked up. "She's sound asleep, as is Nathaniel."

Olive had already taken the eight or nine steps up to the Jared Coffin House before I could recover myself. When I did, I dashed after her, and through the hotel's front door. I walked into the kind of foyer one would find in a private home during the nineteenth century, with a grand staircase leading up to the rooms. To the right was probably what had once been a parlor, but had been retrofitted into a reception area. To the left were two connected grand rooms decorated with period antiques. I knew Emily was planning to use the rear one as a private dining area for Frank Marshall's celebratory dinners. The back of the hotel had been turned into several beautiful dining rooms and bar areas, which were filled with lunchtime visitors, none of them Olive. With a second look at all of the rooms on the main floor, I accepted that she had likely returned to her room. I walked directly to the front desk.

"Olive Tidings," I said to a woman with JAN written on her nametag. "What room is she in?"

"I'm sorry, but for the privacy of our guests, I'm not at liberty to say," she said.

Jan returned to her computer.

Reimagining Rex Laruam as the kindly lady who had presented herself to us at Café Bonne Chance in Paris, I remembered how Olive had waved and nodded to so many people. Playing the part of a coat check lady at the World Perfumery Conference would have been an easy way to gain access to both the attendees and the inner workings of the event. In addition to having access to bags and other personal items, she had made an impressive number of acquaintances outside of me and Millie.

Jan looked up at me, probably wondering why I was still loitering, so I headed back down the steps of the hotel. My cousin, Liz, and Emily were on the sidewalk below, smiling and chatting as if the world they lived in was safe from all harm. Their brightness filled me with warmth for my loved ones and a steadfast commitment to succeed in my mission.

Emily was holding the large bag she used to transport supplies for parties. It was almost as big as she was.

"Hi," I said.

"Is Millie feeling better?" said Liz.

"She's still sleeping," I said.

"I'm so tired I could sleep for a week. Between the baby and the Marshall party, I'm a zombie," said Emily.

"Well you look gorgeous," I said, and I was serious.

For a busy woman with a baby at home, she looked fabulous in a tan knit sweater with a furry trimmed collar, tan pants, and her signature high heels.

"What about your new Parisian look?" she said.

I took a bow in my jumpsuit.

"I love it," said Liz. "How's Millie's friend, Nathaniel? Let him know I'm available for house hunting if he wants to settle down here. I heard he sprained his wrist in their accident, so I haven't bothered him. Yet."

"He hasn't left my mom's side," I said. "Speaking of houses, can you check an address for me to see its sales and rental history?"

I gave her the address of the house that I'd seen John Pierre enter. Fingers crossed she'd find something for me.

"You know, Nathaniel's done pretty well for himself over the years," said Liz. "He owned a car dealership in Maine, was married for thirty years."

"Wow, you're thorough," said Emily.

"I was looking out for Aunt Millie," she said, and then gave us a look like she knew she'd been busted. "OK, I confess that I look into all my potential customers. It's part of the job."

Emily and I marveled at how thorough she was, but I realized Liz's bio about Nathaniel was probably the most I knew about him outside of what Millie had told me. In truth, Nathaniel was technically new to Millie's inner circle. Lennie Bartow, too. Since they had grown up on Nantucket and were former schoolmates of my mom's, we did not think of them as strangers, but neither of the two men had been back to Nantucket in twenty years.

I had no idea what Lennie had been up to early this morning. He might have pinned the note to my door.

I now wondered if even Nathaniel could have slipped out of the hospital and back, undetected.

Emily looked at her watch.

"I've gotta scoot," she said. "I have dozens of photos and trivia questions to organize. Tonight's theme is 'This Is Your Life.' Tomorrow night, the last dinner, is themed 'Whiskey.' Frank wanted it simple, and to the point."

"I like Frank's sense of fun," I said.

"Too bad you didn't want a birthday party, Stella," said Emily. "I could've thrown you a good one."

"I know. Love you," I said.

For the heck of it, we all hugged. As we did, I thought I saw Peter's car pass us, but he did not stop. I fancied he even ducked a little as he drove by, but I had a lot to do, and worrying about Peter was not on my list right now.

"I love how young women always find an excuse for hugs," said a familiar British voice, coming back down the stairs.

Chapter 12

"Hi, Olive," I said as Liz and Emily went off in different directions.

"It's a lovely day," said Olive when she reached the sidewalk.

I noticed she had changed back to her standard skirt and jacket. Today's tweed was a deep mustard. Call me crazy, but whoever she was, she pulled it off.

"I'm going for a walk," she said. "I always say that lollygagging is a folly we should all resist. That's why I like your mother. Her talk about the Amazon was inspiring. I hope she's feeling better."

"She's resting," I said, pointedly. "Not to be disturbed."

"As well she should," said Olive.

"I know my mom will be so sad not to have had more time to spend with you," I said.

"Don't worry about me. Laura Morton and I had a lovely breakfast this morning at a little café. We met another lady at the counter and got to talking about the Cranberry Festival. She even gave me her Gram Scully's cranberry pie recipe. You know me. I always love to hear people's stories."

"Did Laura tell you anything interesting about

herself?" I said. Suddenly, my suspect was becoming an informant.

"She's an artist and a farmer," said Olive. "Fascinating combination, don't you think?"

"I do. I wonder what kind of farmer she is," I said. "She doesn't strike me as a milk maid."

"My dear, I see you know little about farming. Take your cranberry harvests, for example. That's farming."

"Point taken," I said. "I'd love to see Laura's artwork."

"I'll bet she's good. I also visited your Whaling Museum and the library," said Olive. "There's an entire section of books at the library dedicated to Nantucket. Authors seem to love to write about the island, don't they?"

"It's the sort of place that gets your imagination going," I said, trying very hard not to let my own imagination get the better of me.

"I also hear the hiking paths are beautiful. On a foggy day, some say they remind them of England," Olive said. "I'm going to walk to Brant Point right now. I hear it has a lovely spot of beach with a very pretty view, a perfect distance from the hotel. Not too far, but a long enough trot to get the blood pumping."

Of course, I immediately wondered if Olive's intention was to observe the *Hatchfield* from Brant Point. I'd be sure to tell Agent Hill that Olive had visited the shoreline.

"Do you have a nice view of town from your room?" I said, still angling to figure out where Olive's room was.

"In fact, I do," she said. She looked up and pointed. "I'm in the one up there with the green curtains. It's small, but it looks right over the street, which I like. Gives me a good view of all the comings and goings.

Mr. Dinks and his pals are right next door to me, however. The men, not Mr. Dinks, mind you, made quite a ruckus last night when they got home. I'm next to that fellow, Lennie Bartow. I don't mind telling you that he's a handful. Not only did he come home late, but he was up and out bright and early, too. There's been no end to the noise coming through our walls. But don't listen to me rattle on. I'm going to get some air while the day's still strong. Ta ta."

I watched Olive walk down the street. I could join her, or I could take advantage of her departure. I decided to visit her room.

With no intention of running into the ever-diligent Jan at the front desk, I headed around to a side entrance of Jared Coffin House and up a staircase that leads to some of the older rooms. There's a large roof space off of this area that guests probably never notice, and I headed there now. I'd worked at the hotel when things were tight with my business in early days, so I am somewhat familiar with the odd nooks and crannies of the old place. The roof space was once a spot for the staff's smokers to sneak a cigarette, until management found out and banned its use. Nevertheless, I knew it connected to rooms in the main building of the hotel via another set of stairs on the opposite side of the deck.

I took these stairs and opened a door into a hallway at the back of the hotel. As I did, an older couple rounded the corner. I turned back to the door I'd entered, as if I was admiring the view through its window. The moment I heard their room door open and close, I scooted down the hallway, around a housekeeper who was searching through her cart, and passed the grand stairs from the lobby. When I reached the room Olive had pointed to from the sidewalk, I noticed a "Do Not Disturb" sign hanging from her doorknob.

Casually retrieving a bobby pin from my hair, I slipped it into an old lock. I'd only recently stumbled upon this new skill, and so I was delighted when I heard the click and knew I'd succeeded in opening the door.

"Excuse me?" said the housekeeper from her cart.

I kept my hand steady on the doorknob, and turned to smile at a woman with the name Marcia on her tag. I started to think of ways to explain my use of a bobby pin to enter my room so that I would not have to face Jan downstairs.

"Do you need clean towels?" she said.

Relieved that I had not been caught, I expressed a level of satisfaction with my bath items that she probably had not expected. Then, I stepped inside Olive's room, shutting it quickly behind me.

The first thing I noticed was that Olive's bed was made, in spite of her "Do Not Disturb" sign. Either she was fastidious about her housekeeping, which admittedly fit what I knew about her, or she'd been too busy in Nantucket for a good night's sleep.

In Olive's closet, I found three tweed suits, hung in a row, next to three silk blouses, each almost identical. The mysterious shovel lay against the wall. I wondered why it was covered in fresh dirt. I really wished I could take photos of this item, but I resisted turning my phone on.

Instead, I opened her dresser drawers to find an impressive collection of shape enhancing undergarments. Moving to the small, tidy bathroom, I found bottles of Sir Bumble's Spirit Gum, both adhesives and removers, which I assumed she used for her wig. There were other beauty products, mostly cover-ups and foundations and lip pencils, which could certainly do a lot to alter a person's looks. Given Olive's simple, arguably uncreative style, I was surprised at how much work she put into herself each day. Unless, of course, Olive was not really Olive. No one would ever give a second look to a charming old teacher on sabbatical, whether she was the coat lady at a perfume conference or a visitor to my hometown.

In spite of Olive's theatrical beauty products and the dirty spade, there was no concrete evidence to suggest that she was Rex Laruam. Although the Jared Coffin House likely offered business services to type and print a note like the one I'd received this morning, I felt the absence of accessories that a spy like Rex Laruam might need. I looked out of Olive's window, fairly certain that I'd broken into a sweet old lady's room.

I was ready to turn on my heels and resume my search for Laura Morton when I heard some noise in the next room. I remembered that Lennie Bartow was next door and had kept Olive awake at all hours of the night. I wondered if he had tacked the threatening note to my door this morning.

I pressed my ear against the wall to see if I could hear anything. There was noise, but I could not determine its nature. I grabbed a glass from Olive's bathroom and pressed it against the flowered wallpaper, hoping for better audio. The trick actually worked. Listening carefully, I heard the sound of fingers pounding against a keyboard. The clamor from inside the room stopped when Lennie's phone rang.

"What have you come up with?" he said.

There was a pause.

"It could mean something," he said. "It's probably worth pursuing. I'm running out of time."

Then, there was silence. I no longer heard speaking or typing. Whatever Lennie was up to, I wasn't going to learn more now.

After putting the glass back where I'd found it, I returned to the room where I noticed a small, white cardboard box poking out from under Olive's bed. I knelt down, and opened the lid. Inside, I saw smaller boxes, each about the size of a soda can, packed tightly together. They were taped shut, so I could not open one without Olive noticing that someone had snooped around her room. I wished I could see their contents, however, because more than half of the boxes had the name of a different country scribbled across them.

Suddenly I heard Olive's voice.

"Young man," she was saying from what sounded like the elegant front stairs leading up to her floor, "you should treasure those shells. If you lift one to your ear you can hear the ocean."

"You can?" said a little voice. The gentle laugh of another woman, presumably the boy's mother, followed.

I pushed the box back under the bed. Without time for grand plans, I boldly opened Olive's door. If she were right in front of me, I'd have to wing it with something like "your door was open, so I thought I'd stop by," or "fancy meeting you here." Fortunately, she was still engaged with the young boy on the stairs, who was now riddling her with questions about how the sea could fit into a shell.

I decided my best bet was to bump into Olive

before she bumped into me. I'd only taken one step toward the stairs, however, when I saw a note on the opposite door. Across it was one word, *Nathaniel*.

I lifted it, carefully. The name and note were typed. In the same font and line spacing as the note I'd found on my door this morning.

When you get your butt back from the hospital give us a call. We'd like to help you numb the pain in much more creative ways at the bar.
—Lennie

"Hello?" I heard Lennie say from inside his room. Apparently, he'd made another phone call.

I wished I could stay to hear more, but I was out of time. I headed to the stairs.

"Hello," I said to Olive who was only three steps from the top of the staircase.

"Oh," said Olive, straightening up from her new young friend, and looking up at me with a surprised expression.

"I thought I'd see if Nathaniel was home, but he isn't," I said. "He's still at the hospital as it turns out. Oh well. Not much of a party weekend for him, is it?"

I said the entire monologue in one breath. I suspected I was red in the face, but at that moment the boy cried out that he could hear people swimming in the ocean from his shell.

"I forgot my camera," Olive said to me, "so I came back to get it, but now it's getting chilly."

"Let's have some tea," I said.

"I'd love to," she said, "but I have a couple of things to do before supper."

And with that, she touched the brim of her fedora

and passed me to head to her room. Fortunately, Marcia and her cart had moved on. I smiled to the little boy and his mother who followed.

Passing Jan and the bellhop I'd met yesterday without attracting undue attention, I exited the hotel and saw Emily peering into her car's trunk, which is always filled with extra decorations and supplies for any event she was working on. I gathered she must be looking for an extra bit of magic as she was starting to coordinate her supplies for this evening's event.

"What're you still doing around here?" she said to me.

"What do you know about Lennie Bartow?" I asked changing the subject.

"Not much," she said. "Why? Because he's a little flirty with your mom?"

"You noticed?" I said.

"On the van to golf, I noticed," she said. "Every time Nathaniel talked to Millie, Lennie butted right in. Millie seemed to get a kick out of it. I wouldn't worry. She can handle herself."

"But what's his deal?" I said.

Emily shrugged.

"He lives in Florida," she said, "but he travels a lot. I had to track him down because he was away when the invites were sent. I think Frank said he works in venture capital. Something like that. He's very polite. The other guys are mostly drinking up a storm this weekend, but Lennie's a little more serious."

"Everyone's commented that he's aged a lot, and no longer looked like his old self."

I hoped Rex Laruam was not impersonating Lennie Bartow this weekend, but it was a possibility I had to consider. I hated to imagine where the real Lennie

Bartow was if my investigation led me further down this road.

"We need to have lunch next week," said Emily, slamming her trunk shut. "Let's have some fun after Frank's party is over. I still haven't heard about Paris except that you saw a dead guy, which I still can't believe. Actually, I guess I can believe it, knowing you. Anyway, I want to know about the food and the people and all of the good stuff."

"I know," I said. "And I'll be thirty by next week. We'll have a 'Ladies Who Lunch' kind of outing—a real mature woman sort of affair."

We laughed and Emily headed upstairs. I, on the other hand, noticed a couple of kids on the sidewalks and realized that school had probably let out. Seeing the kids, it occurred to me that the Nantucket High School might have an old yearbook, or old trophies that could enlighten me on the two other newcomers to Millie's inner circle: Lennie Bartow and Nathaniel Dinks.

I jumped into my Beetle and headed to school.

Chapter 13

Classes were finished for the day, but the Nantucket High School campus was filled with kids. On a field behind the building, the Whalers' soccer team was practicing. I waved at a coach, a regular at the Wick & Flame, and then headed into the school building. Since I was looking for an old yearbook, I decided that the library would be a reasonable place to start my search.

I was impressed when I walked the familiar halls of my alma mater and entered the Gardner Library, which had been impressively renovated since my school days. The library was both comfortable and high tech, and I enjoyed seeing it in action. I'd followed stories about the recent renovations. In fact, Peter had written a story about their interest in adding a café-style coffee service. The kids here were hard at work, many on computers, many in groups at tables; others were studying quietly.

I walked to the main desk and smiled at the librarian.

"I went here," I whispered. "The renovation is amazing."

"Isn't it?" she said.

"I'm wondering if you can help me with a project. My mom, Millie Wright, also attended NHS. She's visiting me right now, and I'm making her a photo collage to reminisce about old times. I thought she'd get a kick out of some pictures from her old yearbook, but she lost it during a move."

"I think your best bet is to go to the principal's office," she said. "They have a collection of them. Someone even donated one from the '40s a couple of years ago. There's also an alumni website if you want to check that out. People post pictures all the time."

"Thanks," I said, appreciating her consideration.

I felt way too old to be sent to the principal's office, but off I went. If I said I knew the way by heart because of the hard work I'd done on student council, I'd only be telling half the truth. During my high school days, I'd found my way to the Head's doorstep on a couple of other, less noble, occasions.

I arrived at a small reception room by the principal's office where I walked to the seating area. The latest edition of *Veritas,* the school's newspaper, was on the table beside a small sculpture made by a student. I quite liked it. The latest yearbook was beside it, but I went straight to a bookcase where the older yearbooks were lined up with the years neatly listed down their spines.

Nathaniel had said he was two years ahead of Millie. I counted from my birthday, back to what I thought her graduation date would have been, then took an extra two years off. I found the book easily and began to browse the pages. Back then, the yearbooks were significantly slimmer, which was helpful. I flipped forward and back, until I found the Seniors section. Deciding to conduct my search alphabetically, I scanned the senior photo page for Leonard Bartow.

Turns out I'm great at balancing an account book and running a business, but not so hot at counting backwards. I was a year off. I went back to the shelf and pulled out the next one.

There he was. A young Leonard Bartow, looking uncomfortable, as we all do, in his formal school photo. Millie was right. Lennie had really put on the pounds over the years. In his photo, he was a skinny kid who led the track team. I studied his eyes, and the shape of his nose. I could see some similarity, but ultimately it was hard to conclude that he was the same man who was attending Frank Marshall's party.

Next, I followed the photos until I reached the letter D, to find a photo of Nathaniel Dinks. Compared to his photo, Nathaniel's youthful dark hair was grayer now, but his ears stuck out in a way that was familiar to me. The slight hooding over the boy's eyes was now heavier, but I could see how the young man in front of me could have aged into the gentleman by my mother's side at the hospital. Both Lennie and Nathaniel had some resemblance to the men I'd met. Nathaniel more than Lennie. Time had done a number on Lennie.

Curious, I looked through the yearbook to find other photos of Nathaniel in club and sport photos. Honestly, I wanted some scoop on the man who was more likely courting my mom than planning an act of anarchy. He did, after all, have an alibi for this morning. And he'd even had Millie's bag in hand when we'd arrived on Nantucket. If he'd been after the bag, he could have grabbed it then.

I found one of him in the Whalers' football team

photos. I also learned he was on the debate team and in the French club. All in all, he was a very likable kid.

When I put the book back on the shelf, I saw my mom's graduation year, two books down. I decided to take a quick peek. Her photo was beautiful, and I could see from the glint in her eye that she was already looking to what lay beyond Nantucket's shores. I would have been happy to spend more time looking through the pages, but I heard a familiar voice from behind the closed door to the Head's office.

"Thanks so much for meeting with me," said Peter, who sounded as if he was getting close to the door. "The wind turbine is an amazing program, and it's time for an update on the fine work you've done to lower electricity costs and engage students in clean energy projects."

I really didn't want to explain to Peter why I was there. I didn't want to lie to this good man, but I knew Agent Hill might threaten to use one of her seventeen methods of torture if I revealed to him the reason for my visit.

I skedaddled down that hallway like a young Lennie Bartow running on the track team. Out the back door and onto the athletic fields of the campus. I looked back through the glass doors I'd exited, hoping they hadn't noticed me. They had. Peter had followed at a distance and was looking right at me.

I can think quickly on my feet on most occasions, but this wasn't my finest moment. I gave Peter a wave, all fingers and jazz hands, and then suddenly found myself doing a sort of jig, which ended with me shuffling out of view before I picked up speed to my car, where I jumped inside and took off. As I looked back, I saw Peter walk outside, his head tilted, his jaw askew, and his eyes following my receding car. I felt badly, but not too badly. After all, he'd driven by me in town without so much as a hello earlier today.

I realized my phone was still off. Helpful in terms of blocking Laruam's ability to track me, but not a great idea given that my mom was still in the hospital. I powered it up. After two stop signs, Peter hadn't called. How could he not know I was up to something interesting after our four months together? Andy had been able to tell I was distracted about something from a twig in my hair. I shook off my frustration with Peter and focused on my list of suspects.

John Pierre's access to an abandoned house seemed more sinister than Olive's boxes with the names of countries scrawled along the sides, but both were unusual. I still didn't know anything more about Laura Morton, but I'd also gone from three suspects to five. I knew I shouldn't dismiss the fact that Laruam might be posing as Lennie Bartow or Nathaniel Dinks. The prospect of finding Rex Laruam before we had to leave tonight was becoming difficult to imagine, but I was not ready to give up.

When I returned to town, I kept my eyes open for Chris's Canadian visitors. I parked my car and strolled up Main Street before weaving my way through the town's other streets. The day was pleasant, and the walk felt good. I saw many familiar faces and a couple of "Sale" signs in anticipation of the fall lull in business, but there was no sign of the Mortons.

When I opened the door to the Wick & Flame, there was no sign of Cherry either.

Chapter 14

"Hello?" I said, immediately concerned for Cherry's safety. I hadn't thought my store would be in danger in broad daylight, but perhaps I had been naïve not to worry.

"Hello," Cherry said as she popped up from behind my counter.

I'd never been happier to see her, until I remembered that my safe, containing Millie's perfume samples, was back where she'd ducked down. I died a little inside, remembering Lennie Bartow's phone conversation. He'd told someone that something was worth looking into. Would Cherry Waddle ever be in league with an anarchist? The idea was more than I could handle.

"What are you doing down there?" I said, peeking over my counter.

Cherry held up my basket of sugar packets.

"Dropped these," she said.

I smiled, but with a heavy heart I knew I had to cover all the angles. I slipped behind the register and lifted the tapestry that covered the safe. With three clicks of the dial, the door was open.

The black bag was still there, and I decided right then that I would not put Cherry Waddle on my list of suspects. This was a woman who once nursed a butterfly back to health.

"What're you doing?" said Cherry.

"I'm sniffing out lingering scents," I said.

"Why?"

I took my head out of the oven, so to speak.

"I have no idea why," I said, taking a peek inside Millie's black bag at the remaining eleven vials. "I'm having a rough day."

"I see that," Cherry said. "And I'd like to make a pitch—so, keep an open mind. Your mother is in town, she's had an accident, and you haven't stopped moving since you got home. Part of that is my fault. I pushed you this morning to hold your class, and maybe I shouldn't have. Anyway, I'd like to offer my help to work here again tomorrow. It's good for me too. I read that it's very healthy for a woman my age to work if she can. So, what do you think?"

"I think that's a great idea," I said.

"Really?" she said, sounding genuinely surprised by how easily I'd acquiesced to her proposal.

"I could use the help," I said, returning the bag and closing the safe's door.

"You also look like you could use a little food," she said, and rummaged through her bag until she handed me a Snickers candy bar.

She was right. I realized I'd only eaten some cheese this morning, while on Peter's boat. Her offering was as good as a meal at a Michelin restaurant.

"Thanks," I said, unwrapping the candy bar. I work around the corner from Sweet Inspirations, a mouthwatering, artisanal chocolate store. I usually satisfy my cravings with their chocolate-covered cranberries, especially in the fall when the cranberry bogs are harvested and everyone has cranberry on their mind. But this Snickers was heaven.

"Interesting things in the store today," said Cherry, all business.

"What do you mean?" I said. I had the bar halfway to my mouth for a second bite.

"First," she said, "there's a run on pink candles of all shapes and sizes. I believe my window display planted pink into people's heads, and it's created a demand. You'll need to make a few more when you get a chance."

"Will do," I said, enjoying my snack.

"Then the fifth-grade Girl Scout troop leader popped in and asked if you'd be able to help with a Halloween event next month. I told her of course."

"Of course," I said.

"The Canadian lady staying with Chris stopped in," she said.

I stopped chewing.

"She loves your candles," said Cherry. "Then a very pushy man came in, and she scooted out. Dark-haired guy. Probably a tourist from the Jared Coffin House. The hotel seems packed right now. Anyway, he walked all around, touching everything. When I asked if I could help him, he smiled but completely ignored me. You know I never trust someone with a shifty smile. If you're not smiling with your eyes, then I say you're not smiling at all. See what I mean?"

She gave me two versions of a smile. One with the eyes, one without.

"What was he looking for?" I said.

"Who knows?" she said, wiping the counter indignantly. "The worst was that he stuck his head into your workroom, and I had to tell him it was off limits. He was respectful, but after all of that he left without a purchase. Your chocolate is melting, stop squeezing it."

I looked at my hand, which had smooshed my candy bar. I ripped off a piece of paper towel from a roll at my tea stand as calmly as I could and wiped my hands clean. As I did, I wondered if I should add a sixth suspect to my growing list. Could the man that Cherry had described have been Laruam?

"Sometimes we get clunkers in here," I said, tossing the paper towel into the bin. "Sorry you had to deal with him. In case he comes back, what did he look like?"

"Oh, you'd know him," she said. "Dead eyes."

"Yuck," I said, trying not to look too interested. "Why don't you get going. Let me close."

"Honestly, I wouldn't mind meeting Flo around the corner," said Cherry, picking up her bag without an argument. "We're finishing a quilt to raise money for the fire department."

As the door closed behind her, my phone rang.

"She's awake," Kate said when I pressed Accept.

My heart filled with joy.

"Is she OK?" I said.

"She's telling Nathaniel stories about a trip she took to Bangladesh."

"I haven't even heard those stories," I said, grabbing my bag.

"I do need to tell you one thing," said Kate.

I stopped in my tracks.

"The doctor can fill you in more, but your mother seems to have lost some memory of the events that happened between leaving Paris and when she fell. Although she recognized Nathaniel, he discovered the lapse while they were talking. He's been asking her questions to help her jog her memory, but nothing yet. This is usually a short-term condition. We'll keep her here one more night, but she can most likely go home tomorrow."

"No. She needs to come home tonight," I said. I knew I sounded unreasonable, but I was supposed to take Millie to Agent Hill for protection.

"Doctor's orders," said Kate. "You can ask him more when you see him."

I knew Kate was doing her best for my mom, but after I hung up I called Peter.

"Hi, beautiful," he said. He sounded like he was as tired as I was about the tension between us.

I was glad I'd called.

"Sorry I couldn't stop and chat before," I said.

"I couldn't either," he said, sounding somewhat defensive.

"I'm on my way to the hospital," I said. "Want to meet me there?"

"I do," he said. "I'm finishing my article about the Culinary Center, then I'll meet you."

"I'd love that," I said, glad he hadn't pressed me about our afternoon encounter at the high school. I wished he had more of an inkling that something was up, but I couldn't complain. I was sworn to secrecy.

Less than ten minutes later, I was bounding through the Cottage Hospital doors for the second time in a day. Up to the second floor and down the hallway, I did not wait for a doctor, nurse, or relative to debrief me. I opened the door and practically jumped for joy when I saw my mother sitting up, wide-eyed.

"Mom," I said, and flew toward her with open arms.

"Stellie!" she said, hugging me in return.

"And how are you?" I said to Nathaniel, who was still by her side.

"I'm strong as an ox," he said, pounding his chest to prove his point.

I was happy to hear my mom laugh.

"You got a big concussion," I said to Millie.

"I know," she said. "But it's nothing compared to the way my head felt when I celebrated Carnival in Rio last year. But there I did not have this kind man to give me a glass of water and hold my hand."

She smiled at Nathaniel, who was, in fact, offering her a glass of water.

"Nathaniel, how can you enjoy Nantucket if you're cooped up here? You need to get out," she said.

The man turned a crimson red at her comment. He was on one side of the bed, clasping her hand. I was on the other side. I budged closer to her, but they had moved on to mushy conversation. I let it slide given that my mom was in the hospital, under threat of death by forces we knew little about.

A doctor joined us to give me an update on Millie's improving health. I argued for an earlier release, but the doctor was adamant that we take the extra precaution. Agent Hill wouldn't be happy. The truth was, however, I needed to know that Millie would be one hundred percent well. Once we boarded Agent Hill's boat, we wouldn't be able to leave it until we arrived at a safe house, wherever that might be.

There was, of course, one silver lining. I hoped Agent Hill would at least appreciate that I could use the extra time to follow up on anything we discussed tonight.

"I forgot to tell you," Millie said. "Andy stopped by today to say hello."

I wasn't surprised. He and my mom have always had a soft spot for each other. He would certainly make time to pop in.

"He said I looked great, and then he said you're up to something. I told him you were worried about me, but he didn't look convinced."

She gave me a questioning look. Even with a memory lapse, she was still my mom. I gave her an innocent smile, but she looked at me thoughtfully.

"That man could always read her," Millie said to Nathaniel. "I always hoped they would get together."

"Oh my God," I said, standing. I knew her memory was foggy, but forgetting about Peter was too much. "Mom!!"

"Hello?"

We all turned our heads. Peter was in the doorway. I had no idea how long he'd been standing there, but from the look on his face I suspected he'd heard enough.

"Mom," I said. "You remember Peter?"

"Oh," she said. She held her chin in contemplation for a moment, then cast him a big smile. "Of course, I remember Pete."

"I'll wait outside," said Peter. "Glad to see you up and at it, Millie."

"You too, Pete," she said.

He gave me a smile before heading out to the waiting room. Kate took his place in the door frame.

"Let's let Millie sleep," she said, intervening in our dysfunctional family moment. "If we're going to discharge you in the morning, Millie, you should rest as much as possible. Nathaniel, that means you too. Time to go."

"I haven't slept this much in years," said Millie. "I'm fine."

"I think you should listen to the experts," Nathaniel said, politely moving to the door. "Millie, I'll come see you in the morning—showered, clean shaven, and in a change of clothes. Meantime, good night, ladies."

"Stella?" she said when Nathaniel left.

I went to her. The doctor closed the door so that we had a moment to ourselves.

"How are you?" I said.

"I think someone, or something, is in danger," she said. "But I don't know what, or why."

I was excited that her memory might be coming back, but I treaded carefully. I didn't want to scare her.

"Is there anything you want to tell me about your formulas?" I said.

Millie frowned, and shook her head.

"Should I be worried about them?" she said.

"Not at all. I've got things covered," I said, and I squeezed her hand. "Get some sleep, and you'll be back to feeling yourself tomorrow."

I lowered the light and gave her a kiss on the forehead.

"Stella?" she said.

I looked back at her, hoping she'd remembered something.

"*Bonne nuit, ma chérie,*" she said.

She leaned back and closed her eyes. In about ten seconds, I heard her begin to snore. I wondered if perhaps Nathaniel's hearing wasn't the best when I shut the door.

Millie Wright wasn't the home-cooked-meal, get-all-your-homework-done, no-way-are-you-going-out-in-that-outfit kind of parent, but she was no slouch either. When I was a child, my mom set up a perfume store to pay the bills while she was raising me. She was no businesswoman, but she had an endless imagination, which included a game she'd invented for me as a child—to match one of her perfume scents to her customers in the store. When I was older, she encouraged me to find a summer job at the Whaling Museum, where I learned about our island's history of lighting the world with clear burning candles made from whale oil. By encouraging me to find my passion, and forcing me to balance her business's books, her least favorite job, she set me up for my calling, a candle maker and small business owner. Now, it was my turn to help her. Nothing was going to stop me from saving my mom.

Chapter 15

"Hi?" I said to Peter when I entered the waiting room.

Before I knew it, his arms slipped around me. Even a crime-fighting super-spy deserves a good kiss. I let myself thoroughly enjoy the highlight of my day.

"Millie didn't scare you off?" I said with a final tug to his lanky body before letting him go.

"Millie is a hoot," he said.

"You've got that right," I said. "Where's Nathaniel?"

"He left," he said. "Something about a 'This Is Your Life Dinner' for Frank."

"I wouldn't mind some dinner," I said.

"You're in luck. Chris sent me a text," he said. "They defrosted a lasagna if we want some. And he said something about a big salad that his Canadian guests were making. And that the British lady, Olive, is there too. They bumped into her at the market."

I had to thank Chris and Peter. In one swoop, they'd managed to organize a dinner with three of my suspects: Olive, John Pierre, and Laura. Seeing them all together, I could compare and contrast their behaviors in a way that might help me focus on one person over another.

Thirty minutes later, we were gathered in Chris's

large kitchen. His boys were wrestling in a corner over a football. Tinker had joined the contest and was jumping on them, as if he thought he had any chance at getting the ball. In an office space at the corner of his kitchen, Chris was showing Laura and John Pierre the plans of a house he had been working on. It was a beautiful scene of family and friendship, except that I had my eyes trained on the Mortons and Olive for murder. Every gesture, every comment, every question about my mom or the island, seemed to take on a hidden meaning.

The main challenge to my concentration, however, was the cheese that Laura and John Pierre had bought. Whatever else they'd been up to today, their cheese excursion had been a hit.

"It's all in the nose," said John Pierre as I melted into a bite of an unfamiliar, but heavenly, soft cheese. "You have a good nose of your own, Stella. I suspect your mother passed hers to you. I bet you can break any scent down to its basic components."

Like the locations of security along the path to the Peace Jubilee?

Cryptic comments abounded.

"I'd never have found this at the Stop & Shop," I said.

"He knows what to look for," said Laura, with a pat to her husband's arm. "For one thing, the rind of this Parmesan says Reggiano, so you know it's authentic. Forget about Brie or Camembert. America doesn't let you make unpasteurized cheeses, which is a crime."

Her disappointment in our Brie made me miss the samplings I'd had in Paris.

"No politics," said John Pierre. "Cheese should never be political."

At the end of dinner, I decided to break John Pierre's rule, and bring up politics.

"What do you all think about the upcoming Peace Jubilee?" I said.

"I think they should focus on technology. It's the root cause of all our problems today," said Olive. I imagined Cherry Waddle would cringe at such a blanket accusation. If it weren't for Facetime and Facebook, her relationships with her West Coast grandchildren would be much harder to maintain.

"I think the only way that the Jubilee will succeed is if there is no more violence," said John Pierre. "Already that dead man at the perfume conference has shaken people's faith. After that, it's a domino effect. One more setback and 'boom.' The whole thing will be an utter failure."

"You are a cynic," said Laura, affectionately.

"Yes, I am," said John Pierre.

I decided it was time for a look in the Mortons' room.

"'Scuse me," I said, and headed lightly down the hallway toward a bathroom, which was also attached to the Mortons' room.

I shut the bathroom door, locked it, then opened a second door leading to their room, an inviting suite in a beautiful, rosy shade of pink. If John Pierre and Laura had stayed at one of our island's bed and breakfasts they could not have asked for a more welcoming chamber. On the wall above their comfortable bed were two sailor's valentines, which Chris and his wife had each made for the other when they got engaged. A sailor's valentine is a collage made of shells and encased in a hardwood box, and theirs were of nautical knot designs. The décor was pulled together by a pink and beige braided rug which covered painted floorboards. A huge bowl of shells sat on the dresser. It was lovely, but I'd still have stayed in the full house John Pierre had visited over a small room in someone's home.

I could hear the conversation continue in the kitchen, and I calculated that I had only about two minutes before I would be expected to return. Looking quickly around the room, I could see that the Mortons had been respectful of their lodgings. Their bed was perfectly made, and their suitcases rested on two benches at the bottom of the bed. Nothing seemed out of place.

To start, I scanned the tabletops, searched under the cushions of two club chairs, and behind the curtains. Nothing caught my eye. Under the bed, I found a matchbox car and a stray goldfish that had escaped the vacuum cleaner. That was about it.

Next, I approached the Mortons' suitcases. The bags were both unzipped, and I flipped open John Pierre's. He had only a few items, which were neatly folded. Corduroy pants in a shade of wine for the fall, a few button downs in soft cottons, and undergarments in the back pocket. Nothing screamed enemy spy or murderer. Unless his spy gear was at the other house, John Pierre's most nefarious possession was a pack of Zantac, which only proved that his body and his affection for cheese were sometimes at odds. I didn't know what I should expect to find in Rex Laruam's bag, but if the contents of Agent Hill's knapsack were any example of what a spy packs, I felt I should have at least found a stash of passports, various currencies, and a gun.

I moved on to Laura's bag. She also had a minimal wardrobe, skillfully packed. There were scarves and other, simple accessories to change a look from day to night. Black pants, a few pretty blouses, her flowered dress. There was a pocket in the back, and I tucked my hand inside to see if there was anything interesting. I found stockings and her dragonfly hairclip.

I also found a small, red gift box which had fallen to the bottom of the pocket. I lifted it out. It was pretty, and just about the right size to fit one of Millie's perfume vials. I'd never noticed any of the stores in town use this kind of box, and I know how everyone wraps their goods. I opened the box. It was empty. I wondered if the Mortons planned to pass off the formula as a perfume gift in a humble exit through customs.

Aside from Laura's mysterious box, I was most struck at this point by how simply the Mortons travelled. Laura had supposedly been shopping in town today, but there were no shopping bags. I knew from personal experience that it is impossible to walk the streets of Nantucket without making at least one purchase.

I decided to look inside John Pierre's bag from Marine Home Center, which was shoved between the bed and the wall. In particular, I was curious to know if his laptop was inside. As I started to open the bag, however, I realized the sound of the crumpled brown paper was loud. I knew it was risky to make so much noise. I'd have to forgo my last opportunity to investigate if I wanted to avoid any suspicion.

Outside, I heard a swell of laughter rise from the dinner party, and I knew I'd be expected back. I returned to the bathroom and flushed. Under the whoosh of the water, I opened the bathroom door.

"Whoa," I said.

Laura was standing right in front of me. She looked the tiniest bit loopy from the wine.

"Oopsy daisy," she said, letting me pass. "I hope you are enjoying dinner. I fear we're imposing on your family after Millie's accident."

"Anyone who cooks is not imposing," I said, letting her pass after a quick look at the bathroom to make sure I hadn't left anything amiss. "Thanks for feeding us. I heard you visited my store today."

"I did," she said. "Your candles lingered in my imagination after I heard Millie's lecture yesterday morning. They are lovely."

I wanted to ask her if Millie's bag and the memory of my safe had lingered in her imagination as well, but I smiled. She shut the door, and I headed back to the kitchen.

"His face was desperate," Olive was saying to Chris's boys.

The boys, in turn, were looking at her with eyes as round as Tinker's.

"How big was the knife that killed him?" said Chris's oldest, while his younger brother took a step backwards.

I realized they were talking about the murder in Paris as if it were a bedtime story.

"It was small," said Olive, "but it was sharp, for sure."

"How do you know about the knife?" I said.

I hadn't seen Olive anywhere near the murdered

man when he'd crawled through the crowd, so I found it hard to imagine how she knew what the knife looked like. I hadn't mentioned it to her, and there had been no description of it in the newspapers. I knew for a fact that Millie would not speak of the murder, so she hadn't learned about it from my mother.

"A friend from the conference told me," she said, patting one of the boys on the head as she spoke.

"I saw a woman on a bike today who looked so much like you that I almost waved," I said to Olive, raising some of the questions I'd have asked if she'd accepted my invitation to tea earlier today.

"I used to be an excellent biker in my day," she said. "My dear, we've all missed your mother at the table tonight, but this is one of those cases where it's important to follow the doctor's rules."

I believed what she'd done was evade my suggestion that I'd seen her biking and deflect to a different topic.

"You must have to follow rules carefully as a teacher," Laura said to Olive as she returned to the kitchen.

"Actually, my dear, when you've worked at an all-girls school for as long as I have, a little anarchy is good for the bones," Olive said.

"Speaking of anarchy, boys, why don't you jump into your PJs?" said Chris. "No showers tonight—if you don't tell Mom!"

The boys cheered like true rebels and ran upstairs with their father before he could change his mind. We all took the hint, too. I cleared our plates. Peter invited Olive to the front lawn to point out the Big Dipper, and the Mortons began to wrap leftovers. Chris's kitchen is a loft-like space with an island in the middle. Their kitchen table, however, is behind a partitioned wall. I'd gone back to the table to clear some odds and ends, piling items onto a small tray, when I heard Laura and John Pierre lower their voices on the other side.

"I hate this endless wait," said Laura. "All of this sitting around when there's real work to do ahead. Let's just hope she comes through tomorrow."

"All will work out," said John Pierre. "Whatever it takes."

The salt and pepper shakers were in my hands, but I'd forgotten all about clearing the table. Instead, my mind was racing as it tried to figure out what Laura had meant. I wondered who "she" was, but of course I was sure it was me.

"Boo," said Peter, wrapping his arms around my waist.

Startled, I tossed the salt shaker behind me and across the room.

Chapter 16

"Jeez," Peter said, turning to pick up the salt shaker as Tinker licked up the spill. "You could blind a guy like that."

"You should go home and get a good night's sleep," said Olive, who had stepped back inside the house with Peter. "All of us should."

"We've got this," said John Pierre, removing the tray from my hand.

"I'll walk you home," said Peter.

I suddenly felt that everyone wanted me out of the house, but I didn't mind. I had a date with Agent Hill, and a lot to share with her. I let Laura pack me a bag of leftovers, and then I headed home.

Crossing the yard, both Tinker and Peter were true gentlemen. With Tinker riding on my shoulder, Peter took my leftovers and held my hand. I thought about the tension I'd perceived between us earlier today. There were things to be said, but before I could start, I yawned. It was out before I knew it.

"Long day," we both said together. We looked at each other, then laughed.

"I should drive Olive back to town, don't you think?" Peter said.

I nodded. Dinner had been nice, but now I felt like we were on a first date and not sure what to do with each other.

"Peter," I said. "Can you do me a favor?"

I know. Asking a favor of Peter in the middle of a delicate moment in our relationship might seem like an unusual choice, but in that moment, I wanted nothing more than for him to join me, in any way, as I puzzled out the identity of Rex Laruam. I couldn't give him details that would jeopardize national security. I'd promised Agent Hill I would not. I knew, however, that I'd feel stronger knowing he was somehow connected.

"Any time," he said, his hands shoved into his pockets, his old smile returning.

And like that, I think we both knew we were on each other's side, even if we didn't know exactly what the other was up to.

I realized, however, that I wasn't sure how to engage Peter.

I looked back at Chris's house. The lights were still on in the kitchen, and I could see the Mortons at the table with my cousin for one last glass of wine. I considered the five suspects we knew. The Mortons, Olive, Nathaniel, and Lennie. I picked the Mortons. They were a two-for-one opportunity.

"Can you put on your reporter's hat and do a little snooping on the Mortons? They seem nice, but don't you think Chris should research people a little before letting them into his house?"

"That's all?" he said, with a laugh. "you've got it."

I might have been tired, but I was no fool. I pressed my lips against Peter for the kind of good-night kiss a couple of four months—and a couple of awkward

days—deserves. I also felt better knowing that once
Peter had a job, he'd follow all leads to the end. If
there was anything fishy about the Mortons, he would
figure it out.

After a reluctant good night, I slipped up to my
apartment, turned out the light, and looked through
the window over my kitchen sink until I saw the light
go out in Chris's kitchen. I put my phone on my coffee
table so that Rex Laruam could not use it to track me.
I grabbed my car keys and the bag of leftovers, locked
the door, and left to meet with Agent Hill.

A few minutes later, I parked two blocks away from
Brant Point, and made the rest of the way by foot.
With the sun now set, the evening picnics had ended.
I had the beach to myself. I fished out the small emer-
gency flashlight I kept in my glove compartment, and
then headed down to the chilly beach.

Following Agent Hill's instructions, I flashed the
light three times in the direction of the *Hatchfield*,
dimly lit by the rising moon. I waited. No one came. I
couldn't see anyone on board the boat, but I was
afraid to send my message again.

I swallowed hard. Driving around town to learn
more about our suspects had been important work,
but now I considered the more dangerous side of the
job. I thought of the murdered man in Paris with a
knife in his back in a whole new light.

Finally, I heard the motor of a boat, and I searched
the harbor waters to identify its source. Unfortunately,
sound has a tricky way of bouncing off of the water. In
the dark, I could not tell if the boat was coming from
the *Hatchfield* or somewhere else. To play it safe, I
crept to the Brant Point Lighthouse, a familiar land-
mark which people love to use as a backdrop for family

or engagement photos. It has a long, wooden walkway leading from the beach to the lighthouse's entrance and is flanked on one side by huge rocks to protect the building from the waters. At the lighthouse, I hid behind one of these rocks in hopes I could get a view of the boat heading toward me.

The sound of the engine cut out. I peered over the rocks. I could hear the lapping of small waves at the shore. I could smell the salt in the air. But, I could not see a boat. I was squinting into the night, debating whether I should make a run for it or try my signal again, when I sensed something to the other side of me.

"What are you doing?" said Agent Hill.

"What the hell?" I said, jumping a couple of feet, and almost dropping the leftovers in my hand.

I hadn't even heard her get off the boat.

"I thought you might be Rex Laruam," I said, coolly.

"Good instincts," she said. "Where's your mother?"

"I have some bad news. She's still in the hospital until tomorrow morning," I said. "She's having some issues with her memory. If you have to leave tonight, I understand."

Agent Hill cursed under her breath. She looked at the sea and then back at me.

"I'm not leaving you," she said. I suspected from her tone that her answer was driven entirely by duty. I knew she was desperate to remove the formula from the island and that every extra moment she remained on the island put her mission at risk.

To break the tension between us, I handed her the bag of food.

"I also have an update for you," I said.

"Come on," she said. "We've got work to do."

I wished we could have had our meeting on the sandy beach, but I knew we needed the safety of the boat to make sure that no one could hear us. Dutifully, I boarded the *Hatchfield*'s dinghy and we crossed the waters. I've motored across Nantucket harbor's waters at night dozens of times in my life, but never for a clandestine meeting with a secret agent. What usually felt enchanting to me, now felt obscured by danger. If a shark had swum by us, I wouldn't have blinked twice. I took comfort in the fact that Agent Hill was ever alert. She wore a black wetsuit, I assumed for warmth, or maybe for cover, with a sweatshirt thrown over her.

In silence, Agent Hill tied the dinghy to the boat, and we climbed up the ladder which bobbed in our wake. Once on deck, we continued to the cabin, where Agent Hill turned on the light above the small table. She gestured me to sit. Still without a word, she went to the galley and opened a drawer. Then, she sat across from me with a fork.

"What did you find out?" she said, opening the bag of food I had given her.

"Olive Tidings wears a wig," I began, immediately feeling that I hadn't led with my best shot at establishing credibility. "And I saw her hauling a shovel around town with fresh dirt on it. Plus, she took a walk to Brant Point this afternoon."

I looked at Agent Hill for a reaction. She wiped her mouth.

"Next," she said.

"There's John Pierre Morton," I said. "He bought gloves and twine and hedge clippers. He also broke into a house. On so many levels, that is not OK."

"Did he use a key?" she said.

I nodded.

"Then maybe he has a right to access it," she said, shooting me down again.

"I figured since we now have extra time before we leave Nantucket I'd keep digging," I said in my defense. "My cousin Liz is checking up on the house for me. She's in real estate. And my boyfriend, Peter, is a reporter. He's looking into them too."

I could see Agent Hill was impressed, by the way she plunged her fork back into the pasta bowl.

"What about Laura?" she said.

I described the small, red gift box I had found in her suitcase.

"Also, I overheard her say to John Pierre that she couldn't wait for tomorrow and hoped 'she' would pull it off. That could be me."

Agent Hill seemed nonplussed by Laura's comment, although I'd thought it was a doozy.

"Anything else?" she said.

"Yes," I said. "The list is longer than we'd first considered. Nathaniel Dinks, my mom's new friend, and Lennie Bartow, are guests at a party in town. They grew up on the island, so I didn't focus on them at first, but they've now reappeared after twenty years. My best friend, Emily, is organizing the event, so maybe Rex Laruam figured out that our paths would cross. Could Rex Laruam have taken one of their places?"

"Do you think Nathaniel could be Laruam? Is that why he's so anxious to spend time with Millie?"

"I'd say yes, but he had Millie's bag in hand when we arrived on Nantucket, before you took the formula," I said. "He could have easily taken off with it then."

Agent Hill nodded thoughtfully.

"Tell me about Lennie," she said.

"Leonard Bartow. Emily said he was flirting with Millie before the accident. He also typed a note and tacked it to Nathaniel's door, telling him he wanted to take him out for a drink when he got home from the hospital. My note was typed, too. Maybe he wants to get Nathaniel drunk to find out if Millie said anything interesting in her sleep."

"This is quite a list," she said. "An old lady, two old men, and a couple of well-mannered Canadians. I want your mom on this boat the first minute she gets out of the hospital. We're not wasting any more time on these leads. We have to protect the vial."

"A man visited the store today, whom my assistant Cherry did not recognize," I said, ignoring Agent Hill's skepticism. "She said that he was interested in my scents and walked around my store as if he owned it."

"Fine. Tomorrow, see if you can find out something about him," she said. "I actually don't like the sound of that."

"Do you think he's Rex Laruam?" I said.

At that moment, we felt a bump against the boat's starboard side, strong enough to make us both stop talking.

Chapter 17

Agent Hill reached into her wet suit jacket and handed me the vial.

"Take this," she said, looking at the door. "Keep the vial safe."

"Let's call for backup," I whispered. "I think it's time we broke protocol. I can call Andy. Our police can be discreet."

"If you think a local policeman can help, you're crazier than I am," she said.

The cabin doors began to break. Agent Hill pushed me into the berth and slammed the door on me.

From the small, dark room, I heard the doors to the cabin burst open. I pressed myself into the wall, ready for gunfire, but instead I heard a resounding crash in the cabin, as if two people had tackled each other head-on. My hands clenched into fists, and I wondered what I should do.

Before I could decide, I heard a loud whack, followed immediately by a thud on the floor.

Someone had won the fight, but who?

As I stayed hidden in the berth, hoping Agent Hill would be the one to open my door, I heard the sound of the cabin doors open again, followed by the sound of a body being dragged across the floor. Heavy clunking noises filled the cabin. I decided the sound was from the winner of the fight dragging the loser up the stairs. Soon, I heard footsteps on the deck above me. Then, I heard a splash. I leaned against the wall, clutching the vial to my body.

The *Hatchfield* was silent for what felt like hours. When I finally decided that I had to make a move, I slipped the vial inside the top of my jumpsuit. I was about to take a step forward when I heard the door to the cabin open again, followed by footsteps descending.

I had only known Agent Hill a short time, but it was long enough that I could tell the footsteps were not hers. These were heavier. Angrier. And they were coming toward me.

The door to the berth where I was hiding opened. It blew right into my stomach, but I caught the knob in my hand, so it did not bounce back to reveal me. A person I could not see from my hiding place, but who I knew was Rex Laruam, grabbed the knapsack. I heard him look through the bag, and then throw it onto the floor. I heard him open each drawer, and then the closet as he looked for the vial I was holding. Failing to find it, he grabbed the door and slammed it behind him. I remained, glued to the wall, keenly aware that I had just been in the same room as one of the world's worst public enemies, but unable to take action with the vial in my possession.

Outside, I heard the clanging of pots and pans, the slam of the refrigerator door, and the contents of a drawer clatter to the ground as he searched through the galley. When all failed, I heard him rip open the cushions of the bench, likely with the same surgical expertise he'd used to kill Agent Hill's partner. Realizing he might likely do the same to the mattress in the berth, or worse, to me, I took a chance. Laruam had left the closet door ajar. I now leapt across the dark room and into the small enclosure he'd already searched, hoping it would offer me protection.

My leap was almost simultaneous with Laruam's reentry to the berth. I landed in the closet with both arms and legs outstretched for balance, a stance I hadn't adopted since about second grade when I'd been obsessed with cartwheels. I remained stuck in this position for the duration of Laruam's search, wishing I had Agent Hill's gun for protection. I was dying to peek into the room, to get a good look at the man, but I knew if I moved an inch, he would hear me.

As I'd predicted, he tore the mattress to shreds as well. When Laruam finally gave up his search of the berth, I heard him pick up Agent Hill's backpack and head up the stairs to the deck. I allowed myself the luxury of lowering my arms, which had lost all circulation, as he performed a similarly exhaustive search of the plush seating on deck above me. Then, I heard him jump off the starboard side of the boat and into the sea.

Rex Laruam had come and gone.

Eager to find any clue about the man that he might have left behind, I opened the berth's door with a steady hand. I was not afraid. In fact, I was getting to the point where if Laruam had appeared again, I might have tried to pop him one.

There were spatters of blood in the cabin, and the mess I expected to find from Laruam's search. Unfortunately, I could not make out footprints to ascertain the size of the man. Nor had Agent Hill conveniently tugged out a lock of her assailant's hair for me to find. At the stairs to the deck, I noticed Agent Hill's gun. I knew in a million years I could never use it, but I picked it up and added it to my belongings. I was into something now. It was deep. I realized I had likely been present at my second murder in less than two days. There was no way I'd let Millie be Laruam's third victim.

Climbing up to the deck, I heard the *Hatchfield*'s dinghy bobbing in the water behind the stern. Laruam had not taken it. I crawled on hands and knees to the starboard side of the boat, and I peeked over the railings to look at the harbor. I could not see any motorboats or people swimming into the distance, but I remained vigilant.

I took the small motorboat back to shore alone, and then I ditched the boat and ran to my car. Even though I had parked away from the beach, my red Beetle stood out. I decided Laruam had not seen it. Otherwise, he would have looked for me on board the ship.

"OK, Stella," I said to my reflection in my rearview mirror. "What now?"

I squinted at myself, then retied my ponytail. I thought about Millie and her yearning to see the world, and I was reminded once again that one didn't have to step far ashore from Nantucket for adventure.

"OK," I said into the mirror. "You're on, Rex Laruam."

It was Friday night. Agent Hill had said that she had been instructed to protect the formula on Nantucket until Sunday. Assuming help would come Sunday if she didn't turn up, I had two days to protect the vial and catch the fiend.

I had no idea where Laruam had disappeared to tonight. I drove past the Jared Coffin House. I could see a light on in both Olive Tidings and Nathaniel's rooms, but I could not see any movement inside. Lennie Bartow's window was not visible from the street. I drove by the house John Pierre had entered today. No lights were on.

I parked out front and stared at the house. No one seemed to be home. I decided to take a look inside. I grabbed my flashlight. When I reached the front door, I shook the doorknob, hoping it was as loose as some of the shingles, but the lock was in good repair. It wasn't the kind of model I could open with a bobby pin either.

I walked around to the backyard in hopes I might find another way inside. There was a kitchen door, but it was locked too. The windows were a little high for me to see through from the yard, but I did my best to open the sashes of those I could reach. They didn't budge. I looked under a rock for a key. On my fourth rock, I actually found one. I stuck the key in the door and easily opened it into the kitchen.

The smell of the house immediately struck me. I could tell that no fresh air had come in or out, aside from John Pierre's visit, for a long time. I flashed my light across the kitchen whose floor was covered in bright yellow vinyl tiles. The cabinets were yellow metal, and the table was yellow Formica. The room had seen its heyday in the mid-seventies.

Stepping out of the kitchen, the house looked like the nineteenth century antique it was. The ceilings were low and beamed, the floorboards were wide wood planks, and the rooms were grouped around a fireplace. I headed into the dining room where John Pierre had been this afternoon.

Outside, I heard a car. I stood still, listening. It passed. The person who had been on the *Hatchfield* tonight was clearly not racing here for cover. I forged ahead, nonetheless.

John Pierre had left the newspapers on the dining

table. Underneath the *Inquirer & Mirror* were the day's *New York Times* and *Boston Globe.* Both of their headlines had a story about the Peace Jubilee. With less than a week until the event began, more and more dignitaries had arrived. So far, there had been no more violence related to their arrivals.

In the absolute center of the dining table, I saw the ball of twine John Pierre had bought today. Isolated as it was, with no other context, I could not help but wonder why he had left behind this one item from the Marine Home Center. It seemed like a clue, but I didn't know what to make of it.

The next room included a pale blue sofa that sagged in the middle. It was framed by two cane-backed chairs with a couple of holes in the caning and floral cushions. The pieces could actually be quite nice if they weren't so neglected. I imagined with a paint job and some fresh curtains that the whole place could be transformed into a happy home. After a thorough investigation I found nothing to prove that John Pierre was Rex Laruam. In particular, I did not find the body of Agent Hill.

I returned to my car. I remembered the policeman from Paris. He'd given me his business card. I wondered if the French police could help me track down Agent Hill's agency. They'd clearly had no idea that the murder was related to a perfume sample when we'd first spoken. Otherwise, most everyone's belongings would have been confiscated. Perhaps, however, they had been privy to some information about the mission as time went by.

I was tempted to call the officer, but I resisted. It occurred to me that I could have been speaking to Rex Laruam himself, as he developed his list of who might have had the formula. If I thought about it, the

man had had the same sort of unsmiling eyes that
Cherry had used to describe the stranger who came to
my store today. Realizing that I could not be sure
who to trust, I put the card back into my wallet and
drove home.

When I arrived, all of the lights were out in Chris's
house, including the Mortons' room. I walked across
the lawn toward the house with the intention of confirming they were home with my own two eyes, but
then I thought about the consequences if I caught
them with Agent Hill's knapsack, or worse, her body. I
had to respect that my cousin and his young sons were
at home too. I would have to watch their room from
my apartment window. My own sort of stakeout.

I was careful when I entered my apartment. I even
had my hand on the gun, now stashed in my bag, in
case there was someone waiting for me.

There was.

Tinker. I sat beside him and took many, many cen-
tering breaths. Tinker purred sympathetically and
nestled into the comfort of my mother's soft sweater.

"Do you miss Millie too?" I said to my little guy.

I lifted her cardigan, looking at the big, black
buttons and sinking my hands into her pockets. I
brought it to my nose. Admittedly, it was not as fresh
as it might have normally been, but it had travelled
home with us, suffered with Millie during her fall,
and subsequently been used as Tinker's cushion over
the last two days. The scent of my mom, however, a
mixture of her rose-scented eau de parfum, still lingered heavily and gave me comfort. My mom was a
master craftsman but wore the simplest scent for herself. Her philosophy is that every scent reveals itself
differently on each individual, and that the memory

a scent produces is as important as the scent itself. Roses produced a profound sense of happiness for my mom, so she decided she never needed more than that. She also felt that anyone who was drawn to the scent, would also be drawn to her since they were so intermingled. It had served her well for years because she had the nicest friends scattered all over the globe.

And yet, among her newest friends was Rex Laruam.

Tinker nuzzled against me. He could try and try but I feared he'd never find a clue about how to make friends with Millie. Some things just weren't meant to be. I gave him a sympathetic pat on the head and turned on my phone. A text from Peter lit my screen with a photo of a house.

The Morton House, Peter had typed below it.

It was really swanky. It was the kind of place where people who could afford the Jared Coffin House would live, not the kind of people who would choose an Airbnb. I googled the address on a website and found that it was valued at two million dollars. My fingers flew to Peter's name, and I called him.

"Hey," I said when he picked up.

"I wasn't sure you'd be awake," he said.

"I can't sleep," I said.

"Nice house," said Peter.

I could hear him typing in the background.

My palms were sweating. I was so glad we were having this conversation over the phone and not in person, because he would definitely know something was up, no matter what signs he'd missed this morning. I couldn't hide my excitement at his lead. I felt as if I was closing in on the identity of Rex Laruam. It made sense. John Pierre had access to a house on Nantucket. In spite of that fact, he and Laura had appeared conveniently as guests across the lawn from me on the day of Millie's and my return. They'd had easy opportunity to pin the note to my door, and they'd talked about their anticipation about tomorrow.

"Are you there?" said Peter.

"Yes," I said. "I mean no. I'm hitting the hay. See you in the morning?"

"See you tomorrow," he said.

Hanging up, I pulled out the unnumbered vial that Agent Hill had handed to me during her last moments on this earth. It was a pale-yellow shade, the consistency of water. Turning it over and over, I wondered how it held so many secrets and had such power. I felt humbled to be its guardian and tempted to know more. I suspected I shouldn't, but I twisted open the small metal cap and took a whiff.

My mind was running wild about what I might find, but nothing prepared me. I inhaled once more before admitting it.

The formula had no scent at all.

I wondered if the formula needed to be warmed in order for it to work. Sometimes heat can release scents, and in the case of a secret code, it seemed like a good idea to have an extra layer of security. I struck a match from a supply I kept by my sofa and which I use often for my candles. Holding it carefully under the vial, I sniffed again. Still, I could not detect a scent.

Suddenly, however, the room began to fade. I tried to keep my eyelids from drooping, but it was impossible. A haze grew around me like a wave, ready to consume me. I sat on my sofa, unable to move and unable to fight the growing lethargy that was beginning to overtake me. The last thing I managed to do before I passed out was reseal the lid on the vial.

Chapter 18

On the morning of my thirtieth birthday, I opened my eyes feeling like I'd been drugged. Then I remembered I had been. Tinker, who seemed to have slept on me, leapt off my lap as I dropped to the floor on hands and knees to recover the vial that had knocked me out last night. While I was on all fours, I also noticed the gun I'd taken from Agent Hill's boat. Seeing it, the room began to sway again. I dropped the weapon in my bag and covered it with Millie's sweater.

Rolling onto my back, I lifted the sealed vial up to the sunlight which was streaming through my window. Agent Hill had told me that the formula contained scents unique to locations where secret operatives were at work to protect the queen's journey, and thus, the success of the Peace Jubilee. Call me crazy, but it seemed like a "scent" with unique aromas would smell like something. Call me even crazier, but I decided that Agent Hill had not recovered the correct formula from Millie's black bag.

Tinker twitched his ears, perhaps assuming my prone position on the floor would lead to a game.

"No such luck, mister," I said.

I lowered my arm to the floor and studied a couple

of dust bunnies. My goal had been to help Agent Hill
find Rex Laruam, while she protected the formula.
Now she was dead, and the formula I had was the
wrong one.

I hadn't panicked after Agent Hill had been killed,
so I wasn't going to panic about this new turn of
events. You might be surprised, but I decided that her
mistake actually wasn't the worst thing. Sure, I had no
idea where to find the formula. I was back to square
one in that department, but I was also hopeful that
Millie might know where it was, assuming her memory
had improved. When she was released from the hospital, we'd have a good long chat.

Meanwhile, I realized I had a formula that had
been good enough to fool Agent Hill. Now, at least, I
had something that I could give Laruam, if push came
to shove, that would not endanger the queen's journey to the Peace Jubilee. I felt a little like I was playing
Three-card Monte, but it was nice to feel I was the
dealer rather than the mark.

There was a knock on my door. I went to my kitchen
window where I saw Olive Tidings standing on my
stoop.

"Coming," I said through the window. I slipped the
vial behind my sofa cushion and headed downstairs.

When I opened the door, I found Olive holding a
baking tin.

"I come bearing pie. I see you like that lovely jumpsuit. It's very becoming on you, but a bit of advice. A
change of clothes is good for the skin. Helps it breath."

Olive took a step inside and headed up the stairs.

"What a pretty kitty," she said at the landing.
"Tinker's your name, little fellow, isn't it?"

Tinker sidestepped away from her. Olive followed.

"Here pretty, little kitty," she said, following him about my apartment.

Each time she reached out her hand, Tinker would hold his pose until she was about an inch away. Then, he'd sidestep another foot or so.

"You're a bit of a terrorist, aren't you?" Olive said to Tinker. "I like that about you."

She put her pie tin on my kitchen counter, removing the foil. The pie was home baked by the looks of it. Cranberry.

"You mentioned you saw a woman who looked like me on a bike yesterday," she said, opening a drawer in my kitchen from which she pulled my sharpest knife. She put it on the counter.

"She looked almost exactly like you," I said, sitting on my sofa, next to my bag, aka my gun tote.

"In fact, it was me," said Olive. "But I think you knew that."

Olive opened a couple of cabinets. I stayed silent.

"I was on an excursion I wanted to enjoy for myself," she said, stabbing the pie into slices before plating them. "And it paid off in spades."

I shuddered at her word choice, remembering the dirt on her shovel. It made me sick to think of it, but I had to consider that the dirt might have been from a freshly dug grave, one perhaps made in anticipation of Agent Hill's murder. Olive grabbed two forks before joining me.

"The cranberry bogs are more beautiful than the description in the old Fodor's Nantucket I checked out from the library," she said, sitting down with a slice of pie for each of us. "I had a good chat with a fellow at the bogs, and he let me harvest my own, before the Festival today. I was able to bring home two pints. The chef in the kitchen of the Jared Coffin House took a shining to me when I told him I had a local recipe I wanted to try. He let me bake a pie in the hotel kitchen after they closed last night. I made one for him, too, of course."

I wondered if she was giving me an alibi.

"Is that why you went to the market yesterday? To get ingredients?" I said, remembering that Chris had invited Olive to dinner after he'd bumped into her at the market.

"You know a lot about people's comings and goings, don't you?" she said.

"Small town," I said with a shrug.

"Chin-chin!" she said, raising her fork, and popping a bite into her mouth.

She clasped her heart.

"As good as I expected," she said.

Based on the speed with which she ate that pie, I concluded it was not poisoned.

"Come on," she said. "Don't be shy. There's no harm in a slice of pie for one's birthday breakfast. I wanted to be the first to bring you wishes, knowing that your mother is not home this morning."

I ventured a bite. It was off-the-charts good, and I told her as much.

"I'm glad you like it. Now, I'll be off so you can start your day." She rose, bringing our plates to my sink and rinsing them. "I'm sure I'll see you later."

I wondered if that was a threat.

She picked up the knife, then she rinsed it, dried it with one long sweep of my tea towel, and put it back in the drawer.

"Now then," she said, drying her hands. "I trust you'll tell no one about my bike ride to the bogs. There are some things that one likes to do alone. I think your generation calls it mindfulness. I call it the quiet joy of independence. Here's another secret: I'm off for a snooze. Don't tell a soul. I don't want to get a reputation for that sort of laziness, but my neighbor is a handful. He was on the phone all night. I even heard his fingers pounding the keyboard. Those walls. I have a good hearing gene, but it can sometimes be a curse."

Olive gave me a hug and headed down the stairs. I watched from my living room window as she mounted her bike and headed back toward town.

I realized that with each twist and turn I felt less like James Bond. I also realized how much I wanted to take off my jumpsuit. I hopped into the shower and scrubbed and scrubbed until I was ready to face the day. I dressed quickly in jeans, a light blue sweater, and gray high tops. I rolled up the jeans to create a fashion statement with my shoes, but the strategy behind my attire was purely functional. If I needed to make a run for it today, I wanted to be ready. I pulled my hair into a high bun and fastened it with a few bobby pins and my hair tie. For a last bit, I threw on some lipstick in a shade of Millie red to give me some confidence.

As I did, the scent of bacon wafted through my window. Eggs and cheese mingled with the siren smell, too. I walked across the lawn and knocked on Chris's screen door, wondering if the Mortons would have an alibi as good as Olive's.

"Smelled the omelets all the way across the yard?" said Chris with a smile.

"I couldn't resist," I said.

"Happy birthday," he and the boys all said when I stepped inside.

Chris handed me a cup of rich coffee as good as anything I've had at The Bean, which is a huge compliment. The boys brought me a plate of food.

"Where are the Mortons?" I said.

Chris shrugged.

"Don't know," he said. "They were out early. They have their quirks, but John Pierre's been gardening for me so I can't complain. If this is the upside of Airbnb, I think I like it."

At least I knew what John Pierre had done with the other two items he had bought from Marine Home Center.

"Do you have anything wonderful planned for your birthday?" said Chris.

"Dinner with Peter," I said.

My answer was greeted with loud raspberry sounds from the boys, and laughter from Chris. With a slice of pie, an omelet, and three slabs of bacon in me, I waved a good-bye to my family and headed out the door.

Two steps toward my apartment, my phone rang.

"Happy birthday!" said Emily.

"Thanks," I said. "How's the Marshall party going?"

"I'm going to miss these old guys," she said. "I'm taking them out to Great Point to look for seals in a few minutes. Except for Nathaniel of course. He's already out. I assume to check on Millie. And Lennie is sleeping like a log. We may leave him behind too."

"Em?" I said. "Can I call you back?"

"Sure," she said.

I hung up. As I got closer to my apartment, I noticed my front door was ajar. I was sure I'd closed it before I'd left.

Chapter 19

I pushed my front door open, gently, and crept upstairs. When I'd climbed high enough that I could see the living room floor, I peeked over the landing.

I couldn't see a thing because Tinker stared me in the face. I motioned for him to move aside. When he didn't budge, I took another step up. Tinker followed me. Worse, he pushed his irresistible pink nose through the two rails and purred at me. I lifted the palm of my hand to the top of his head and gently lowered it so I could see over him.

"Oh my God," I said.

Peter was seated on my sofa.

"I thought you were an intruder." I said, entering my living room.

"Happy birthday," he said, rising from the sofa and offering a single rose to me.

I'm such a sucker for a single rose.

"I used my key," said Peter.

Peter and I had traded keys before I'd left for Paris. It was a big deal. We weren't living together. We hadn't talked about marriage. But trading keys is a big step. It basically says you can come and go as you please. Except this was the first time I'd ever arrived home to find him already here. I was feeling a lot of emotions in that moment, and I wanted to share them all with Peter. Instead, I sat on the sofa, buried my head in my hands, and took a deep breath.

"Oh boy," he said. "Maybe we should have waited to trade keys?"

"No," I said. "I'm glad you're here. I am."

But I also have to leave, I thought. Sometimes a girl just has to find a secret formula she doesn't have.

"Can't you tell?" I said, sheepishly.

He laughed.

"I like the rose," I said.

"I have more than a rose for you," Peter said, leaning his forehead against mine. "Your reporter's been at work."

"You know the way to my heart," I said. "What did you find out?"

"The Mortons' house in Quebec is part of Laura's family estate," he said. "They run a Christmas tree farm. I checked out their net worth. Their income lines up with that of a modest business. Although they must have some savings. They seem to be at the tail end of a world tour. They've posted loads of photos on their Instagram feed."

I wondered if a world tour could be a cover for a spy.

My phone pinged and I saw a text from my cousin Kate.

Millie's up! And sharp as a tack. She's itching to leave.

"Nice!" said Peter.

"I hope her memory is back," I said. "See you later?"

"Sure. Listen. Tell me if I'm reading into this too much," Peter said. "Since you've come back from

Paris, you've seemed different. I know I'm a small-town reporter and you've been to Paris and have had adventures with Millie. I hope you don't feel like Nantucket, or me, are too small now. In comparison."

"You're worried about me being bored?" I said, incredulously.

He nodded, and I almost laughed. Truth was, I was worried he would get bored once the winter hit.

I was about to tell him as much, but my hand had sunk into my sofa cushions and I realized that the vial was gone.

I threw the pillows onto the floor. There was no vial. I looked on the floor, then under the sofa. No vial.

"Um, Stella?" said Peter, standing to the side with Tinker as I searched.

I stood up and smacked my head. I realized that anyone might have had the opportunity to enter my house in search of the vial, after I'd left for breakfast at Chris's house.

"I think I might have allowed an enemy spy to steal something right from under my nose," I said.

I knew it was a mistake to confess anything to him the moment the words left my mouth, but I couldn't stop myself.

"Seriously, Stella," said Peter, walking to my stairs. "I meant that Paris was a big trip. That's all."

"You don't understand," I said as the door opened and shut below.

I followed him. When I stepped outside, Peter was already in his car. Then I noticed something else.

A note was pinned to my door.

I opened it. The contents, typed, were short and to the point.

Today's the day.

I'll be by the Wick & Flame after five, when your store closes, to pick up the formula. Hide it in a purple candle and place it among your pink window display.

Don't mess with me.

For one brief moment, I'd thought I was a step ahead of Laruam, but whoever had taken the vial had quickly figured out it was a fake. Now, I was back to square one. Worse. I had no formula and still no idea who Laruam was. Sunday was around the corner. When Agent Hill's colleagues came, I would have nothing for them. And in the meantime, my mother's life was still at risk.

I checked the time. It was almost ten. The clock was ticking.

My phone rang again. My mom's name lit the screen.

"My baby is thirty!" she said, as if I were three.

"Thank you," I said, happy to hear her voice. I knew she'd lost her memory, but fingers crossed she might have remembered where she'd put the missing formula. If not, we were in trouble.

"Don't be mad," my mom said. "I've already left the hospital. I took a taxi to town. I have errands including getting you a birthday present."

"No," I said. "What errands? I need to talk to you. Alone. It's really important. Can you meet me at the Wick & Flame?"

"Sure," she said, but I knew her. She was more interested in my birthday than my urgent invitation. "Happy, happy. I love you. Don't call me, I'll call you. I feel great, and we have much to celebrate this afternoon."

And then she hung up. I grabbed my bag and my car keys and headed to the Wick & Flame. On the way, I received one more call.

"Did you find out anything interesting about the house?" I said to my cousin Liz, whose name had lit my screen.

"First, happy birthday. Second, the house lead was a dead end," she said. "But I'm happy to contact the owners if you think there might be interest in a sale."

"So, it's not on the market?"

"Nope," she said. "It's owned by a partnership. Not sure who they are."

"Like a sleeper cell on Nantucket?" I said.

"I hope not," she said with a laugh. "But let me know the minute Nathaniel's ready to look. And have a fun day."

"Thanks," I said, parking not far from my store.

Entering the Wick & Flame, I kept my store's sign at CLOSED, and went right to the safe.

You will find the vial, and everything will be fine, I said to myself.

I lifted the tapestry and turned the dial. I looked through every pocket in Millie's black bag. I'd looked through it yesterday, when Cherry was in my store, but now I looked again. As I suspected, I found eleven vials, each with a label on it in Millie's handwriting.

I did not find an extra vial with a pale-yellow liquid.

A new question occurred to me. If Agent Hill had mistakenly given me a vial which had been Millie's, how come it hadn't had a number on it like all of her other ones?

Chapter 20

I waited for Millie.

And waited.

To keep busy, I opened the closest thing I had to a high-tech, spy-catching gadget. My phone. I flipped to the photos I took in Paris. Millie posing at the Eiffel Tower. A selfie of us in front of the *Mona Lisa*. At the end of the album I saw a video I had not watched. It started with the back of Millie's head.

"How does it feel to be a scent extractions expert?" I said to my mom, off camera. *"Look at the camera."*

It was the video I had taken when we'd entered the World Perfumery Conference.

"Hi." She waved.

I watched my mom, smiling, as she turned toward me. Then, the video stopped. I played the short sequence again. I had forgotten that a man had bumped into her when we'd entered. I'd forgotten that I'd stopped taping because of it. Reviewing the film, I now noticed that as he brushed against my mom, his hand graced over her bag. His actions had been so subtle. I wouldn't have noticed unless I was looking for it, but now I could see that he'd slipped something into her black bag. I zoomed in on his hand and watched the video frame by frame. Sure enough, he had deposited a vial, the same size as Millie's standard perfume vials, and the same shade of pale yellow.

It was confounding. I saw with my own eyes that he'd slipped the object into her bag, and yet it was not in her bag now. I made the assumption that Millie had arrived to Nantucket with twelve sample scents. Eleven had been marked, and one had not. Agent Hill had stolen the unmarked vial during my first night home. It was the sleeping scent I had now lost. What had happened to the vial containing the secret formula?

Aside from the stranger who had visited my store and spoken to Cherry, all of my suspects had been at the lecture—John Pierre and Laura Morton, Olive Tidings, Nathaniel Dinks, and Lennie Bartow. If any of them had seen the formula then, there would have been no need to send me the letter. Millie's presentation would have been the perfect time to grab the formula and run. None of us would have been any wiser about the identity of Rex Laruam or the vial's connection to the Peace Jubilee.

Challenged by this puzzle, I extracted the page of notes that Millie had slipped into a side pocket, describing all of her scents. Like the vials, which were lined up neatly in two rows, each tucked into a safe space, the notes were broken into columns and numbers. The scents were described by their Latin names, which meant little to me, but I looked them up, nonetheless. The layman's versions of the extracts were little help as well. Compounding my confusion about the unmarked sleeping scent, no twelfth vial was listed on her page of notes. At least I understood

Agent Hill's mistake. There was nothing to indicate that Millie had had a sleeping scent with her.

I needed to talk to my mother. I called her again, but there was no answer.

I took out each vial and opened them to test out their scents. The first one smelled floral, but not a flower I recognized. It was light, and yet it had a smoky tone to it that I wouldn't have expected from a flower. It was really nice. The second and third vials gave off a more herbal smell. The last one was putrid. I've heard about flowers that blossom once a year and smell like a corpse. I had no idea, thankfully, what a rotting corpse smelled like, but I was willing to bet that this scent was close. The extract was a testament to Millie's passion for scents, no matter what they were. If it was unique, she loved it. If I knew my mom, this one probably had nutritive properties that interested her, or something else of value.

When I finished investigating each vial, I was relieved to find that none of them had made me pass out, throw up, or sprout a new limb. I heard a knock on my door and looked up in hopes that Millie had arrived. Instead, I saw Cherry. I looked at the time. It was almost ten.

"You should give me a key of my own," said Cherry, striding into the store with high spirits. "Oh, you have a lot of smells going on today. Were you looking at Millie's Amazon scents?"

I was impressed she remembered the aromas. I picked a simple base note votive candle from my collection, Lemon Citrus, and decided to make it my Candle-of-the Day. It was a perfect choice, both lovely and effective at killing the scents I'd unleashed from Millie's vials.

Cherry pulled out an apron from her bag with the logo of my store embossed across it. She tied it around her waist.

"What do you think?" she said about her newest accessory for working in my store. "I got one for you too. Happy birthday."

"Thank you," I said, genuinely touched. "I think I couldn't ask for a better helper."

While Cherry got busy for the day, I gathered my bag and decided not to wait around for Millie any longer. I headed out the door, and walked to the Jared Coffin House to see if Nathaniel was in, hoping that my mother would be with him. Jan informed me he was out.

I looked in the garden of the library. I looked in the Hub. I walked down to the docks, and I gave a quick look inside the town's Stop & Shop. My search, however, was getting me nowhere. I called Millie again, but there was no answer. If she were any other woman, I would have jumped to the worst conclusions by now. I knew, however, that she was as easily celebrating her first day of freedom in some unique Millie fashion.

When I passed The Bean, I stopped in, hoping that some caffeine would help.

With a cup of coffee and a seat at the counter in front of the window, I saw Liz talking to Emily across the street. Andy's girlfriend, Georgianna, passed by with a huge green smoothie. I remembered she was bringing her honey a nutritious concoction to the town's station every day. I imagined it would go straight down the sink after she left, but Andy was a good sport. He'd probably take a few honest sips before he did.

I tried Millie's phone again, but there was no answer.

I need you, ASAP, I texted.

I started to miss my mom. Not the way I sometimes did when she was travelling and I hadn't seen her for a while. I missed her like I'd lost her.

I watched the video of the man slipping the vial into Millie's bag again. By now, I'd searched my mom's black bag inside and out many, many times. I closed my eyes and traced the bag's travels since Paris. The bag had been with Millie, or me, or in the safe, at all times except for three times I could remember. First, when the policeman had looked at it in Paris. Second, when the bellhop had taken it at the Jared Coffin House. And, third, when she'd given her lecture in my store.

Then, I remembered that Millie had opened her bag one more time, before we'd left Paris. I had only focused on a period of time after Agent Hill's partner had been killed, but Millie had opened her bag at the conference, right before I'd made her Vanna White video. If Millie had found the formula at that moment, she might have put it into her navy sweater's pocket to examine during our trip home. In her daze after the murder, she'd packed the sweater as we'd left for the airport. The vial could have travelled to Nantucket in her small suitcase, rather than her black bag.

"Oh boy," I said.

The theory came to me in a flash, but once it did, other things began to make sense. For example, I realized that Agent Hill could have only confused one of Millie's scents from the Amazon with the one for the Peace Jubilee if it was the only unmarked, pale-yellow formula in the bag when she'd broken into my store our first night back.

I put down my cup and absently retied my hair. I had not found the vial in her sweater pocket when I'd looked through it the other night, but Millie had been carrying the sweater the night of her accident in Nantucket. I realized that when Tinker had scared her at the Wick & Flame, the vial could have slipped out of her pocket and onto my workroom floor. I hadn't seen it lying around, nor had Agent Hill or Rex Laruam, but it could be there. I must have looked somewhat crazed because I noticed two women next to me glance over, but I didn't care.

I hurried back to the store and straight into my workroom. Cherry was helping a woman choose an array of tapers for her dining table.

"That's Stella herself," I heard Cherry say as I tore by them. "She makes each candle by hand."

I shut the door on the two women and sank to the floor, where I proceeded to inspect the room for the missing vial.

It was nowhere to be found, but another idea hit me.

"The accident," I said aloud.

Nathaniel had brought Millie's sweater to her before they had both fallen. If the vial had not slipped out of her sweater in my store, it could have fallen out of her pocket any time from when Nathaniel had collected the sweater for her to when their accident had occurred. It had been two days since the accident. Sidewalks had been swept. Streets had been cleaned. The chances of finding the small vial were slim. The chances of finding it in one piece were even slimmer.

Composing myself, I opened the door gently and

smiled at Cherry who was rearranging a display. Her customer was gone.

"How's business?" I said.

"If you can believe it," she said, pulling herself up an extra inch. "That creepy man came in again, while you were out. Pale gray shirt today, but same black jeans. He tried to put a little smile into his eyes, but I didn't buy it. He said to tell you he'd be by later to talk to you and your mother, but I told him I had the store covered today. He left looking put out. Flo came in, too, and bought a gift."

Hearing her reference to the dead-eye guy, I headed to the door.

"I gave her the friends and family discount. Is everything OK—?" I heard her say as I left.

If the vial had fallen from Millie's sweater while Nathaniel was heading down the sidewalk, I suspected it might have been swept by a store owner into the street curb by now. I walked along Centre Street with my head down, scanning both the bricked sidewalk and the curbs beside them.

When I turned the corner onto Main Street, I kept my eyes peeled to the ground. By the time I'd made it halfway down the block, to where Nathaniel had crossed the street to my mother, I was still empty-handed. At the spot where Millie fell, I stepped off the sidewalk, and I studied every stone in spite of a few horns honking at me.

Last summer, a newcomer to the island had filed a petition to get rid of Main Street's cobblestones. Every year, someone probably does, but I love those cobble-stones, even if they sometimes wreak havoc on my car's muffler.

Unfortunately, the nooks and crannies I'd hoped

might protect my missing vial had not done their job. As hard as I looked, I could not find my treasure. The more I searched, however, the more convinced I was that the vial had fallen from Millie's sweater, somewhere between the Wick & Flame and where I now stood. It was the only thing that made any sense.

Fortunately, I had a secret weapon when it came to the streets of Nantucket: my cousins, Docker and Ted. These two lovable brothers own a carting business. It was amazing how much guys in trash removal knew about places, and people. From a pile of garbage, they could tell whose marriage was on the rocks, whose business was booming or tanking, or who'd had a birthday. The Wright Brothers Carting Company had purchased a smaller dump truck over the last couple of months, which had brought new business opportunities, including extra help this fall to keep Main Street and other key streets in town free of fallen leaves.

On my phone, I opened my Favorites and flipped to Docker's name. Feeling one step ahead of Rex Laruam for the first time, I hit Docker's name and waited while the phone rang. And rang.

"Hello?" I finally heard my cousin say.

"It's Stella. I need your help," I said.

"Whatever you need."

Chapter 21

"I need your Main Street trash from the last two days," I said.

My family spends a good amount of time at Chris's famous barbeques, so we're fairly up-to-date on each other's work and personal lives. For example, I knew my cousins' new truck was big enough that they stowed their haul for seven days, before making their trek to the dump at the beginning of each week. If I remembered correctly, they brought the bags to the dump on Mondays. It was Saturday. A break!

"My trash is your trash," said Docker, no questions asked. He actually got these kinds of requests, every now and then. Once he went through ten bags to search for a kid's lost retainer, and he actually found it. If I'd asked him to dive through it all to find the vial he would have, but I wasn't going to ask.

I headed to my car. When I opened the door, I found a surprise. Tinker, with a stealth that even the best-trained spy would admire, had followed me to my car, and was now in the passenger seat, taking a nap. He looked up at me and purred.

"Have you been trying to tell me about the missing vial this whole time?" I said to my furry friend, as

I remembered he'd been guarding the sweater for two days now.

I knew he felt badly about the entire debacle with Millie. He'd tried to make a friend and had instead landed her in the hospital. If there was anything he could do to help the humans in his life, he would. I had missed his cue.

I drove out to Docker's garage in good time with Tinker perched beside me.

When I pulled into Wright Brothers Carting Company, neither Docker nor Ted were out front. I parked my car and got out with Tinker.

"Hello?" I said, hoping someone inside the office would hear me. There was an eerie quiet to the place.

I walked across the lot, telling myself to relax. Rex Laruam wouldn't know to come here, I reminded myself.

It didn't help.

I didn't like the emptiness of the place. Usually I could at least hear a radio playing or Docker and Ted talking from behind the garage.

Tinker walked straight ahead, his tail waving leisurely, then darted behind the garage.

"Tinker," I said in a yell-slash-whisper that was neither a yell nor a whisper. "Psst."

"Yeeeooooww," Tinker screeched.

I ran in the direction of my cat's scream, across the parking area, past the side of the office building, and to the back of the garage. There, I found Tinker on all fours, tail perpendicular to the ground, nose extended at the same angle. I think my yoga teacher from the three classes I took last year would call it Warrior One or Two. Something Warrior.

The focus of his gaze? Across from him, a large gray

cat lay low to the ground, looking for an opening to escape my maniacal pet. Docker was leaning against his truck, arms crossed, one leg over the other, as if he'd just turned on the TV to watch Bugs Bunny.

"My money's on Sugar," he said, watching the two of them size each other up. "She may look like a scaredy-cat, but she's a genius."

"Tinker," I said, with my sternest voice.

Tinker dropped his tail and looked at me with an expression that reminded me of the night I'd caught him with a salmon filet in his mouth. It was the first dinner I'd ever made for Peter, and he'd eaten it.

"I have zero time for drama right now," I said to him. "Be friendly, or it's back in the car for you."

Tinker looked miffed by my lecture, and although he backed down, his chest stayed puffed.

"You, too, Sugar," said Docker.

Sugar stood, casually, and a little mouse scurried away for its life. I burst out laughing.

"I thought he was screeching at Sugar," I said to Docker. "Had I known Sugar was sitting on a mouse, I'd have understood. Tinker hates mice more than I do."

"Sugar lives for mice," said Docker. "That's why we keep her around. She guards the trucks. The bags inside are like winning the lottery for those vermin. There's a lifetime's worth of food for a mouse in each one of them."

Frankly, I was grateful to learn about Sugar's skills. As long as I was digging through the bags of trash my cousins had collected, I was happy to know I wouldn't have any creatures jumping out at me.

"What're you looking for?" said Docker, opening

the hatch to the back of his truck. Black trash bags were piled up, one beside another.

"I need to find something for my mom," I said.

"First in, last out," said Docker. "Monday's in the back, today's up front."

The phone rang in his office.

"Let me get that," he said, "and I'll come back to help you."

He was off before I could answer. Tinker and Sugar now sat shoulder to shoulder, a few feet away, watching me in the same way that Docker, moments ago, had watched them. I could hear Docker in the back, speaking politely to someone who sounded like they needed to hire him to move some wood from a fence that had been replaced. He didn't sound like he'd be off the phone any time soon, and I had no time to waste.

I climbed onto the truck and tried to size up the number of bags inside like a kid tries to guess how many jelly beans are in a jar in hopes of winning a prize at a school fair. I estimated ten, and assumed the bags in the back had been collected on Tuesday, since the guys dropped their load at the dump on Mondays. I did some quick math. Five days had passed, ten bags had been collected. I decided two bags a day sounded about right. Since Millie had fallen on Thursday night, I needed bags five and six. I pulled out the bags in front and laid them on the ground beside the truck until I reached bags five and six, which I removed as well. I ripped five open and got to work.

Given how much lighter the autumn foot traffic in town is compared to the summer, I was surprised by how much random debris they had collected. Paper napkins, cups, receipts, cigarette butts. Nantucketers

smoked more than I realized. There were lots of
leaves because of the number of trees along Main
Street. The leaves slowed me down. They served as the
proverbial haystack in which I was searching for a
needle. They were slimy, too, and my jeans were
quickly getting dirty.

Deep in trash, I opened the next bag, whose contents were almost identical to the first except for a
bag of buttons and a couple of empty mini bottles of
vodka like you get on an airplane. I swear if they'd
been full, I'd have wiped them on my dirty jeans and
taken a swig or two.

In the end, neither bag held the vial. I couldn't
bring myself to accept it, but the truth was that the vial
could have easily broken, and I'd never find it. I'm
not a nail biter, but if there'd ever been a moment for
it, right now was it in spite of the bubonic plague I'd
have gotten from the muck on my hands.

I looked at the bags I'd already removed, wondering if I'd misjudged which ones to open. The problem
was that I could no longer remember which of them
had been first or last in the pile, so I was flying blind
on these. Eventually, Tinker's curiosity began to get
the best of him. He left Sugar, whose interest in
garbage remained firmly tied to mice, and he started
to poke around the bags as well, sniffing and pawing
here and there. When the smells failed to produce
anything as interesting as the Tuna Delight I serve
him at home, he curled on top of a bag, in the shade
of the truck, and dozed off. Tinker has the most
Zen-like ability to nap anywhere, anytime. At least his
presence confirmed that there were no mice ahead.

I was halfway through my third bag, sweat forming
across my brow and a level of filth in my nails I feared

might never wash away, when Docker returned. He handed me a pair of latex gloves.

"Gross," he said. "You went through these without gloves on?"

I did feel gross. I'd gone from sexy spy goddess yesterday, to garbage diver today.

He looked at the bags outside his truck. Six in all. Then he looked back into his pickup.

"I thought you said you wanted something from Thursday," he said.

"I did." I straightened up, holding a Styrofoam cup in one hand and attempting to push aside a tendril of hair that had slipped over my cheek with the forearm of my other arm.

Docker walked toward his vehicle.

Lesson learned. Wait until Docker gets off the phone.

I joined my cousin as he studied the identical black bags in both the truck and in the pile I'd created. He was like a Jedi Knight, letting the Force guide him to the right bag. When he finished his calculations, he reached for one bag, and then decided on another. It was the bag upon which Tinker was sitting.

Lesson number two. When Tinker chooses a bag upon which to take a nap, consider his decision carefully. He'd spent the last two days curled up on my mother's sweater. Of everyone I knew connected to this case, he was likely the only one who had had access to even a trace of the formula I was seeking. I went right for the bag, pulled it open and dumped its contents onto the ground.

"Cool," said Docker. He picked up a penny. "How'd we miss that?"

"This must be our lucky bag," I said as I studied the ground.

Docker joined my gaze, perhaps looking for another penny.

Leaves. Obligatory foam cup. Leaves. Straw wrappers. Leaves. A receipt. Leaves and more leaves. My heart leapt for a second, but it was only a pen cap.

I got on my hands and knees and started to feel around.

"Put on the gloves, Stella," said Docker, dangling them before me.

"I need my hands," I said.

I knew the shape and feel of the vials. It was my turn to channel the Force. I felt through the mess. I climbed into the mess. I let the mess climb over me.

I was lying flat across the pile of trash, moldy leaves in my hair, when my fingers hit upon the treasure I'd been seeking. I grabbed hold and lifted a vial, about three inches long and filled with the same shade of pale-yellow liquid I'd seen the dead man slip into my mother's bag.

"Bingo," I said, and sat in a puddle of old coffee.

Chapter 22

"What's in there?" said Docker, looking at the liquid. "That's a very suspicious color."

I rose and wiped a few leaves off of my pants.

"Honestly, I have no idea," I said, trying to sound casual. "You know Millie. You never can tell what she's up to."

I went to hug Docker, but he backed off.

"Oh man," he said. "I feel like I should hug you because it's your birthday, but you are so disgusting. How about I clean up this mess you've made and we'll call it even?"

"I am disgusting, aren't I?" I said, joyfully.

I gave him a big bear hug, slime and all. He yelled in protest, but he then laughed and let me.

"You're getting weird in your old age," he said.

As a truce, I helped him pick up the trash I'd strewn about his truck. As we worked, Tinker and Sugar found a new activity, chasing a butterfly. Tinker looked very happy, and I knew once he saw Millie again, he'd try to win back her friendship. Unfortunately, today was not the day for such futile efforts.

"How'd you like a playdate, my furry friend?" I said to Tinker.

"Cool," said Docker.

"Thanks," I said. I threatened another hug, but let Docker off the hook this time and headed to my car. There, I threw an old beach towel I kept in my trunk onto the driver's seat. I waved to Docker, Tinker, and Sugar, and pulled away with the vial.

My confidence was running high. In one morning, I'd found and lost a decoy, but, more importantly, I had succeeded in Agent Hill's mission to recover the secret formula. I now had until five o'clock to continue my search for Laruam. I had six suspects, but, to Agent Hill's point, they were a quirky bunch. Whoever Laruam was, he had done a good job at keeping me guessing as to his identity. At five o'clock he would be coming to my store, but I knew I couldn't hand over the formula. I had to protect it. I'd have to find another way to catch him.

As I continued to town, I ran through everything that gave me a home-field advantage over Rex Laruam, King of Shadows. I did not have a fast car or a black belt in karate. I didn't even know how to use the gun in my bag. If it weren't for my cat, Rex Laruam might have found the vial in Millie's sweater. The thought made me shiver.

Thinking of Tinker's leap that had fortuitously knocked the vial out of Millie's sweater, I realized my greatest advantage. I had my own army. My friends and family on Nantucket. Agent Hill had had to go it alone, but I had no problem with teamwork.

Liz and Peter had given me some information about the Mortons already, and I hadn't had to tell them anything about the mission. I had promised Agent Hill I would not divulge national security threats, and I would not go back on that promise, but I decided I could make some allowances.

First, I would show the Peace Jubilee code to Millie. Since Agent Hill had planned to take it with us to a safe house, I decided Millie would have eventually gotten her hands on it, even with Agent Hill around. The only difference now was that she would hear about it in my store instead of on a boat.

Having made this one decision, I was able to make another. With all of the obstacles he had met with over the last couple of days, Laruam had not been fooled this morning by the sleeping scent as Agent Hill had. She'd been on a grab and go mission. He'd been on a treasure hunt. With my mother's help, however, I knew we could make a credible copy to give to Laruam. If anyone could make a scent he'd believe was real, it was Millie and Stella Wright and our excellent noses.

Secondly, although Agent Hill had been opposed to my calling Andy when Rex Laruam was boarding the boat, she could never object to Andy arresting him on other charges. If Andy, for example, was on the scene when Laruam took my candle from my store window, he might just have to arrest him, and keep him locked up until Sunday.

I felt my inner Secret Agent returning.

When I reached the cranberry bogs I remembered it was Saturday, the day of the festival. I also remembered that Georgianna was running a smoothie table there, which would feature her newest creation, Cranberry Delight. Georgianna took her hobbies seriously. Over the summer, her interest in maritime sculptures had overrun the island for a short time. I took a chance and figured Andy might be there with her. I'd rather speak to him in person than over the phone if I could.

The festival was in full swing with food markets, a band, and a puppet show among the activities. Up until World War Two, cranberries were a significant part of the island's economy. Now there were only two commercial bogs left. Each fall, the bogs were flooded to harvest them. I thought of Olive and her cranberry pie. I realized that she may have visited the bogs, but she hadn't used her spade there, since the cranberries were flooded, not picked.

I hopped out of my car, and walked into the food tent where I spied Georgianna. Sure enough, Andy was about four tables away at the Sweet Inspiration's booth, buying chocolate covered cranberries. I headed straight to him.

"I heard you visited Millie," I said to him.

"Of course," he answered, offering his box of confection to me.

I took a couple of pieces and popped them into my mouth.

"What have you been up to?" he said.

"I'd tell you, but then I'd have to kill you," I said, trying to keep things light but failing. "Actually, I need your help."

I looked over to Georgianna who waved me over as she held up a pink drink. I waved back with a smile and a nod, as if we were greeting each other, not negotiating a taste test.

"I can't explain everything," I said. "You'll just have to trust me. It's one of those Millie things."

"That woman drives you crazy," said Andy, putting the lid on his box. "Is that why you've been acting so weird since you came back from Paris?"

"I'm not acting weird," I said.

"Hmmm . . . first you were convinced you had a break-in, then I find you wandering the streets with twigs in your hair. Don't think I didn't notice you walking aimlessly down Main Street this morning. And then there's this." He motioned to my entire being, and although I was filthy, I felt he was crossing the line. "If I didn't know you better, I'd be worried. To be honest, I think you're just scared."

I realized his accusation had nothing to do with my mission.

"I'm not scared," I said. "What do you think I'm scared of?"

"I don't know," said Andy. "You tell me."

Georgianna was heading our way with a smoothie. My plan to build an army was not going as planned. Andy began to walk towards her.

"Hey, Southerland," I said.

Andy turned back to me.

"I need your help," I said.

At that moment, there was a cry from outside the food tent. Along with an officer on duty, Andy headed toward the noise. I followed to see some people shouting from the shoreline and out into the bog. I had a horrible thought that maybe Agent Hill had been found. Olive had certainly scoped out the place. If she were Rex Laruam, the bogs she'd found would be quite a handy place to stash a body.

Fortunately, the commotion had nothing to do with the discovery of a dead body. A tourist had fallen into the bogs while trying to take a selfie. By the time we arrived to the scene, the young woman was laughing with her friends and drying herself off with her sweatshirt.

"Andy," I said, as he cleared the area and began to head back to the tent.

I walked straight to him until we were eye to eye.

"I don't care what you think my problems are," I said. "At least, right now I don't. We can discuss that later, because right now I have bigger problems. I need your help. What if I could tell you that sometime around five o'clock tonight there would be a break-in at my store?"

"You can tell me that?"

"Yes, I can. With certainty. At least, with certainty that someone is going to steal something from my store."

"You told me yourself that Tinker made the mess. Why do you think you'll be robbed? And why five o'clock?"

"Andy, baby," Georgianna said from her smoothie stand.

Andy turned and waved at her.

"I can't explain, but I need you to dress in your plain clothes and watch my store at five o'clock to arrest someone who I feel certain is going to rob my store. I can even tell you what he's going to steal. A purple candle from my display window."

"Your window is pink," said Andy.

"Exactly. I will have a purple candle in the window, just to make this easy for you," I said. "And I'll meet you there. You'll need my help."

I knew the suspects better than anyone. Even if Laruam arrived in a disguise I had not seen, I'd be familiar with his quirks and traits. No matter how disguised he might be, it would be possible to identify him since I knew the characters already. Even if he got away, I'd know which locations we'd likely be able to find the thief. Between me and Andy, we would have him in handcuffs in no time. By tomorrow morning, when help arrived from Agent Hill's agency, I'd send them over to the jail to pick up their killer.

"I'm a real police officer, Stella," Andy said. "I can't hang around your store in case it's broken into. I know you've had a rough couple of days, but I just can't."

"Have I ever steered you wrong?" I said.

Andy laughed.

"You're never going to let me forget you helped me catch a murderer, are you?" he said, referring to my help in solving one last May.

"Best time we ever had," I said.

"A definite meeting of the minds," he said.

"Andy," Georgianna said again.

Andy smiled at me, and headed to the tent.

"Come at five o'clock," I said to his retreating figure. "Please, trust me. This is important."

Andy raised his hand over his head and turned his palm toward me. I smiled in relief. I knew I could count on my army.

As I walked to my car, Millie's name finally lit my screen.

"I'm here, but you're not," she said.

By "here," I was sure she meant the Wick & Flame. I heard Cherry in the background.

"Is Nathaniel with you?" I said.

"No, but I can call him if you'd like," she said, sounding pleased.

"No!" I said. "I need to speak to you alone. Do you feel well enough to sit tight for ten minutes? I'll be there soon."

"I feel great," she said.

"I'm glad to hear it," I said, and I hung up.

When I finally entered the store, Millie and Cherry were settled on my counter stools and enjoying a cup of tea. I noticed a shopping bag on the counter from Vis-à-Vis, my favorite store.

"Hi," I said.

"What happened to you?" said Millie.

The door opened behind me. Unable to greet a customer as I was, I raced to my workroom, waving to my mom to follow me.

Once we were inside, I shut the door. I locked it. I locked the window too. Then, I pulled down the shade. I could not risk anyone hearing my story.

"How do you feel?" I said.

"How do *you* feel?" she said.

She had a point. Of the two of us, I was probably the one who looked the worse for wear.

"What's going on?" she said.

I pulled out a stool for each of us around my work-table.

She sat.

"In a nutshell, here's what's happened since you hit your head," I said.

As simply as I could, I began to tell my mom about Agent Hill, the death of her partner in Paris, and Rex Laruam's interest in the coded formula.

"I remember the Peace Jubilee," she said. "That elephant."

"Before the elephant we were at the perfume conference," I said. "That's where the murdered man hid the formula with you. One which looked exactly like the twelfth, unmarked vial in your bag."

"You must be thinking about my sleeping scent. I never had time to label it. I'll tell you the truth. I was going to use it on the airplane, but then I remembered I'd have to heat it up. I couldn't do that on a flight."

Suddenly, she grabbed my wrist.

"I just remembered. At the conference, I did see an extra vial in my bag that looked exactly like my sleeping scent. I thought the crew in the Amazon had given me an extra sample, because we had a joke about how it could come in handy if I ever needed to knock myself out. Where's my sweater? Your formula will be in my pocket."

She instinctively looked around her.

"I found the secret formula," I said, patting my bra.

"Then how do you need my help?" she said, looking forlorn.

"I'm hoping we can make an imitation of it, using your scents from the Amazon and my fragrance collection at the store. It needs to be good enough to trick Laruam into thinking he's got a hodgepodge of oils from around the world that are a code."

"We can do that, but why not use my sleeping scent?" she said. "That'd be a funny scene. Knock him out and we'll tie him up."

"He took it from me this morning, actually," I said. "But then he figured out it wasn't the correct formula. What we make has to be really, really good."

Millie frowned.

"I can't tell you how rare that sleeping scent was," she said.

"And effective." I added.

She rolled up her sleeves and took out her reading glasses from her pocket.

"Mom," I said, reaching my hand to hers. "This is dangerous stuff. If Laruam discovers the scent is a fake, there's no telling what he might do to us."

"We can do it," she said.

In spite of the circumstances, I was happy we had the opportunity to work together. My mom's spirit was infectious, too. Millie Wright is great under pressure, as long as there are no cats or dead bodies to distract her.

"What happens after we make this formula, and Mr. Laruam steals it?" she said.

"You're on a need-to-know basis," I said, feeling like Agent Hill.

"Fine, but I'm not doing anything until you clean yourself up," she said. "I've felt great all day, but being near you is giving me a headache. I don't care which secret agent is waiting for us to hand things over. We're not doing a thing more for anyone until you pull yourself together. Really, Stella."

Millie opened the door to my bathroom and handed me a towel. I couldn't argue with her.

Chapter 23

I usually use my tiny shower at the Wick & Flame as extra storage space, but after removing the box of silicone tubes, and a few other pots and containers from the stall, I rinsed off the muck that was beginning to set on my skin. When I opened the door, clean and spiffy, I was thrilled to see Millie at work, sniffing one of her scents, with the Vis-à-Vis bag beside her.

"I need a whiff of the real formula," she said without looking up at me.

I retrieved the vial from my small bathroom and handed it to her. Still wrapped in a towel, I stood beside her as she twisted off the cap.

"Good lord," she said.

I took the vial from my mother and smelled it.

"That's an understatement," I said.

From a perfumer's perspective, the aroma was a disaster. I don't have the nose of my mother, but I surely know when a scent lacks sophisticated, well-defined notes. A good scent has a maximum of three, notes, rarely more. At first scent, I could detect at least five, ranging from woody herbs, to floral tones, to minerals from land and sea. It was the sort of fragrance someone in my basic candle class would make as a first attempt at mixing, when the aromas in my workshop were all too tempting to choose from.

"I need a pen," said Millie, reviewing the samples in her bag and eyeing the scents I collect in jars along my back wall. "And paper."

My mom, ever the professional, closed her eyes and breathed in the formula.

"Try on the stuff in the bag while I start working," she said, rhythmically breathing while I peeked at my gift.

"Oh, thank you!" I said, looking in the bag. "This is just like the outfit we loved in Paris."

"I was hoping you'd get the connection," she said. She lowered the vial and smiled.

On our first day in Paris, on the Boulevard St. Germain on the Left Bank, we'd seen a woman on a bike with a baguette in her basket. What captured our attention was that she was wearing high heels, a black chiffon blouse, and palazzo pants on a bike. So chic. The outfit Millie had found was similar. It was a matching blouse and wide-legged pants, with all the sophistication of the chiffon, but in black with a red and violet flowered pattern that suited me.

"It screamed 'Stella' when I saw it," she said, returning to her project and jotting down her notes. "Ooh, this one's from Indonesia. Very interesting. I hope the government doesn't end up killing me for cracking their code."

"Maybe they'll end up hiring you," I said.

"I might like that," she said. "Let me see that outfit on you. I thought you could wear it to your dinner with Peter tonight."

I took the bag back to my bathroom, shoved my candle supplies back into my shower, and changed.

Both top and bottom fit me perfectly. It showed off the parts of my figure I liked best, while leaving enough to the imagination. The pants were also loose enough that I could sit and enjoy a good dinner with Peter in comfort. The two pieces were linked by a flowing sash which I wrapped around myself twice and tied into a bow. Also inside the shopping bag was a red cashmere cape that made me feel like a queen. It must have cost a fortune, and I was deeply touched by her splurge.

"I L-O-V-E it," I said, opening the bathroom door into the workroom so that I could enjoy the outfit from farther than the three inches of space my bathroom afforded.

"I knew it," she said with an approving once-over. "Perfect. Something special for a special night."

I still had a lot to do before I could enjoy a special night.

While the wax hardened, I took a few fragrances from my shelves and joined my mother at the table where she had stationed her black bag. We worked together, mixing certain oils, liking some, rejecting others.

Rex Laruam had asked for a purple candle, and I'd give him one. I decided I wanted to make a statement. Inspired by my candle mold class, I looked through the collection of molds I'd amassed over the years. I found the one I wanted. It was of a fist. I'd made it years ago, from a small statue a friend had.

Blending blue and red dyes until they reached the perfect hue, I poured the melted wax into the mold. Finally, I took one of Millie's empty vials and dipped it into the pliable wax so that I'd have my secret compartment ready for her formula.

"Can you believe I'm supposed to be enjoying a special dinner tonight?" I said. And a surprise party, I thought. If things went according to plan, I'd be able to catch a murderer and make my birthday celebration.

A tear sprung to my mom's eyes, and caught me by surprise.

"My baby," she said, and hugged me.

"What?" I said.

Millie winked at me and went back to work.

"It's a special night," she said.

There were many words that had terrified me over the last couple of days, but the way she said those particular words was the most terrifying of all. Suddenly, I thought of Cherry's gentle teasing about Peter's affection for me, and Emily's spontaneous hugs over the last couple of weeks. I also thought about Peter's edgy mood over the last couple of days.

I couldn't believe I had been so blind. I had thought for the last two weeks that I was walking into a surprise party tonight, but I realized I'd had it all wrong. Peter was going to propose. And if my mom already knew, my dear Peter had been the true gentleman and had asked for her permission for my hand.

I relived every ambiguous comment about a surprise party that I had heard. In a new light, they could all have easily been hints about my engagement, and not about a surprise party.

"What are you hiding from me?" I said to my mother.

"My lips are sealed," she said. "I won't say another word, and you know that's true."

The woman could keep a secret. On the other hand, Emily couldn't, and she was only a block away, setting up for Frank Marshall's last event, the "Whiskey

Dinner" at the Jared Coffin House. I needed to see her. Right now.

"I added a dash of number three. I think we're getting to the same olio, although, of course, from completely different locations than the original," she said.

She handed it to me. I nodded with approval.

"How about a drop of this, too?" I said, handing her a vial from my shelf.

"Nice," she said with a smile. "I think we're almost there. I just need a few more minutes."

I calculated how long it would take me to get to the Jared Coffin House and back and decided to take advantage of her final touches to find Emily.

I grabbed the real formula, not willing to let it out of my sight, stuck it into my bra, and threw on my sneakers.

"Slingbacks will look much better," she said.

I opened and closed the door to the workroom.

"Oh, that looks much better," said Cherry as I headed straight out of my store. I dashed down Centre Street to the Jared Coffin House, where Emily was finishing up her decorations for Frank Marshall's dinner party.

In spite of my shock and, yes, a little panic, I realized one important thing. If Peter was asking me to marry him, then he'd decided he could live on Nantucket through thick and thin. A surprise engagement made me a little queasy, but the idea of him staying on Nantucket was beautiful news.

Before I reached the end of the street, Nathaniel appeared at the entrance of a new gift shop that had opened.

"You look beautiful," he said, stopping me in my tracks. "Your mother knew that outfit would be perfect for you."

"Thanks," I said, straightening the sash. "I'm going to show Emily."

"I just saw her feverishly at work in the hotel. I wouldn't bother her right now. But maybe you can spare me a minute?" he said, guiding me into the store. "I'd love your approval on a gift for Millie."

"How sweet," I said.

Even with my burning questions, I knew how focused Emily could be when she was working. I'd take Nathaniel's advice and give her a few minutes. Nathaniel held up a felt hat with a flower on it, a beautiful shade of burnt orange that would look amazing with Millie's red hair.

"What do you think?" he said.

"Lovely!" the saleslady and I said together.

Looking very pleased, Nathaniel handed over his credit card.

As he did, I got a text from Millie.

Your candle has hardened. I've hidden the vial in it. Where are you?

I checked the time. It was four o'clock. I still had time to catch Emily, put the candle in the window, get Millie to safety at my apartment, and return in time to meet Andy. I'd keep my eye out for the arrival of my suspects, including anyone with dead eyes. By dinnertime, I hoped to have Rex Laruam behind bars in the local jail.

Stay put!!! I'll be right back, I texted.

Little text bubbles flashed and disappeared a few times. Finally, the bubbles stopped bubbling.

"Everything OK with Millie?" said Nathaniel.

"She's great," I said.

When we left the store, I counted my lucky stars. Emily was getting into her car. I hadn't missed her.

"Do you know something you want to tell me?" I said, sprinting ahead of Nathaniel.

I thought she looked suddenly desperate to drive away.

I remembered that when Emily got engaged, she'd had a feeling it was going to happen. She'd made sure her nails were perfectly manicured for a month. I'd had slime in mine less than an hour ago, and no idea this was coming.

"Are you OK?" she said.

"I don't know, am I?" I said.

We both looked at each other, waiting for the other to say something. I broke first.

"I can't walk into tonight without a clue, and Millie won't tell me anything," I said.

"You know?" she said, looking both excited and disappointed that I knew.

"Oh my God," I said.

We both laughed, and Emily hugged me.

"Stop. I'll get weepy," she said, opening her car door. "And don't make me say anything. Let's keep some element of surprise, You know, Peter's a really special guy."

"Have fun with Frank and the guys," I said as her car pulled away.

When I returned to the Wick & Flame, Cherry was packing her bag to leave for the day.

"I can close up," I said.

"You should be getting ready for your dinner with Peter," she said.

"I will," I said. "I just need a mother-daughter chat with Millie before I close up."

"Millie left," said Cherry. "She told me to tell you good night and not to worry about her. She has plans."

"She left?" I said. I'd been clear with her that we needed to stick together. "What plans does she have?"

Cherry shrugged.

"Was she alone?" I asked, wondering if Nathaniel had come to the store for her.

"Yes," said Cherry.

This was not the time to disappear on me.

When I entered the workroom, I had another unexpected surprise. The candle I'd made was gone.

"Cherry, did my mom take the candle we were making?"

"The purple one? I wish she had. I don't think that goes with your current product line. But no, she left it on your worktable. I saw it a moment ago."

I went to the window of my workroom. The lock was now undone. How had Rex Laruam taken the candle without anyone seeing him?

I had let Rex Laruam slip from me, as he had with everyone else who'd tried to uncover his identity. I was furious with myself, and worried too. If Laruam discovered that the formula was a fake, Millie would be in danger.

I called my mother again, but the call went to voicemail.

I called Nathaniel, but his phone went to voicemail.

"Happy birthday," said Cherry as she shut the door and left for the day.

I left a moment behind her. I drove home on autopilot, wondering what my next move should be. I'd let the world down, and I feared for Millie's safety. It was just like her to disappear at the worst moment. Our entire relationship, it seemed to me, revolved around her taking off on a whim. I never knew where she was.

When I pulled into my driveway, I noticed Peter's car. He was early.

"Hello?" I said, as I opened my door.

One step inside my apartment and it hit me. My knees began to sink. I took a huge lungful of the evening air outside before I climbed the stairs.

My living room lights were turned off. The low sun shined through my windows. On the small dining table in front of my kitchenette, I saw Peter. He was seated at the table, which he had covered with a red paper cloth, my favorite color. His head, however, lay heavily on top of one of two fancy china plates we'd bought on sale when an antique store in town closed up after the summer. Both of his arms dangled to his sides, and I could tell from the way he was breathing that it would be a good while before he'd be himself again.

I knew why, too. In the center of the table, beside a covered pot filled with Peter's other infamous dish, his rice and beans souffle, were two candles. They were different widths and heights, halfway between a thin taper and a fat hurricane candle. The wax wasn't particularly smooth, and the wicks, I could see, were wildly off center. Had any of my students crafted them, I'd have sent them back to the drawing board.

These, however, I loved, because these had been made by my guy, Peter Bailey. I realized what had happened to my missing vial of the sleeping scent. When I'd caught Peter in my apartment, he'd likely been grabbing what he'd thought was a scent to finish his candles. His efforts warmed my heart. This was the sweetest dinner I'd ever been invited to. It was perfectly planned, despite his accidental use of sleep-inducing oils.

I blew out the candles, and opened the window for another breath of fresh air.

"Peter," I said, and shook his shoulder while I covered my nose with Millie's sweater to filter the air.

"Mmmm," he said, a smile spreading across his face, despite the fact that his eyes were still closed.

"Peter," I said, shaking him.

With some effort. He lifted his head and flashed me a smile. I could see an indentation across his cheek from where the china dish had dug into his skin. The guy was really out of it.

"You look pretty," he said. "Can I tell you something?"

"Sweetheart," I said. "You've been poisoned."

"Poisoned with an arrow from one of those little cherubs. Like in the movies," he said, nodding emphatically. "I'm really tired."

He put his head back on the china plate.

"Have you seen or heard from Millie?" I said, persisting.

"Hmmm?" he said in a deeply groggy state. "Oh, she left whiz-a-man."

It took me a moment to figure out what he'd said.

"With a man?" I said. "She was here? And there was a man?"

He nodded. "She said . . ."

"What did she say?" Sleep was beginning to take hold of me.

"Not to worry about," he said, and drifted off.

"About what? Not to worry about what?"

"'Bout her. She said. Take care of you. Then she left."

"With the man?" I said, clutching his shoulder and feeling wide awake.

"Mmhmm," he said.

"Did you know the man?" I said.

"I don't trust him," he said.

"Who?"

My phone pinged. I looked down to a text without any number attached.

39 Cross Road. Bring the vial.

I could have passed out right then and there, without the aid of Peter's candles. My worst fears had come true.

My grand plan to catch the thief who would steal my purple-fisted candle had gone terribly wrong. Rex Laruam's note had been clear. He had threatened to kill my mother if I messed with him, and I had. He had discovered that the formula she'd inserted was a fake. My only hope was that he was holding her alive until I handed over the real formula.

The address in Rex Laruam's text struck me as familiar, but it wasn't the address for John Pierre's house. Then, I remembered where I'd seen it before.

"I've got to go," I said to Peter. "You probably can't hear me, but this was a great dinner, and when you wake up, hopefully I'll be back."

I kissed Peter's sleeping head. I looked at his dead weight and didn't know whether to laugh or cry. Fortunately, the circumstances didn't leave room for either. This was not the engagement a girl dreams about, but duty called.

Chapter 24

I left my apartment, windows open for Peter's recovery, and ran across the lawn to Chris's house. There were no cars in the driveway. The Mortons were out, as were Chris and the boys. The house was quiet as I opened the kitchen door and went straight to his workspace. On the counter were the floor plans Chris had shown many of the guests after my dinner party. They were of the house he'd been constructing, where the owners had gone bankrupt halfway through the project and had halted work.

The address was 39 Cross Road.

I realized that by now all of my suspects had seen these plans and had likely heard that the house was abandoned. A remote and empty house was a great place to hide a kidnapped victim. It was even better than the house I'd seen John Pierre use, since no one would be able to hear a scream.

The first floor outlined a kitchen, living room, dining room, bathrooms. The plan suggested a large home, definitely the type that seasonal residents liked to build for their summers, with porch space and sketches for a pool. I noticed a plan for a semi-detached garage.

I flipped to another page below, which showed the second floor to the house.

Then, I turned to the last page, at the bottom of the pile, which outlined the basement of the house, finished with a media room, a wine cellar, a rec space, a laundry room, and a workout room. The wine storage area was as big as my apartment. It looked amazing.

I still hated to abandon Peter, but I headed to my car. I called Millie's cell phone. It rang. No answer. I left a message. I texted her. Then I stared at my phone screen, but there was still no response. Instead, I got a text from Andy with a simple question mark. It was now after five, and I knew he'd arrived to my store without seeing a purple candle.

Only a couple of hours ago, I thought I might be close to letting Andy in on my mission. With my mother held hostage, I now knew I couldn't. I felt in my bag for Agent Hill's gun. I took it and shoved it into my sash. Then I thought of one more weapon I had at my disposal. I dashed into my house one more time and grabbed one of Peter's handmade candles. I wasn't a trained spy like Agent Hill, but I had a gun and a sleep-inducing candle in my sash, and a vial of liquid worth my mother's life stuck into my bra.

Game on.

I jumped into the car and headed to 39 Cross Road. I needed one more bit of help—Siri. She gave me directions to the place. It was all the way out toward Sciasconset, a small outpost of a town at the other end of the island.

I decided to park at a distance from the house and find a place to hide until I got my bearings. I knew I should have been terrified, but I felt like a warrior. I'd been casting around for answers for the last two days, and I was ready to go head-to-head with this villain.

When I reached the Milestone Road that led to Sciasconset, I was careful not to exceed the speed limit, but it was hard. I was toying with picking up my speed when I saw a police car coming toward me from the other direction. I kept my eyes straight ahead and hoped that the fog was strong enough to hide my license plate: CNDLADY.

We passed. The driver did not flash his lights in greeting. I exhaled, and took it as a good sign.

About a mile later, however, I heard a funny noise in my car.

"You've got to be kidding me," I said to my steering wheel.

I pulled over to the side of the road and got out of the car. Sure enough, I'd gotten a flat tire. I pulled at the cape my mom had given me for warmth, and considered my next steps.

In the distance, I spied the Old Sconset Golf Course, known to those of us who have been on Nantucket a while as Skinner's. I'm not a golfer, but the few times I've played, I've come to this public course. I realized that if I cut across the course by foot, I might be able to shorten the remaining distance to the house. I'd hoped to park closer to my destination in case Millie needed assistance escaping, but given the circumstances, this seemed like a good substitution to my plan.

From my car, I grabbed Millie's sweater, and put it on under my red cape for extra warmth. Securing the gun and candle in my beautiful, flowery sash, I locked my car door and headed to the golf course, grateful I'd never changed out of my sneakers.

Unfortunately, Skinner's has no golf carts, which would have been the ideal mode of transportation, and, I'll admit it, I know how to jump-start a golf cart. When we were seniors in high school, our senior cut day had ended at the island's fanciest golf club where we'd all "borrowed" the carts to play golf cart tag on the course. Let's just say that the entire budget for senior brunch covered a couple of dents the carts encountered. Now, without a cart to speed my journey, I decided that I should try to find a map of the course to make sure I took no wrong turns in the growing darkness.

The small clubhouse was straight ahead. In the front of the building, which overlooks the sixth hole, was a porch. The rocking chairs that invite visitors for a relaxing drink from the bar after a long game, were stored inside for the night. Thinking someone might have dropped a map on the deck, I stopped there first.

The porch was completely tidied, not a map or a piece of trash anywhere. I risked Laruam tracking me for a moment, and put on my phone's flashlight as I rounded the clubhouse and passed the putting green. Like everything else, the flags were down for the day. Stuck into a bench by the putting green, I noticed something that could pass for a folded map of the course or a scorecard that had not been worth keeping. I powered down my phone, and, with the dimmest light of the sky now leading me, I ran across the green.

Halfway across the field, I took a leap, but when I landed my body dipped farther than I expected. My foot immediately sank into the earth. I pulled, but found I was immobilized. My foot was in a hole. Stepping backwards, I got my foot out with ease, but my sneaker was jammed. As I leaned down to pull it out, I saw the beam of a flashlight coming toward Skinner's.

I looked around for a spot to hide. The bench I'd been heading toward was the only coverage near me, so I abandoned my shoe and scurried to safety. Halfway there, I heard a familiar voice.

"Stella?" said Andy, his flashlight beaming directly on me so that there was no chance of escaping.

"Hi," I said, covering my eyes from his blinding light.

Andy headed toward me.

"What happened to meeting me at five o'clock?"

"Andy," I said. "I'm sorry I left you stranded, but there are things I cannot tell you. I've been sworn to secrecy."

"Stella," he said. "You've either lost your mind or you're really caught up in something. I can't believe I'm saying this, but I hope you're caught up in something. And it's time to let me in on things."

"You know I would if I could, right?" I said.

"My car's down the road," he said. "Come on, let's go. Don't you have some birthday plans, by the way?"

"You know about my birthday night too?" I said.

"No," said Andy. He said the word too slowly.

Even in the dark, I could tell he was lying.

"You like Peter, right?" I said.

"Sure," he said, but his image was obscured in the darkness, and I couldn't entirely read his expression.

"*Sure*? That's it?" I said.

"Come on," he said. "Your birthday will be over before you know it, and you'll have spent it with me on this golf course."

We should have moved, but the sound of the crickets and the rolling fog made time stand still for a moment.

"I can't go with you," I said.

I pointed across the putting green.

"I lost my sneaker."

Andy walked toward the hole and pulled out my sneaker.

"Thanks," I said. "The thing is, I think I sprained my ankle. Any chance you can drive your car up here? I'd rather not walk down the path."

I sat on the bench and noticed that the map I'd hoped to find was no more than a leaf. As I dropped it to the ground, I noticed a whoosh of light across the black sky, and realized it was coming from the Sankaty Head Lighthouse, which was in the vicinity of Cross Road. I knew if I followed the direction of the beam of light, I'd reach the location of the house.

"Don't move," said Andy, as he turned his flashlight back on and headed down the path.

"Where would I go?" I said.

In the dark, I silently puffed my cheeks out to keep from exploding. The minute he left, I put on my sneaker.

I hated to ruin Millie's beautiful gift, but the bright red of my cape would surely catch Andy's eye. I ran about twenty yards in the opposite direction of the path I planned to take across the course and threw my cape on the ground.

I turned and ran back toward the putting green. I found a few stray golf balls sitting at the bottom of a bucket, neon balls which the kids loved during clinics. I grabbed two and continued toward the first hole. About fifty paces down the path, I heard Andy's car pull up to the clubhouse, but I stopped for nothing. Behind me, I heard him shut his car door and then call my name. I knew he'd be worried about me, but I couldn't stop or explain.

I kept running, as fast as my feet could carry me.

Chapter 25

The darkness was growing, and the fog was thick as I moved in the direction of the lighthouse, but each time its beam blazed across the fields, I had a moment to see the path ahead of me. My feet were soaked within minutes from the dewy ground. The night was getting chilly, but I could feel myself beginning to perspire. I took off Millie's sweater as I ran and wrapped it around my waist. The crisp air on my free arms gave me a second wind, and I could feel myself pick up speed.

Every step I took brought me closer to Millie. Closer to my mom. Every tree or bush, however, took on a sinister form in the night. At one point, I stopped dead in my tracks, sure a bear had blocked my path. Rather than remind myself that there are no bears on Nantucket, I thought about how I'd once read that if you encounter a bear you are supposed to stand very still, and not provoke it through any means of self-defense. I challenge anyone to stand still in front of a bear, real or imagined. I pulled a golf ball from my sash and threw it. As a kid, I'd learned how to throw a good fast ball from a family friend. I took advantage of the skill now and threw hard. The ball, however, bounced off a tree and into my shoulder. It was nothing compared to a bear attack, but it hurt. I moved on.

At the end of the course, I had to climb through thick, uneven brush. I tried to pull up my palazzo pants, but learned at this inopportune moment, that they don't roll. Holding them up as best I could, I crunched through branches and brambles. I knew my legs were getting scratched and bruised, but eventually, perhaps miraculously, I made it to the partially paved road which was about fifty yards from the house. I was breathing heavily, and I'd lost a good twenty minutes due to my car's breakdown, but I was close.

I slowed when I saw a stake in front of what seemed like a freshly made, circular driveway. There was no mailbox out front since the house was under construction, but the stake had the number thirty-nine painted on it. I leaned against the wooden post while I caught my breath and scoped out the property.

I could tell that the house would be a beauty when someone finally got around to finishing it. The two stories, with room for a widow's walk on top, were positioned at a slant on the property, likely to take advantage of the sunlight. The outside of the house had been fully framed and almost completely shingled. The front door was formal but not overbearing.

There was one light on in the house. I felt my sash and found comfort in the protection I had brought with me: My gun, my sleep-inducing candle, my phone, and the remaining golf ball. I realized I had another weapon—my knowledge of the floor plans to the house ahead of me.

I closed my eyes and envisioned what I'd seen in

Chris's kitchen. Specifically, I tried to remember where the entrances to the house were, and where the best place to hide someone might be. The first floor had a side entrance by the kitchen. From my angle, I thought that the shining light came from the kitchen, so I had no desire to use that door.

I tiptoed across the edge of the driveway, where a Jeep and a motorcycle were parked, and headed to the end of the house, where I knew a porch extended from the master bedroom on the second floor. As I passed the kitchen windows from afar, I tried to catch a glimpse inside, to see my mother or Laruam, but I saw no one.

When I reached the end of the house, I could see that the porch was built, but would require an ambitious climb. Untying my sash, I decided to use it as a lasso around the posts supporting the second-floor porch. I realized that I would not be able to climb it and also carry my assorted weaponry, but I had no choice. I put the items on the ground along with my mom's sweater, and forged ahead unarmed.

Tossing my sash as high as I could to gain some leverage, I used the edge of the post to balance my feet as I began to ascend the house. Each time I shimmied the scarf up the post, I climbed a little higher. I was amazed at the progress I was making, and honestly, on any regular day I have no idea if I'd actually be able to achieve the same feat, but foot by foot I made my way to the top of the post until I'd reached the railing of the master bedroom's porch. At the top, I used my right arm to support my weight. I knew my arms would be feeling the burn tomorrow, but I was able to fling myself over the rail. I crept across the deck and peered through the window.

Although the outside of the house was mostly finished, the interior work seemed to have stopped at a much earlier stage. The walls were framed with two-by-fours, but only a couple of them had been finished with drywall. All of the tools were packed up, aside from a few screws scattered across the flooring. My mother was nowhere to be seen. My heart sank at the thought that she was downstairs, perhaps in the kitchen with Rex Laruam.

I decided that by entering the house from here, I'd be able to listen to whatever was going on between my mother and Rex Laruam downstairs. Duct tape covered the space where a lock should be on the door of the porch. The missing lock was likely a casualty of the fact that the work had halted quickly, but Chris's team had secured the doorknobs with a rope. It took a few moments, but I untied the rope, peeled off the tape, and pushed open the doors without making a noise. Softly, I stepped into the unfinished house, which greeted me with the comforting scent of sawdust.

Through the master bedroom, I saw the main staircase. From the floor plans I'd looked at, I knew it led down to a vestibule and the front door. To the left was the living room. To the right was the dining room. Behind was a family room that connected to the kitchen. I heard noise below, but I knew I'd have to get to the staircase to hear anything clearly.

I took a step, then paused. I waited. If Rex Laruam heard me, I'd be in big trouble. There was no place to hide. I took another step, and paused. The walk seemed interminable, but I was not willing to take any chances at revealing myself. Plus, the slow journey produced one immediate benefit. On the ground, someone had left a pack of matches. I realized that Peter's sleep-inducing candle was useless without them, so I picked up the matchbook.

When I got as close to the stairwell as I dared, I heard a phone ring below. The ring was the sound of an old-fashioned phone, but maybe more European than American. That sort of short, double ring our phones had made in Paris instead of the single, longer rings of American phones. After a couple of rings, I heard the person below me answer.

"Laruam." It was a man's voice, low and gruff.

I tried to determine if it was anyone I knew, but the voice was not familiar to me. It was foreign, but I could not figure out what country it was from. The accent itself was more British than American, but there were other accents mixed with it that could be from anywhere.

"I've got her," the man continued.

My hand flew to my sash, but I remembered that I'd left my armor outside.

"The stupid girl messed with me," the man said when I was close enough to hear. "Her policeman friend was hanging around. His girlfriend gave him away, yelled out his name. I realized it was a set-up immediately. But I have the hostage. I'll get the formula and get rid of both of them."

Georgianna had joined Andy on his stakeout. So, my army wasn't perfect.

I wanted to run down the stairs, without a thought to the danger that lay ahead of me, but I suddenly realized that I couldn't hear my mom. I knew that if she was awake, she'd be screaming. And, if Rex Laruam had knocked her out, she would be snoring.

I heard Laruam open a door.

I'd forgotten about the basement, a cold, damp, and inhospitable place for someone recovering from a concussion.

I made the path back to the porch in two silent leaps. There was a storm door by the side of the house, near the kitchen. As long as I could open it without Rex Laruam noticing me, I could slip down into the cellar. Sticking the matchbook between my teeth, I grabbed my sash and flung myself over the porch's railing.

Once I'd made it back down, I retied my long sash around my waist, rearmed my makeshift holster, and crept toward the cellar. As I reached the lit windows of the kitchen, I fell to my hands and knees, and crawled along the side of the house.

I had no idea about my mother's condition, but I did not want to risk her calling out to me when I found her while Laruam was inside and could hear us. Therefore, I decided to create a distraction to lure him out of the house. Then, I could enter the basement through the cellar doors, and figure out the situation. If I could get Millie up and out the cellar door, we could hide in the fog until we got back to the golf course. There, I would have the upper hand.

I gripped my other golf ball, and I decided what my distraction would be. The Jeep's alarm. My aim had been good with the tree, so I reckoned it would be successful with the surface area of the Jeep. Perhaps I could set off the Jeep's alarm. I wound my arm back and went for a fast ball. As the ball left my hand, I could feel the speed. In the dark, I could not see its flight, but I held my breath, waiting for the car alarm.

Instead, I heard it land softly, as if on a pillow.

"You've got to be kidding," I whispered to myself.

Crouching back down toward the earth, I ventured into the open, in hopes that I might find the ball and try again. I made it across the driveway in one piece to find that the neon ball had landed in the exposed back end of the Jeep. It lay on one of two bags, piled on top of each other. The bag on top was filled with scuba equipment. At least I now knew how he had arrived to and left from the *Hatchfield*.

I also noticed a can of gasoline beside the bags. A fire would take more time to contain than a car alarm. I was getting used to revising my plans on this mission, so I grabbed the gasoline can instead of the golf ball. Out of sight from the kitchen windows, but still crouched low, I began to pour the liquid from the Jeep, toward the motorcycle, and then back toward the house. About six feet from the cellar door, I pulled out the matches from my sash. I struck a light and threw it on my propane trail.

The flame expired immediately.

I lit three more matches in a row, and dropped them onto my gasoline trail without success. On my fifth try, I finally saw a small flame. I scurried to the cellar door only to find a strong rope was tied around the handles, similar to the one I'd struggled with on the porch. If I didn't move fast, Rex Laruam might notice the fire before I made it to the basement. I was thinking about lighting the rope on fire, too, but then a piece of the knot loosened at the expense of my nails, which would look absolutely terrible with an engagement ring later on tonight.

I got the knot untied as a small blaze took hold of my gasoline trail. I flung open the door to the basement and peered into darkness.

"Millie?" I said, as quietly as I could while breathing heavily.

I heard no snoring. I heard no breathing.

I took a step down. Then another. Then another. When I had both feet firmly planted on the cellar floor, I let my eyes adjust. I could make out foundation work, the base of the brick chimney, and a pile of cement bags in the corner of the room.

"Hello?" I whispered again.

There was no answer, but I wasn't a quitter. I picked up a shovel a builder had left behind and slowly walked to the middle of the cellar. Until I had had a look on the other side of the chimney and behind the cement bags, I would not give up hope that my mother was here, and alive.

When I reached the chimney I stood still, suddenly afraid that Rex Laruam might already be down here too. I raised my shovel, and held it aloft, ready to smash it against him if I had to. I took a step around the corner.

"Ooooph." I started to scream, but a hand covered my mouth.

I'd been simultaneously kicked in the gut and gagged. I knew Millie had learned a lot of tricks as a female travelling alone around the world, but this seemed way above her skill set, especially with a concussion. I struggled with all of my might, but one arm of my assailant was over my face so I could see nothing as I was dragged across the room. I knew, however, that Laruam had me.

I felt my body thrown against something, which I decided was a cement bag. During the push, I felt my assailant's grip around me loosen for a second, and I realized I might have only one chance to fight back. As I fell, I kicked behind me, toward what I hoped would be a very painful spot on Rex Laruam. I made contact, but the figure dipped behind the chimney before I could make him out. I still had no idea who he was.

The shovel lay on my side of the chimney, so I grabbed it. I held it up and peered into the darkness, my only cover, in hopes that my other senses were sharp enough to detect movement. After a moment, I thought I heard or sensed a human being to the right of me, and I swung blindly into the dark. I continued swinging and heading into the darkness.

"Mom?" I said. "Are you OK?"

I took another step forward. I could tell from a slight change in the temperature that I was reaching the open storm door.

"Millie?" I said loudly.

That's when it happened. The small fire I'd lit outside had reached the Jeep. The sound of an explosion outside caught me off guard. In the light that burst forth, the cellar lit up.

I found myself staring directly into the face of my assailant.

"Agent Hill?" I said.

Chapter 26

I stood, frozen, for as long as I dared, my mind trying to process the figure before me. Was Agent Hill actually Rex Laruam? Had I helped bring the real formula to her?

"Where is she?" I said.

I raised my shovel in the most threatening way I could, but without the darkness to shield me, I had no chance. Agent Hill grabbed the shovel from my hand.

"You're crazy," she said.

"That's right," I said, raising my fists.

"Do you have the formula?" she said, calmly. "Hand it over if you have it. This is a case of national security."

"How do I know I can trust you?" I said. "I thought you were dead."

"Rex Laruam brought me here after our fight. He put a safety vest on me and threw me overboard. After that I blacked out and woke up here. And when he decides he doesn't need me, he'll kill me."

I noticed she was disheveled and still in her wetsuit from the night of the fight.

"Where's Millie?" I said, deciding to trust her.

Agent Hill looked at my sash. Before I knew it, she

had the gun in her hand. I was down to a candle for my personal protection.

"Rex Laruam will be downstairs in less than one minute," she said. "He's likely out there now, checking out your explosion, which was brilliant thinking, but it won't keep him for long. He's probably checking the perimeter right now, thinking I've escaped. But he'll soon check down here. When he sees you, we'll both be dead. So, I will ask you one more time. Where's the formula?"

I stared at the gun.

"Where's Millie?" I said, my heart pounding.

"She's not here."

Another explosion burst from outside. I figured the motorcycle was now on fire.

"If I can help you find your mother, I will," said Agent Hill, "but right now you need to give me that formula before Rex Laruam comes for us."

It seemed like the moment for a salute, but instead I handed the formula to her. I wanted to explain that she'd had the wrong formula, and that I'd recovered the right one, but I figured now was not the time to fish for compliments.

Agent Hill climbed the stairs and looked outside.

"OK," she said. "We have cover. Let's go."

At that moment, we heard the door open above us. Agent Hill pushed me behind her and took aim. Rex Laruam took a step down the kitchen stairs. We could not see him clearly in the dark, but he opened fire.

Agent Hill fired back.

"Go!" said Agent Hill, pushing me toward the stairs of the storm door.

I felt the whiz of Rex Laruam's next bullet fly past me. I didn't need her command. I soared to that exit at about the same speed as the bullet. I was up the stairs and heading toward the end of the house before either of them had the chance to fire again.

When I reached the end of the house, I realized that the explosions we'd heard weren't quite what I'd thought they'd been. My small fire had gone all of about two feet before burning out in the dewy earth. The can of gasoline I'd thrown next to it, however, had been in its path and had exploded. The fire was burning brightly, and the breeze was pushing it toward the house. The second explosion had been from one of two fire extinguishers on the ground, near the house. The Jeep and the motorcycle were still intact.

Behind me, I could hear a brutal fight underway in the cellar. Using my one last chance to find Millie in the house, I ran to the front door and went inside.

"Mom? It's Stella," I said.

The first floor was also unframed, so I could see through most of the space. Millie was not there. I could hear fighting continue in the cellar. It was like nothing I'd ever heard. I ran toward a plywood wall which blocked the kitchen area. My last chance.

The room was empty.

Below, I now heard footsteps heading up the cellar stairs. I ran out the front door to see the silhouette of Rex Laruam leaping into his Jeep. Agent Hill was not behind him. The flames from my fire were getting closer and closer to the house. Chris was going to kill me if these two didn't first. I grabbed a fire extinguisher by the front door and sprayed it at the open flame as I headed to the cellar.

Agent Hill was climbing the stairs and rubbing her head.

"He got the formula from me," she said, then she looked at the now-smoldering fire.

I grabbed her arm and pulled her toward the motorcycle as Rex Laruam sped off the property and out into the street. There was no key in the motorcycle, but the ignition was not much different than a golf cart's. I found a piece of wire lying in the construction site's debris. In a moment, I had it hot-wired.

"Jump on," I said, grabbing the helmet and giving it to her. She looked like she needed it more than I did. As an islander, I've spent a good amount of time on motorbikes and on the path we were about to take. I knew I was ready for the job.

"Get off," she said. "This is a matter of national security."

"I'm going after Rex Laruam," I said, revving the engine. "If you want to come, jump on. Otherwise, you're on your own."

It wasn't entirely reassuring that the woman who had only moments ago moved with a speed that would humble Tinker, climbed on with a few curses and mutters. I took it as a sign that she'd had a bad fight and needed a moment to recover. We pulled away with her arms around me, down the driveway, and with the smoke behind us. I heard the sound of a fire engine coming toward us. I knew the neighbors must have heard the explosion. Hopefully they'd thought the gun fight had been part of the blast. Either way, I wasn't going to wait around.

Ahead, I saw Rex Laruam's Jeep lights in the fog. I could tell he'd slowed enough so that he wouldn't attract the attention of the fire truck passing him. It gave us time to catch up a little bit, but not enough. After the truck passed, we all hit the gas again.

"Careful," Agent Hill said, shouting over the motor.

"I've got this," I said, equally loud. "I'm used to fog."

We were quiet for a moment as the sound of the motor and the wind filled the night.

"Sorry tonight isn't going as you'd planned," Agent Hill said.

Did everyone know about Peter's proposal?

"I'm sorry about your partner," I said.

"Donny."

We were quiet again as I sped down the road. I kept my eyes on Rex Laruam's taillights.

"Did he ever propose?" I said.

"Watch out for that curve!" said Agent Hill.

I hugged the curve, gaining on Laruam as he turned onto the Milestone Road, toward town. Following him would be trickier now. There would be more traffic.

"I think if I can get back to town, I can find my mom," I finally said. "If we're chasing John Pierre, he might have stashed her in his other house."

Agent Hill did not answer.

I gunned the motorcycle as fast as I dared and surprised even myself when I came up on his tail. The guy didn't slow down for even a second, and I figured he had a specific destination in mind. When he reached the rotary, which has exits to all of the island's main thoroughfares, I knew what it was. "He's heading to the airport," I said.

"Makes sense," she said. "Slow down. Let him think he's lost us."

"Element of surprise," I said. "I get it."

"I'll do what I can to help once I recover the formula," she said. I desperately tried to ignore the tinge of sadness in her response. It suggested a conclusion I did not want to consider.

At one end of the airport is an area for private planes. I parked the motorcycle at the edge of Airport Road so we could make the last bit of our journey on foot. I was suddenly cold. Instinctively, I reached for my waist and realized, that in all of the action, I'd lost my mother's sweater.

Ahead of us, we could hear the sound of a jet plane. It was a dark silver aircraft with a pointy nose and an engine that roared even while idling. Very slick. I'd always wanted to see what the inside of one of these planes looked like. From behind a fuel truck, we watched as a man shrouded in a black hoodie got out of the Jeep and spoke to an airport employee in a bright yellow vest and headphones.

"Thank you for your service," said Agent Hill. "Now get out of here. Go find your mother. I can recover the vial on my own."

Agent Hill took off on foot toward the plane without another word. I held my breath as I watched her board, undetected. Across the tarmac, I saw the man in the hoodie. Rex Laruam. He must have been confident that he'd lost us, because he seemed pretty calm. As far as he knew, he had the coded formula. His mission was almost complete. He was lucky, too. The fog was lifting, so he'd be cleared to take off.

I watched him reach into the cargo area of the Jeep and removed the scuba bag I'd seen earlier tonight. Then he retrieved the other bag I'd noticed.

It looked like a large backpack. When he threw it over his shoulder, however, I noticed the leg straps dangling from it. I also noticed a metal handle hanging from the wide shoulder straps of the bag. I realized I was looking at a parachute. I knew this because Emily and I had spent hours one day googling skydiving, years ago, when we had decided to start our businesses and we wanted to celebrate with something crazy. Once we read the fun fact that you fall at about 120 miles per hour, we'd opted instead for a beach party, which had been legendary.

Suddenly, I had the feeling that Agent Hill was entirely unprepared for the trip she was about to take. She needed help.

Skydiving is not a pastime on Nantucket because there's a lot more sea than land. I knew of only one person who had ever shown an interest in skydiving here. Georgianna. She had arrived to Nantucket almost a year ago with two chutes in tow, which she had won at a raffle in her town in Florida. She'd even go so far as to bring them to the airport in search of a coach before the land-to-sea ratio became clear to her. Andy had told me the story one morning in town. He'd thought it was sweet. Now, I was glad he'd told me the story, because I also remembered that she had donated the chutes to the airport.

As Rex Laruam focused on his phone, I decided to go for it. I ran along the perimeter of the field, and into a small storage structure. If Agent Hill had been tasked with the hunt she would have lost valuable time, but I located the chutes in no time. I took them both, shot across the tarmac, relieved that Laruam did not look up from his phone as I did, and climbed aboard.

I entered the plane, which was as fabulous as I'd thought it would be. Tan leather sofas ran along each side of the plane's cabin with small lights above. I saw a stocked bar on a wood-paneled back wall with an impressive array of drinks and snacks. To my left, I noticed that the door to the cockpit was open. I peered inside to see a panel of instruments that made no sense to me. There was no pilot. Agent Hill had disappeared too.

"Agent Hill," I said. "Where are you? I think Rex Laruam is planning to meet someone in a boat, not fly somewhere."

At the other end of the plane, the bathroom door flung open.

"In here," she said, pointing to the bathroom.

I dashed down the aisle and into the bathroom. She closed the door.

"I told you not to follow me," she said.

"I know, but I thought I should tell you," I said. "He's got a parachute."

"Crap," she said.

At that moment, we heard the door to the airplane shut. In the next moment, the door to the cockpit shut too.

"We're trapped," I said. In a few hours, I might be crash landing into the ocean, with a terrorist and with no chance of finding my mother.

"What do we do?" I said.

"*You*," she said, "will stay inside this bathroom. *I* will take care of things."

Chapter 27

I sat on the toilet and buckled my seatbelt. A seatbelt on the toilet. On a plane. Does it get better than that?

I'd never been on a private airplane before. Over the two bulky vests on my lap, I watched as Agent Hill opened a medicine cabinet over the sink. In spite of our peril, I continued to be impressed. The cabinet was filled with what amounted to the best of the best from the travel-size aisle in the drugstore. Razor blades, mini-toothbrush sets, a nail clipper, lint roller, shaving cream, Band-Aids. Even dental floss.

I looked at Agent Hill and noticed that blood was dripping from her arm. She was still wearing the wetsuit she'd had on when we'd met in the boat, and she now unzipped the top.

"You've been hit," I said.

"Grazed," she said, examining the wound more casually than I might have.

She opened the mouthwash and poured it on the wound without flinching.

"Antiseptic," she said in answer to what must have been my bewildered expression.

I guessed toothpaste was also an antiseptic because she added a dab of it to the wound as well. Next, she grabbed the dental floss. I caught on to her plan and unbuckled myself to help.

"Sit down," she said.

"Cut it out," I said. "This plane is going to take off in the next few minutes. You need all the help you can get."

I held a washcloth against her forearm as she threaded the dental floss into a needle from a sewing kit and began to stitch her wound. When she was done, she rezipped her wetsuit.

She pulled out a compact mirror from the medicine cabinet and slowly opened the bathroom door. At this point, a lot of Agent Hill's body was shoved against me and my chutes as she leaned down in the cramped space and slipped the mirror out, as low to the ground as possible. Like a dentist examining teeth, she explored the cabin for a moment and then closed the door, a hand on her gun at all times.

"What can you see?" I said from behind her.

"He's in the cockpit," she said. Maybe to me, or maybe not. "No one else is on board." She was in her zone. I could see that.

"Stay here," she said to me.

The last place I wanted to be was strapped to a toilet, alone, in a three-foot-square closet, while a woman with a gun in a plane was on the prowl.

"You're stuck with me," I said.

"I can't protect you," said Agent Hill.

I felt the plane begin to move toward the runway. Agent Hill opened the door and ran up the aisle. I moved more slowly behind her. The plane's starts and stops didn't help my balance as we taxied along the runway while other planes took off ahead of us.

I pressed myself against the back wall, as Agent Hill strapped on her chute.

"I don't know how to jump," I said.

"Hopefully you won't have to," she said, buckling her harness.

I put on my chute, nonetheless.

Next, Agent Hill examined the cabin and the cockpit door. I wasn't sure what her plans were, but I decided it was time I had my own. I grabbed a bottle of whiskey from the bar next to me and held tightly to its neck so that I had a small bat in my hand.

"Are you going to shoot the cockpit door open with your gun?" I whispered.

"I'd rather catch him off guard," she said. "I only have one bullet left. Plus, I don't want to risk a bullet hitting the vial now that he has it."

"Good point."

Instead of waging war, Agent Hill began to unscrew the lightbulbs in the cabin. I gathered that she planned to catch him off guard, maybe get him in a choke hold and use all of her different methods of torture. I liked the plan, except that the plane suddenly picked up speed. We were out of time. The plane was taking off. Before we could count to ten, it shot up into the sky, as if we were in a rocket. I assumed Rex Laruam was trying to gain altitude quickly so that he could safely jump from the aircraft. I grabbed one of the leather seats to keep from slipping back to the bathroom of the plane.

As we quickly gained altitude, I looked out the window, I realized my hopes at saving my mother would quickly be in peril. Once aloft, we'd move out to the open ocean quickly. I needed to return to land to find Millie Wright. Now.

I opened the bottle of whiskey and took a long, hard drink. As I did, I braced myself against Rex Laruam's scuba gear bag which he'd left on the ground in front of one of the sofas. I unzipped the bag. I was thinking perhaps a canister of oxygen would be a better weapon than a bottle of whiskey.

"Hide that in the bathroom," said Agent Hill, pointing to the oxygen tank. "If my gun goes off, I don't want to hit it."

She didn't have to tell me twice. I remembered the fire extinguisher exploding on Cross Road. I hid it in the bathroom and crawled back out, where the scuba bag had slipped down due to the steep take-off. I opened a pocket on the front of the bag, in search of a flashlight. If Agent Hill lured him from the cabin, I could flash the light in his eyes to gain advantage over him before attacking, as Andy had done when he'd found me tonight at Skinner's.

I had begun to search the pocket when I froze.

"Agent Hill?" I said.

She didn't answer. With one last twist of the lights, the cabin was now dark. Only the moonlight lit the plane, and she began to close the window shades too. Before the last one closed, I caught a glimpse of the island below us. I could see the lights of cars on streets. They looked like ants.

"I found the vial," I said.

Agent Hill turned to me.

"Excellent," she said, heading my way. "I'll neutralize the enemy and fly us to Central."

The plane began to level out.

"What about my mother?" I said.

We had no time left before we were out to sea. As dearly as I wanted to help Agent Hill, I had duties as well. I put the vial in one of the parachute's pockets and zipped it up.

"What're you doing?" she said.

"Laruam will come after us if he knows we have the vial," I said.

From the corner of my eye, I saw the airplane door's emergency latch. With one quick turn to the left, I'd be out of the plane with the vial and Laruam behind me. I dashed across the cabin, and turned the latch.

"Let's go," I said.

I saw the handle of the cockpit begin to turn as I jumped into the night air.

As I began to fall 120 miles per hour, in the dark, I tried to remember the videos Emily and I had watched on how to open a chute. My palazzo pants did nothing to help me. Rather than gather air and slow me down, they flew to my chin. I heard a loud rush of wind that was something like the sound of a car window being opened on the highway. I felt pressure on my skin, but I was not freezing. I was also surprised I could move my arms and legs.

I grabbed the rip cord and pulled. Nothing happened. I was falling. And falling. I wondered what would happen to the queen from the South Pacific and how the Peace Jubilee would turn out. I wondered what would happen to Millie. I wanted to scream, but I could not find my voice.

Then, I felt as if I'd been pushed off a diving board.

Agent Hill was on my back. Her arms wrapped around my waist. She turned me around so that I could cling to her like a baby wanting to be picked up, which I did. I had no shame. I held on to that US spy for my life. I had a feeling she was yelling at me, maybe cursing a bit, which was understandable, but the air was too loud for me to hear her as we fell. A moment later, the parachute opened, and everything became quiet, peaceful, and still. The fog had cleared and below us, I could see the ocean.

"Did you get Rex Laruam?" I said, finding my voice.

"No, but he'll be after us," she said. "Our exit was not elegant."

"Can you get us into town?" I said.

"You want a door-to-door lift?"

I might have been imagining it, but I thought she laughed, a little bit. She deserved to. We'd recovered the vial. Tomorrow would be Sunday. She had accomplished her core mission.

At that moment, we heard the sound of a bullet through the night sky.

"He's trying to find us," she said. "Stay quiet."

We heard another bullet go off. It wasn't close, but it wasn't far either.

"Hold on tightly to me," she said. "I'm going to let go of you."

I could feel my fingernails dig into her back as she let go of me and pulled the cords of her parachute to navigate. From over her shoulder, I could see we were heading closer and closer to Jetties Beach, the public town beach. It was empty at this hour and time of year, and I knew it offered a nice stretch of open space for us to land. I was beginning to feel that I'd survive, when I saw Rex Laruam. He had not seen us, but he was also heading over the beach and toward town.

"Over there," I said. I peered carefully into the darkness, hoping to determine his identity, but it was dark, and he still wore his hoodie.

Agent Hill saw him, too. In an instant, my safe

landing on the beach was diverted. We continued over the jetties, over the beach, and on toward town. As we flew over Centre Street, which was lit by street-lamps below. The town looked a little bit like Mr. Rogers' Neighborhood, and I had that happy feeling he always sang about—knowing that I was alive.

In the distance, Rex Laruam stopped in midair.

"What the—?" she said.

"He's landed on the steeple of the First Congregational Church," I said.

We watched as Rex Laruam unhooked himself from his chute, leapt to the spire and began to climb down from the clock to the lintel over the church door. Agent Hill maneuvered as close as she could to keep an eye on him. His face was to the church as he made his descent, so he could not see us.

Agent Hill began to lower us at a house with a good front yard at the northern stretch of Centre Street, across from the church and not far from the Jared Coffin House. I was expecting a lot of bumps and bruises when we landed, but my return to Nantucket was surprisingly pleasant. She had us back to the ground like a gently falling feather. The hardest part for me was letting go of her. My arms and legs had become a solid rock around her body.

"I don't see him," I said, looking at the steeple.

"He'll be hiding somewhere," she said, pulling my limbs from her. "And we're going to take him down. You take the vial and put it in your safe. I'll pick it up after I detain Rex Laruam."

"OK," I said, feeling like my legs were made of Jell-O with each step, and knowing that she was using "detain" in the deadliest sense of the word.

By the time I made it to the sidewalk in front of the house where we'd landed, Agent Hill had disappeared without a trace. Even the chute was gone. I ran past the Jared Coffin House and down Centre Street toward the Wick & Flame. I could hear sounds inside of the hotel, as life moved on, oblivious to the dangers outside.

Down the street, I opened the door to my store and flew to the safe, where I stashed the vial. I looked at the formula only once, as it left my hands, for what I hoped was the last time. I made a wish that everyone protected by the code would live and be well. Then I shut the safe's door.

Just as the light in my store flicked on.

Chapter 28

"I think you lost this earlier tonight," said Andy.

I looked up, expecting Andy to give me my red cape and a stern lecture about ditching him on a golf course.

Instead, he reached his hand toward me and handed me Millie's sweater. I'd lost it at 39 Cross Road. The house where Rex Laruam had been hiding. If he'd recovered my sweater, he'd known I was there. He'd known I'd been part of the fire. He'd known I escaped. He did not, however, say anything to me. Instead, he took a step toward me, and hugged me.

The hug was quite the opposite of the one I'd given Agent Hill as we'd flown over Nantucket. Now, I was in strong, warm arms that held me close and made me feel that nothing could harm me. I could have, might have, melted into them, but they were not Peter's arms. They were the arms of the guy who'd once dropped water balloons on my head from his eighth-grade classroom window, and a host of other things I decided not to think about for this one moment.

And then, the moment passed. Andy let go of me.

"Sorry," I said, putting on Millie's sweater to hide my confusion.

"I thought you'd gone bananas. At least I know you were just in some sort of Stella scrape."

"You make me sound like my mother," I said, horrified.

He laughed.

I looked down at my outfit, my mother's gift to me, which was in advanced stages of disarray.

"I saw you falling from the sky in a parachute," he said.

"You did?"

"I also received a message from headquarters not to intervene. That's unusual," he said. "You going to tell me the story?"

"If I can," I said.

"Right. Only you would fall from the sky after setting a fire and then tell me, a police officer, that you'll tell me the story only *if* you can."

"I still need your help," I said. "I've lost Millie."

"Let's go," he said, and he pulled me out the door. I didn't bother to lock up.

"I was thinking we might—" I began.

Andy continued to pull me down the street at a quick pace.

"Where are we going?" I said as he reached the corner and crossed the street.

He said nothing but headed straight to the stairs of the Jared Coffin House.

"What are we doing?" I said.

Andy ushered me up the stairs and inside. I thought about Lennie. And Nathaniel. And Olive. They were all staying at the Jared Coffin House. I wondered how much Andy had figured out on his own.

We headed past the stairway, however, and toward the back of the inn where Frank Marshall had had his party earlier that night. Now, the room was dark and empty.

"Do you think he has her upstairs?" I said. "Why are we going back here? We're wasting time."

"Can you just come with me?" he said.

"But—"

"But I can help you on at least one of your mysteries if you'll just come with me."

Before I could answer, he opened the door to a room in the back of the hotel, and switched on the lights.

"Surprise!!" A chorus of friends and relatives burst from every corner of the room and into the bright light of the hotel's restaurant, which was decorated to the brim with birthday streamers, balloons, hats, horns, and champagne. In the center of the room was my mother. Docker had even brought Tinker along.

"Mom," I said, hugging her.

I should have known. I'd risked my life jumping out of a plane only to find out my mom had been here all along. I turned to Andy and smiled. He was busy receiving a kiss from Georgianna, but he gave me a thumbs-up.

"Baby," she said. "I'm sorry I skipped out on you, but Andy came to get me for setup while Peter was making your dinner. I knew I would be safe in his hands."

"You did this?" I said to my mom.

"Peter did," she said. "With Emily. I tried to help, but then I spent the last two days in the hospital. Olive did the streamers."

I thought about my mom's comment that Andy had brought her from my house to the hotel. If I remembered correctly, Peter had mentioned in his deep stupor that he didn't trust "the man." I wondered if he was a little less confident than he appeared.

I saw Peter against the back wall of the room. I wanted to rush over to him, apologize for leaving him asleep at dinner, and for ignoring him so much since I'd come home. I was about to do as much when I noticed Cherry. I smiled at her, but realized she was pointing to her eyes and then at someone. I followed her gaze to see a man walking toward me. A man with dead eyes. I got her message. He had been the stranger who had visited my store.

Instinctively, I stood in front of Millie for protection. I began to raise my hands in self-defense when I heard the sound of a phone, with the odd European *ring-ring* that I'd heard at 39 Cross Road. It was not coming from the dead-eyed man. I looked around the room for someone who was checking their phone or talking on it.

I heard the sound of the phone again, and I turned the other way. The ring was receding out of the party room. I could not see the phone's owner over the crowds of birthday well-wishers, but I knew I was close to Rex Laruam. I headed toward the exit.

"Birthday girl," Emily said, blocking my way with a huge hug. "It was either this or jumping out of a plane. Remember that plan?"

"This is much better," I said, with full knowledge of what I spoke. "I need to freshen up though. I had no idea. Cover for me while I'm in the bathroom?"

I was already over the threshold before she could answer, but I could not hear the phone anymore. I stood still for a moment, hoping for a clue.

"Stella?"

Peter came to my side.

"Listen," he said. "I don't know what happened tonight. I made my rice and beans. I guess I had a little too much wine while I was waiting for you and before I knew it, I was passed out and Andy was waking me up to take me here."

"Thank you," I said, squeezing his hand. "We're good. Really good. I just really have to go to the bathroom. OK?"

There was a nudge at my feet. I looked down to see Tinker, who took off down the hallway. I followed him to the front of the hotel. I realized that Rex Laruam could only be in one of two rooms, on either side of the entrance. To my right, I heard a familiar voice speaking into a phone. Of all of my suspects, it was the last voice I wanted to hear.

"I am quite clear about the consequences."

The accent was different from the person I knew, but I'd discovered Rex Laruam's identity. I looked back down the hallway to Millie who was surrounded by her friends. She blew me a kiss. I walked up the grand staircase, pulling a bobby pin from my hair.

Intelligence officials around the globe had never been able to identify Rex Laruam, but I knew that one of the world's most dangerous killers was at my birthday party, in an old whaling captain's home. And I had no idea where Agent Hill was or how to contact her.

Once on the landing, I walked to Room 302, where I knew Lennie Bartow had tacked a note on the door to Nathaniel Dinks's room. Taking a deep breath, I slipped my one remaining bobby pin into the lock and turned.

The room was empty. The small suitcase Nathaniel had been carrying when we'd met him on the ferry was at the bottom of the bed. On the dresser was a hatbox with a small notecard beside it. I opened it.

Millie,
*   You are an extraordinary woman. I can't explain why I had to leave, but please know how much I cared about you. I hope you will remember me with this small token of my affection.*

*   Love,*
*   Nathaniel*

Hoping Agent Hill might be at the store, I called the Wick & Flame and left a message on my machine, telling her to meet me in Nathaniel Dinks's room. I put Peter's candle on the dresser by my mother's gift, lit it, and took a seat.

After a few minutes, Rex Laruam, aka Nathaniel Dinks, walked into the room. He didn't glance at me, but he looked at the lit candle, which didn't seem to ruffle him. I watched his body transform from the small, mild-mannered Nathaniel to the sophisticated spy that he was. His shoulders broadened. He gained at least an inch in height. When he unbuttoned his shirt, he removed a small paunch he had strapped to himself. Under it, I saw the bruises and bashes from earlier in the night beginning to take on their deep, purple hue.

Rex Laruam looked into the mirror where I knew he could see me reflected behind him. Maybe I was already too groggy from the powerful candle, or too much in shock from the evening, but I was not afraid. I pushed my hand into the pocket of Millie's sweater and pointed my finger at him as if I were concealing a gun. He stared at the bulge. Then he looked up at my eyes which I knew were beginning to droop. I opened them as wide as I could, and he quietly sat down on the edge of the bed, maybe out of curiosity about what I was doing.

"One question," I said. "Why didn't you take Millie's bag the first day we saw you on the ferry?"

"Because she let me peek inside of it," he said in his real accent, the one I'd heard at the house on Cross Road. "She showed me a sleeping scent that she was going to use to get over jet lag. I saw that the others were numbered. I knew the vial had been moved."

"So, after the accident, you snuck out of the hospital, sent me the note, and then sat by Millie's side, hoping she'd tell you where it was while you made me run around the island looking for it," I said.

He nodded.

"You rat."

"The job isn't always easy," he said. "Sometimes you meet people."

"How did you find Agent Hill?" I said, cutting him off.

"I know you won't like to hear it, but you led me to her," he said. "At dinner. You said she was a sailor. Didn't take much work to narrow down the yachts in the harbor."

He had me there, but I decided I had the last laugh. Agent Hill had been tempted to leave Nantucket without further investigation until he'd broken on board. My slipup had ultimately led to our current showdown.

He calmly removed his shirt and traded it for the black T-shirt inside his suitcase. I noticed the small laptop in his bag.

"That was clever of you," I said. "Coming back here and changing into Nathaniel's identity so we couldn't find you. You're good at disappearing, aren't you?"

"Coming here was not a good idea for you," he said. "As fond as I am of you, you must know by now that I don't let anyone who's ever seen me live to tell the tale."

"Don't make a move," I said, aware that my voice was groggy. "I've got you covered."

I knew all I had to do was keep him talking for a minute, so that the candle's potion could slow him down too.

The King of Shadows, however, was not shaken by my threat. He switched from his khakis to tight black jeans. He was younger than I had realized, which I understood when he looked into his mirror and rubbed his eyes to peel off the corner of a masterfully constructed mask. In an instant, his heavy lids and wrinkles disappeared.

"Olive would be impressed with your make-up," I said.

Rex Laruam turned around, leaning against the dresser, and crossed his arms.

"Trying to think of how to get rid of me without causing much pain?" I said.

"Trying to think how to get rid of your body without upsetting your mother," he said.

"Ah, the enemy falls in love," I said, winking so slowly I wondered if my eye would open.

"The killing part is easy," he said.

He yawned. As close to the candle as he was, I could see the potion was beginning to take effect quickly. I knew I had to keep talking.

"How're you going to kill me?" I said.

Laruam didn't answer. He sat down on the edge of

the bed and put on a shoe. I noticed as he leaned over to tie it that he leaned a little too far to the left.

"It's OK," I said. "You can tell me. Because you're not going to kill me."

Laruam sat back up and looked at me with a silly, yet unpleasant, smile.

"Are you going to kill me with that gun in your pocket first?" he said.

I giggled. Then I lifted my finger out of my pocket.

"It's not a gun," I said.

"I know," he said. He giggled. "Guess what?"

I could tell we were both good and drugged by now.

"What?" I said.

"I have no bullets left," he said.

"You could strangle me," I said as I watched him lie down.

"That's a good idea," he said, his head on his pillow, his eyes beginning to droop. "But I have to do it fast. I'm picking up the vial at your store. Not so smart after all, are you?"

"How do you plan to leave the island without your jet?" I said, lifting my phone with my last bit of strength. I turned it on, ready to type the only message I could to Andy, in hopes he would intercept Laruam before he managed to escape, but my fingers would not cooperate.

"The *Hatchfield*," he said. "Should work for my purposes. Now, I really have to kill you."

The next thing I knew, a hand was on my shoulder. I pushed as hard as I could to defend myself.

"It's OK," said Peter, falling backwards.

"Where's Rex Laruam?" I said, jumping from my seat.

"Who?" said Peter.

I stumbled to the dresser. The candle was out, but

the wax was still loose. The candle could not have been out more than five minutes. The gift and note for my mom were still on the dresser, but Nathaniel was gone. I couldn't believe I'd lost Rex Laruam again.

"Are you OK, Stella?" said Peter, coming to my side.

"How'd you know I was here?" I said to him.

"A woman told me I could find you in Room 302," he said. "I guess she works here. She was helping a drunk guy out of the hotel. What's going on?"

"What did the woman look like?"

He shrugged.

"I don't know. Blond. Sort of pale. She said I should come up here to find you. I'm thinking I should do a story on the amazing people who work in Nantucket's hotels."

"I like the idea," I said, but I had a feeling he'd never find the woman who had sent him to fetch me.

Peter sat on the edge of the bed where Rex Laruam had passed out.

"I didn't get to finish saying to you what I wanted to before," he said. "Maybe now's not the time, but there hasn't been the right time since you got home and I wanted to say it even before you left for Paris. I know things have been weird between us since you got back. I think you must know what I've wanted to say, and if you don't want me to say it, then I won't."

I sat down. Then stood. Then sat again.

I'd never done this before, but I began to spontaneously hum a random tune. Now that the moment had come, I knew in my heart that I was not ready to get married. To anyone.

"Stella, I love you," he said. "There you have it. I love you. You don't have to say it back, but I can't keep it inside. I know you have fancy jumpsuits and you double kiss now that you're back from Paris. Maybe you want to travel more, but I'm sorry, I love it here on Nantucket. Maybe you want to see the world now, with your mom and stuff. But I love you. And I've done my bit with travelling, but if you want to do more stuff, that's fine with me too."

I smiled.

"You weren't going to propose?" I said.

Peter looked three shades paler in less than three seconds.

"Do you want me to?" he said. "I mean—"

"No," I said. "I mean, maybe. But we've only been dating for four months."

"Right," he said. "I mean, you aren't even used to me having your key to your apartment."

"Given that the first time you used it you stole one of Millie's scents from me, I wasn't out of my mind to be suspicious of you."

"That's true," he said. "Sorry we've had our signals so mixed."

"No, it was me. I thought Millie was trying to tell me that you were going to propose tonight."

"Ah," he said, taking me into his arms. "Millie. The mystery is solved."

He had no idea.

"I don't know why, but I'm getting tired again," said Peter.

"Let's get out of here."

Chapter 29

Turning thirty is an incredible moment in life if your mom is home, safe and sound, your boyfriend says he loves you but doesn't want to marry you (yet?), and you've helped save an international peace conference. Having ticked all three of those boxes, I had more fun at a birthday party than anyone on Nantucket has possibly ever had. We danced until the Jared kicked us out, and then brought the party back to my place.

It was about nine in the morning when I woke up on my sofa with Peter beside me and Millie snoring in my bedroom. For a moment, I wondered if everything had been a dream. If perhaps I'd just awoken from my first night home, after our dinner party to welcome Millie back to Nantucket. When I crept to my door to check on Millie, however, I noticed a box of Kleenex and Nathaniel's gift beside her.

I remembered, then, when Millie had slipped away in search of him last night. I'd been tempted to stop her. To tell her everything. Or at least to tell her he had gone. I realized, however, that she might want to digest the news in private, and so I had watched her go with an aching heart. She'd returned about twenty minutes later, with a knowing look.

"Everything OK?" I'd said.

"Everything is fine," she'd said. "But it's been a long two days."

"I know what you mean," I said.

"Excuse me," said Lennie Bartow. Without Nathaniel Dinks in the room, Lennie seemed much happier. Before I knew it, he'd asked my mother to dance. I knew she was only being a good sport, but she accepted. She smiled politely as he moved without lifting his bad leg, and nodded as he told her about the big business deal he'd been working on all week that had just closed.

When she finally extracted herself, she returned to me.

"When will you be taking off again?" I said.

"Soon," she answered. "I want you to meet someone."

She brought me across the room to the dead-eye man.

"This is Eric Jones," she said. "He works for United Perfumers International and was going to introduce himself to us after the panel in Paris. He's interested in my work on responsible scent harvesting. He's been looking for us here, but we've both been busy."

Eric greeted me with a stiff bow.

"Eric has offered me a job as a scent extractor in the Amazon for a little while," my mom said.

"We'd love to fly you there for at least one trip too," said Eric. "I was admiring your candles at the Wick & Flame. There might be an opportunity to work on something together."

Millie and I looked at each other with hearts bursting. I knew she'd be leaving, but to think that we might have another adventure and a project together was more than I'd bargained for.

The biggest surprise had come later, when the party had spilled into Chris's garden where the Mortons had strung tea lights. When I slipped inside to use the bathroom, I heard Laura and John Pierre talking. I now knew that they weren't international terrorists, but I still had a lot of questions for them.

I knocked on their door. Laura opened it.

"I have a birthday present for you," she said.

She went to her suitcase and retrieved the small red box I'd seen while snooping in her room last night.

"While taking care of our house and farm," said Laura. "I also like to paint."

"Sounds very romantic," I said.

"She could turn the story of our leaky house into a romance novel," said John Pierre.

"Ah, you married me for that house. Don't pretend," she said with a laugh. "I inherited it from my grandma, who inherited it from her aunt. Auntie was a model in the 1930s who married a playboy with a lot of money, which he lost gambling. He took off, leaving her with only the house, but our family has taken care of it for generations, as if it had always been our own. We added the farm. It's right on the property."

"I'm a kept man," said John Pierre with a kiss to his wife's cheek.

"Not anymore," said Laura. "Tell Stella about the house."

"I had a great uncle from Nantucket," said John Pierre. "None of us really knew him, but he passed away last year. His will left everything to me, including a house I checked out this week. I'm not sure what I'll do with it, but I do plan to take home with me a beautiful painting for Laura."

That explained the newspaper and the twine, but not their anticipation about today. Laura handed me the small box.

"I also have some good news to share," she said.

I opened the box to find a pinecone inside. It was painted like the Brant Point Lighthouse.

"I started to make Christmas ornaments from pinecones off our trees back home," she said. "I took my stock to the Hub, and the woman there called today and put in an order. My first real customers."

I held the beautiful gift in the air to admire it.

I was looking at the pinecone again, in the morning light, when there was a knock on my door. Millie was still asleep, but I opened it to find Olive.

"I'm off," she said. "But I didn't give you your birthday gift."

For the second time, one of my suspects handed me a small box. I knew, immediately, that it was one of the boxes I'd seen in her room, even though it did not have a country name written across it. I opened it to find a bobble head of Olive Tidings. It was the best gift. Ever.

"My students gave them to me before I left," she said. "A whole cartload with a challenge to bury one everywhere I went on sabbatical. There's one by the topiary outside the conference center in Paris. And I buried one beside the library in Nantucket."

The dirty shovel.

"They put the names of all sorts of countries they

hoped I'd visit on some of the boxes," said Olive, "but I don't think I'll get to them. I miss the girls. I'm heading home."

"You're always welcome back here," I said.

"Give your mum a hug and a kiss from me," she said. "My plane leaves in an hour."

And with that, Olive Tidings got on her bike, her suitcase tied to the back, and headed to the airport.

A week later, I sipped a cup of tea at the Wick & Flame and scrolled through the news about the Peace Jubilee, which had started. I was happy to see that the queen from the South Pacific had arrived safely, and that her presence had added to the goodwill of the event. As I finished one article, a text popped up on my screen from Millie.

> Arrived safely. You must come visit. The Amazon won't be nearly as action-packed as Nantucket, but I'm sure we can amuse ourselves.

Deal, I answered.

My front door opened. I looked up to see the most unlikely visitor.

Agent Hill.

Her hair was blond. Her outfit was even somewhat stylish. The way she carried herself, however, gave away her military training.

"Here," she said, and she passed me a small pin.

"What's this?" I said, deciding we were forgoing hellos.

"There's a queen from a small island in the South Pacific who wanted to pass along her appreciation," she said. "I think those might be real diamonds."

"Get out," I said.

"Thanks for your service," said Agent Hill with a salute.

"We'll always have Paris," I said in my best Humphry Bogart impersonation.

She rolled her eyes, then turned to the door.

"Before you go, I have to ask you something," I said.

I took a deep breath, afraid but needing to ask the question that had haunted me all week.

"The real Nathaniel Dinks is fine," said Agent Hill, reading my mind. "And none the wiser about the weekend he missed. Thanks to Laruam, he won a free trip to Alaska the day he was setting out to Nantucket. He'd been fishing there all week."

"I'm so relieved," I said. Millie would be too.

And with that, our girly banter ended, and she headed to the door. Her exit, however, was made slightly awkward by the arrival of Andy. He was wearing his off-duty T-shirt, jeans, and baseball cap. For a moment, his off-duty, laid-back demeanor had switched to the sharp-eyed policeman, but he let Agent Hill pass.

"She's just a friend—" I said, but I didn't have to finish. Georgianna entered the Wick & Flame behind him, holding a large bottle of coffee.

"Hey, girl!" she said with a hug. "I brought you your favorite. Coffee from The Bean. Consider it a belated birthday gift."

She'd come up with a great gift. The bottle even said THE BEAN along the side of it.

"Are we all ready?" said Peter, entering the store with a basket of goodies and Cherry in tow. My part-time helper took out her apron and put it on even though I hadn't hired her for the day.

"I'm here, I'm here," said Emily, crashing into my store, somewhat out of breath and dressed in sneakers, which she rarely did.

"Where are we going?" I said.

Peter held up a bag of pennies.

"We're going to the *Yacht*," he said. "And we're all going to throw pennies overboard."

"Why?" I said.

"Yeah, why exactly?" said Andy to Peter.

"Because it's fun," said Emily.

"Because it's an adventure and my lady likes an adventure," said Peter.

I grabbed his hand and smiled, appreciating the sentiment. It had taken him a couple of days to catch up to me, but better late than never.

"I had quite an adventure last week," said Emily, as my friends headed out the door.

I heard her grouse about Frank Marshall's crazy friends, and heard Peter try to one-up her with his story about a new article he was starting.

I slipped my broach into the safe. Then, I grabbed Millie's sweater for warmth, and followed them out the door.

CANDLE MOLDS 201

WHY DIY CANDLE MOLDS?

Make a mold, make it personal.

Right again, Stella. As with every craft, personal designs bring it to the next level.

Gifts, gifts, gifts!

So easy to make a mold, so special to receive a custom, one-of-a-kind candle.

Save money.

Stella reminded us how much money we spent on premade candle molds after our "Intro to Candle Molds" workshop last summer. I wonder if she knows that Flo bought four different dog figures, plus all of those flower designs. Ha-ha! I only bought seven, and I've already used four.

Note: ask Flo if she'll lend me the sleeping-hound mold. So cute.

IDEAS FOR MOLDS

Cast the Lego structure that little Billy made for me. Make one for him and a couple for his teachers as holiday gifts.

My old, bronzed bootie. I owe Stella's friend, Emily, a baby gift. She'll love it. And she'll need a treat after running the Frank Marshall party. What a group!

Stella made a mold out of her teeth from before she got braces. Wonder if she'd like a mold of my dentures. Tell Flo.

SILICONE MOLDS ARE STURDY,
EASY TO MAKE, AND LONG LASTING

Stella says there are kits we can buy to cast an item into a silicone mold.

Fast drying, plus not as smelly as the solution we're going to make in class

Making a silicone solution from scratch.

<u>Pros</u>: Can be cheaper than a kit if we like making molds and plan to design many.

<u>Cons</u>: Smelly. Need to mix in a well-ventilated area or with a mask.

NO SILICONE?
EASY PILLAR CANDLE MOLD HACK

Use an existing cardboard-type container that is wax-lined for a mold—can be from snacks, take-out food, milk cartons, etc. Pour the wax directly into these items. When the candle hardens, peel off the container. Done! Add the personal touch through fragrance and color choices.

Recipe

GRAM SCULLY'S CRANBERRY PIE

Filling Ingredients:
- 2 lbs cranberries
- 3 eggs
- 2 cups of sugar
- 3 tsp almond extract

Place cranberries in a colander and rinse thoroughly to wash out seeds. Set aside. Beat 3 eggs well then add 2 cups of sugar. Continue to beat until well mixed. Add 3 tsp of almond extract. Add cranberries, mixing well. Set aside, stirring a couple of times while rolling out pie crust.

Pie Crust Ingredients:
- 4 cups flour
- 1 tsp salt
- 1 tsp baking powder
- 1¾ cups Crisco
- ½ cup cold water
- 1 egg
- 1 tsp vinegar

Mix together flour, salt, baking powder, and Crisco. Hands are the best tools for this. Add cold water, 1 egg, and 1 tsp vinegar. Mix well. Shape into 4 balls.

Chill for ½ hour before rolling. Pie crust can be made ahead and frozen. Will keep up to 6 months in freezer.

If frozen, the balls will take about ½ hour to thaw enough to roll out.

Line two large pie plates with crust. Divide cranberry mixture between them. Place top crust over mixture, cutting 3–4 slits on top, and brush with a small amount of milk.

Bake at 400° F for 40 minutes.

ACKNOWLEDGMENTS

Many thanks to everyone who helped bring this second book of the Nantucket Candle Maker series to life. Christina Hogrebe, Norma Perez-Hernandez, Larissa Ackerman, Michelle Addo, and Judie Bouldry, your support of Stella Wright's stories has helped make her adventures spring from the page in so many ways.

I'd like to extend my deepest thanks to Chrissie McGrath Iller, from Nantucket, who shared her grandmother Beulah Scully's cranberry pie recipe. There are many wonderful Nantucket cookbooks, and tempting Nantucket cranberry pie recipes. Chrissie, however, found this treasured recipe in her gram's handwriting, and entrusted it to me—and Olive Tidings.

Jonathan Putnam and Michael Bergmann, you are a writer's best editors. I am also lucky that so many of my friends and family, a shocking number of you, actually, are happy to talk murder with me over coffee and during walks in Central Park. . . . Special thanks to Meredith Lipsher and Jennifer Sheehan.

Thanks to my mother, Rini Shanahan, who is always my first reader and indispensable fact-checker; to my father, Tom Shanahan, who is my trusty companion when we scout Nantucket locations; and to my brother, Mark, who should be every mystery writer's go-to. And, to Steve, Tommy, and Carly, who fend for themselves so graciously when I'm in the middle of one of Stella's mysteries. I cherish each of you, and all of us.

Keep reading for a sneak peek at

15 MINUTES OF FLAME

The next Nantucket Candle Maker Mystery.

Available September 2020

**from
Kensington Publishing Corporation!**

Saturday morning, I was lounging on a folding chair in my backyard, enjoying a little sun. My chaise for such luxury was the kind with the plastic straps across a metal frame, where one or two bands always seem to be missing in crucial places. I didn't mind, however. Even though my rear end sank a little lower to the ground than I'd prefer, I was deeply engaged with the clouds rolling above me on this late October day. Thick, fluffy, bright white, and moving fast along an otherwise clear blue sky. As one remarkably beautiful apparition whisked by me, I remembered a game I used to play as a kid. My friends and I would study a cloud, and then we'd compare the images we saw. Mickey Mouse, a choo-choo train, a duck. It was amazing how often we saw different pictures from the same floating cloud.

You'd think I'd have learned from our game that there were a thousand ways to see the world, but it took me until I was almost thirty years old to really grasp the concept. Less than six months ago, I was grappling with the fact that my small candle business, the Wick & Flame, would not make it through another year on Nantucket Island. My dream of making candles and selling them in a store I owned, in my hometown, with the good fortune of being with family and friends, could have vanished like the flicker of a flame when it's snuffed out. But then, solving a murder, of all things, helped me see the world differently. Puzzling out a crime and restoring justice was as fascinating to me as studying the ways a wick might last longer or a flame might burn brighter. I'd jumped in to help before I'd even thought about it, and never looked back. After I solved the case, my business grew like wildfire, and, most surprisingly, I fell in love with Peter Bailey, the town's newest reporter for the local *Inquirer & Mirror*.

To my surprise, it was my fate to find murder one more time, less than two weeks ago. Unlike my first, no one knew I was even on a murder case except for my mom, who'd been home for a short while. Andy Southerland, the town's best police officer and one of my oldest friends, caught on too. It's a good story— spies and national security abound—but that's a whole other kettle of clues.

This morning, my focus was on something much lighter: Halloween, which was only six days away. This year, I'd volunteered to assist with the Girl Scout's *Halloween Haunts* fundraiser for the island's neediest. I'd helped them for the last week build papier mâché cauldrons, bats, and spider décor. We'd carved pumpkins. We'd planned activities for all ages, ranging from crafts and apple bobbing to a scary, ghostly maze. Today, my assistant, Cherry, was covering me at the Wick & Flame, so I planned to check in on the girls' progress.

I raised one leg to the air and pulled it to my forehead as a cloud that looked like a gun, I'm not kidding, rolled by. For one moment I had the witchy feeling that I was too complacent. As its shadow passed, I caught my breath, wondering if the peaceful afternoon, the healthy stock in my store, and the warmth of my relationship with Peter was no more than the calm before another storm. I shook it off. The flip side of having solved two murders is the danger of getting a little paranoid.

Also, I was in close proximity of two boys, all of eight and ten years old, my cousin Chris's sons, with whom I was sharing my patch of lawn. My home is the apartment over Chris's garage. My bucket list includes owning my own place one day, something with room for a studio and a garden out back, but, for now, their company is wonderful, and the modest rent is ideal for my entrepreneurial ambitions. The boys had inched closer and closer to my personal space over the last half hour, however, so I chalked up my unease to their questionable skill set when it came to a ball and mitt.

Chris appeared at his kitchen window as their last throw zoomed over my chair.

"Dudes! Don't bug Stella," he said.

"Hi!" I waved to him as the boys retrieved their ball and continued their game.

"Do you want some mac and cheese? I'm on lunch duty," Chris called out to me.

"That's very tempting, but I can't," I answered. "I'm heading over to the Morton house in about ten minutes."

The Morton house was home to *Halloween Haunts.* The Girl Scout's troop leader, Shelly, had had her eye on the historic place near town, and therefore on me, since it was owned by my friend, John Pierre Morton.

In spite of the fact that I'd briefly considered John Pierre a murder suspect only a couple of weeks ago, we'd left on good terms when he returned to his home in Canada. His visit to Nantucket had been motivated by his inheritance of the musty, forgotten home. After I gave him a call, he graciously agreed to allow the Scouts to set up shop there for the holiday.

"That place is haunted," said Chris's youngest, rubbing his ball into his mitt.

I knew the source of his fears. In an effort to drum up business, the Troop had circulated a few rumors that the house was actually haunted. Given Nantucket's foggy nights and a seafaring past filled with shipwrecks and whale's tales, the town had no shortage of ghost stories. It wasn't hard for the girls' propaganda to take off.

"Things aren't haunted in real life," I said.

"Yes, they are," he said, pulling his arm back for a throw.

"Mwah-ha-ha," I said with my best vampire-slash-ghost voice, my arms held high in zombie fashion.

"Boys!" said Chris.

It was then that I realized how sharp a parent's instincts can be. My eyes were suddenly glued to a new vision of white streaking across the sky. Not a cloud. Nay, it was the white leather of a baseball which flew from the hand of Chris's youngest with the greatest speed and farthest distance of the day. Right toward the closed kitchen window of my apartment. Unable to interrupt its trajectory, the four of us watched, our jaws hanging, as the ball hurtled toward my window and crashed unapologetically through the glass.

The boys took a step back, and then froze, torn between their primordial instincts of fight or flight.

I managed to stifle an *"oh no!"* in spite of my shock. The boys would have enough to answer for without me. The window's glass hadn't even hit the ground before the sound of Chris's back door shot open.

"What the—?" he said, storming across the lawn. "Get inside!"

"It wasn't my fault," each boy said in his own fashion as they both scrambled, defiantly but obediently, toward the main house.

"Sorry, Stella," said Chris, not pausing to stop.

I found enough unbroken chair straps to stand as Chris opened my unlocked door and climbed the stairs to my apartment. I followed him up. Tinker was on the top step, his whiskers peeking over his paws in a way that suggested a combination of empathy for and disappointment in his humans. Indeed, there were glass shards on my countertop and in the sink. The window would need to be replaced. Chris, a contractor, immediately dialed his window repair guy on the Cape, so I grabbed a broom and got to work. I looked at the window as I heard him complain about how long the delivery might take. I figured with a trash bag and some heavy tape from under my kitchen sink, I could probably cover the hole well enough until a new window arrived.

"I got this," Chris said to me, his hand over the receiver. "Really."

I looked at his flushed, red cheeks, and could see his frustration with the boys' shenanigans was at an all-time high.

"Maybe it's a good idea for you to keep busy for a while," I said.

"You got that right," he said. "Scoot."

Chris went right back to his phone call, so I scooped

up my keys and wallet, and traded my broom for a soft blue blanket from my sofa which I planned to drop on Tinker. My cat, however, took one look at me and hopped down the stairs. My pet refuses to limit his role to house cat. Sometimes I think he sees himself as another human, or maybe a faithful dog. I've learned by now not to fight him when he has the urge to join me. Plus, I knew the girls would get a kick out of seeing him.

The two of us jumped in my red Beetle and headed to town. When I pulled up to the Morton house, a gray-shingled antique in the ubiquitous Cape style of so many others on Nantucket, I parked across the street, since there was no driveway. Tinker and I exited the car to a chorus of young girls' voices coming from inside. As I was heading up the stairs to the front door, ready to give Shelly a break, I heard a heavy creak from behind the house, followed by a shriek that sang of pure mischief. Fool me once, as they say. My radar for middle-school hijinks was on red alert thanks to my own family. I headed around the back to investigate.

The backyard was empty, but I wasn't ready to concede that I was alone. I headed across the half acre of yellowing grass toward a dilapidated stone structure behind the main house that had once been a smokehouse, and which we now affectionately called "The Shack." Homes built in the early nineteenth century sometimes had additional buildings behind them, which served as workshops. By now, most of these structures had been razed for garages, or more yard space, but the Mortons' house still had one. It was such a dump, however, that no one particularly relished it as history.

The Scouts were strictly forbidden to enter The Shack, partly because a chain which secured the front screamed tetanus shot. From the girls' squeals and the now-opened door, however, I concluded that some of our Scouts had decided to break a few rules today. I didn't blame them. I'd have likely done the same at their age. The question, now, was whether they'd scrambled back into the house or they were still exploring. I was formulating a plan to give anyone inside a good, haunted house scare as penalty for breaking the rules, when my phone rang.

"Hello, handsome," I said.

"Hello, beautiful," said Peter. "Are you interested in joining me at Crab City later? Low tide is in two hours."

Peter was working on a story about the island's hermit crabs that had lately consumed him. He was having the time of his life studying the hundreds of crabs that emerged at low tide off the shore of the Nantucket Field Station, which was managed by the University of Massachusetts's environmental studies department. He thought they were amazing, but I was still figuring out how I might share his latest passion. Fortunately, I'd come up with an idea this morning.

"Sounds good," I said. "I've been wondering if it's possible to mix a fishy smell with other scents for summer candles."

"Sounds like an impossible challenge, but I'm sure you can figure it out if anyone can," he said.

"I'm at the Morton house," I said. "I can meet you when I'm done."

"I'm happy to carve pumpkins or whatever you need until low tide," he said.

"Your skills with a staple gun and your eye for boyishly creepy things might be of use," I said.

"You had me at staple gun," he said. "See you."

I smiled and figured I had about twenty minutes before he arrived. Half a yard later, I arrived at the front door to The Shack. I heard nothing inside, but I gathered Tinker into my arms.

"Ready?" I said into his soft, pink ear.

With a Cheshire smile, Tinker answered me by jumping from my arms into the small building with one big yowl, which can be deafening when he's in the mood. His cry, however, was followed by a sigh. I gathered that his performance had been for nothing. The girls had not waited around to see what was inside.

I, however, decided to finish what they'd started. I slipped around the thick, rotting door and into the dark, one-room building. After I brushed aside some cobwebs, I found myself in a space which smelled of dried dirt and a few autumn leaves that had blown inside. Although the main house was old and musty due to years of neglect by its last owner, it felt thoroughly modern compared to The Shack. Some daylight crept through the door, but the only other source of light was a small window, across which several weeds had taken root. The floor was made of wide wooden planks, which were warped from damp and neglect. The walls were exposed stone, round and about the size of the cobblestones on Main Street. It was a pleasant day outside, but the room was noticeably cold.

I picked up Tinker and walked toward a hearth at

the back of the dimly lit room, passing a few odds and ends from the last owner. A rusty bike wheel. A spade. A roll of chicken coop wire.

Like many old fireplaces, this one was huge, at least seven feet wide and maybe five feet tall, with a cooking hook on the left, over a space to build a large fire. These household features served as heaters, lights, stoves, dryers, and more. The mantel of the hearth was made of the same stones as the walls and cantilevered over the firepit for protection.

As my eyes adjusted, I noticed a sign hanging above the hearth. Holding my phone up for extra light, I made out the words COOPER'S CANDLES painted in pale blue, faded and cracked in some places, but still clear.

"No way," I said, as much to myself as to Tinker, who whisked his tail and jumped to the ground to investigate.

I realized, with much delight, that I was in a chandlery. The Shack was, in fact, Cooper's Candles. I couldn't believe I had accepted Shelly's explanation that the building had been used for smoking meats when, in fact, the fireproof stone structure with its small chimney was once a place where candles had been made, stored, and sold. The discovery caught me completely by surprise, although, in reality, the business of Cooper's Candles would not have been an unusual one for Nantucket in the early nineteenth century, when the Morton house had been built. Around that time, about a third of the island's economy came from candle making. Nantucket's candles were known to have the brightest and whitest light due to the islanders' access to spermaceti oil from whales.

I couldn't help it, but I envisioned a young me, sitting by the flames in this room, melting wax and forming it into candles that the neighbors might buy. I touched the name on the sign and wondered who Cooper had been. It was likely a family surname, as was the custom back then. My sign over the Wick & Flame was a shiny, black quarter board, framed in silver with silver block letters announcing the name, but Cooper's sign was homier. I imagined its architect with a brush in one hand and a paint can in the other. The sign was the length of the hearth, and about two feet high.

I took a poorly lit photo and sent it to John Pierre. A moment later, he responded with the words I'd hoped to see.

> Amazing! Take it for your apartment. It was meant for you.

I sent back a thank you, and a heart.

Then, I got to work.

First, I pried at the board, gently, so as not to break it. The wood was thick and still strong in spite of years of neglect and the island's sea air. When I decided it wouldn't budge, I searched the items strewn about the floor and picked up the spade. Carefully, I used it to pry the wood ever so slowly from above the wall. Before I knew it, I was building up a sweat, but I didn't mind. At one point, my phone pinged. I knew it was probably Shelly, wondering where I was, but I'll admit I couldn't stop. Although we'd steered clear of The Shack, I was seduced by it now that I was inside. I felt like I had crossed from one world and back into another.

Finally, the wood came free. I slowly lowered it to the floor. As I stood back up, a stone fell from the newly exposed wall, missing me by a couple of inches. Another followed. Then another. I looked above the mantel and pulled the next one free. They loosened like dominoes.

"Psssssst," said Tinker.

Behind us, the room became icy cold for no more than a second. Then, I heard the door move, and, with it, a ray of light entered the room.

"Stella?" said Peter, peeking through the doorframe, first at me and then at the mantel behind me. He straightened at the sight. "Wow. I thought the decorations would be spooky in the house, but that's overkill. Get it?"

"It's not a decoration," I said, staring back at the hole in the wall the sign had left behind.

The two of us faced the mantel, and the human skeleton I'd uncovered, nestled into a carved-out space in the wall.

Connect with U(s)

Visit us online at
KensingtonBooks.com
to read more from your favorite authors, see books
by series, view reading group guides, and more.

for sneak peeks, chances to win books and prize packs,
and to share your thoughts with other readers.

f y

facebook.com/kensingtonpublishing
twitter.com/kensingtonbooks

Tell us what you think!

To share your thoughts, submit a review,
or sign up for our eNewsletters, please visit:
KensingtonBooks.com/TellUs.